The Re

Born and raised in Sheffield, Joanne lives in the coastal village of Laxey in the Isle of Man with her husband, children, dogs and other assorted wildlife. She has worked in print, radio and broadcast journalism in the north west for the past three decades and is now a full-time writer of historical fiction set in nineteenth century Sheffield.

Also by Joanne Clague

The Sheffield Sagas

The Ragged Valley
The Girl at Change Alley
The Watchman's Widow

The House of Help for Friendless Girls

The House of Hope
The Lightfingered Lass
The Rebel Daughter

The
Rebel
Daughter

Joanne
CLAGUE

1℃ CANELO

Penguin
Random
House

First published in the United Kingdom in 2025 by

Canelo, an imprint of
Canelo Digital Publishing Limited,
20 Vauxhall Bridge Road,
London SW1V 2SA
United Kingdom

A Penguin Random House Company
The authorised representative in the EEA is Dorling Kindersley Verlag GmbH.
Arnulfstr. 124, 80636 Munich, Germany

A CIP catalogue record for this book is available from the British Library.

Print ISBN 978 1 80436 804 6
Ebook ISBN 978 1 80436 806 0

This book is a work of fiction. Names, characters, businesses, organizations, places and
events are either the product of the author's imagination or are used fictitiously. Any
resemblance to actual persons, living or dead, events or locales is entirely coincidental.

Cover design by Rose Cooper

Cover images © Arcangel, Shutterstock

Printed and bound in Great Britain by Clays Ltd, Elcograf S.p.A.

Look for more great books at
www.canelo.co | www.dk.com

I

For Florence and Teddy

Prologue

Winter, 1889

If anyone had thought to ask, she might have said the trouble started the day Isaac's mother hurtled back into their lives after a twenty-year absence, that their woes began with a promise fulfilled – and a threat.

And all that remained, the beginning and the end of her world, were the rasping breaths of the occupant of the bed behind her.

She pressed her forehead against the windowpane, welcoming the chill against her skin. On the street below, the pavement and cobbles that had been slickly black under the streetlamps were softer, less harshly outlined, in the forgiving light of dawn. When a blackbird's song pierced the gloom, she straightened and rubbed her eyes and smoothed back loose tendrils of hair from her forehead. The clattering chatter of wheels preceded the entry of the coal cart into the street. She watched the horses slow and halt beneath her before pulling closed the curtains.

The cascade of coal down the chute into the cellar sounded like the rumbles of thunder that had filled the skies during July and August and September. With a shudder, she picked up the poker and stirred the glowing coals in the grate then returned to sit in the armchair by the bed. She caught sight of movement in the shaving mirror that sat on top of the dressing table – a smudge of white in the gloom – and her hand flew to her throat before she realised it was her own reflection she had glimpsed. Too soon for ghosts.

Returning to the chair, she rested her head against one of its wings and closed her eyes, listening to his breathing, grateful her wish to keep this nighttime vigil had been granted.

He slept in his childhood bed, a simple frame with a curved rosewood headboard and no footboard, which was a blessing as the bed was not long enough for the body that lay on it. Even with his stockinged feet hanging off the end, a sight that was heartbreakingly poignant, he seemed somehow diminished, less himself. She imagined she could easily pick him up in her arms and carry him away to some imagined safety. He would allow it, too. She knew that now.

Chapter 1

Summer, 1889

Located a stone's throw from the centre of town, the Crofts had once been a large common, gradually parcelled off and bounded by hedges, the air pure and clean. Now it was a maze of streets, gennels and overcrowded courts where, under the pall of the smoke belched out by factory chimneys, families lived in squalid conditions and there was a thief with a blade on every corner.

Or so her mother told her.

Alice Leigh passed the blackened brick façade of a tool manufactory and glanced into the entrance of a smithy, her ears attuned to the anvil's clang. She nodded politely when a butcher hanging carcasses inside the window of a pork shop caught her eye and wished her a good morning. All the while, she recited in her head the directions supplied, a little grudgingly, by the warden of the House of Help. It stung her that Miss Barlow thought this a fool's errand, although she had not explicitly said as much.

The sign for the Orange Branch public house hung out over the litter-strewn pavement ahead. Alice was to take the gennel beside it, then turn left once she emerged onto Pea Croft. Jervis Court was some five hundred yards along, on the opposite side of the road. If she reached the pawnbrokers on Solly Street she had gone too far and must turn herself about.

'You've no need to do this,' the warden had told her.

'I know,' said Alice.

'All right then. Keep your wits about you.'

The confident stride Alice had adopted faltered when she saw, despite the early hour of the day, a handful of men loitering outside the barred door of the Orange Branch, evidently waiting for opening time. Alice recovered herself, lifted her chin and marched into the narrow passageway beside the pub, the back of her neck prickling. At the warden's suggestion, she had replaced her silk summer cape with a woollen shawl and her straw bonnet with a rough cotton headscarf, both supplied by the House. Her fine suede boots were hidden beneath the hem of her dress and she wore no jewellery.

The high, dank walls of the gennel were piled with rubbish, bulky dregs that stirred and bulged with the movement of unseen rats. Alice kept her eyes on the ground ahead, afraid of stumbling and landing in the rot, her breath held in anticipation of a filthy claw reaching out to grab her arm or seize her ankle, followed by a croaky demand for coin. She had none. Her ears strained for the sound of footsteps but all she could hear was the gurgle of drain water. Emerging onto the next street, she took a breath of the smoky air, relieved to be in the open again, and turned left, her brisk steps echoing along the pavement.

At the entrance to Jervis Court, a small child was crouched over a shallow pool of cloudy water, chasing a curl of potato peel with a stick, intent on the task. An older boy stood above the infant, leaning against the wall, his eyes vacant, his mouth chewing energetically. He straightened up as Alice approached and spat a stream of brown fluid onto the cobbles.

His voice was surprisingly high and bright. 'Spare a coin, Miss?'

'I'm sorry,' she said, averting her eyes from the mess. 'I have nothing on me. Do you know where number fifteen is? Mr and Mrs Bramall?'

But he had lost interest in her, pulling the brim of his cap down over his eyes and turning his head aside to spit again, this time spraying the pool of water with the brown muck. Alice hesitated for a moment, then entered the court. A path of uneven flagstones opened onto a cobbled yard hemmed by dilapidated two- and three-storey houses and festooned with laundry hanging limply from washing lines. She ventured further into the yard. Nearby, a dirty net curtain was snagged on the cracked pane of a ground floor window. Both drawn and repelled by grunting noises and giggles from inside, Alice got close enough to peer through the glass, then stumbled backwards into the middle of the yard. There had been a mattress on the floor, and she had glimpsed bare limbs, and a face turned towards her. A laugh, a raucous sound, rang around the court.

'Who's tha lookin' for, love?'

The voice belonged to a woman leaning on a rail at the top of a small flight of stone steps. She was bareheaded, the sleeves of her housedress rolled above the elbow, her round face flushed. Trotting down the steps, she came to stand before Alice, wiping her hands on a rag. Her hands were swollen, her skin red and mottled to her elbows.

'Look sharp, love. I've a mountain o' washin' to get through.'

Before Alice could speak, another woman emerged from a house to her right. ' 'Ey up,' she called to the first woman. 'Is he sendin' young lasses now?' She pointed at Alice. 'Tell 'im from me that until the 'ole in the roof's fixed he can whistle for his rent.' She jerked a thumb over her shoulder. 'I've got nigh on half a dozen buckets catchin' drips in here.'

Alice shook her head. 'No, no. I've not been sent by the landlord.' How much, she wondered, were people paying to live in such squalor? 'I'm looking for a Mrs Bramall. Mrs Alfred Bramall. Polly. I'm...' she looked around the yard helplessly, '... I'm here to check on her welfare.'

'Her welfare, eh?' said the laundrywoman.

Alice caught the glance that passed between the two women.

'Has Alfie come out o' the nick yet?' the second woman said.

The laundrywoman shrugged. 'No idea. Polly's up there,' she said, pointing to the top of the yard, where another, narrower flagged path disappeared around a corner. 'Last 'ouse before the dead end. I'd tread careful if I were thee.'

'Thank you.'

'An' don't go peerin' in winders.'

The laundrywoman cackled.

'I won't,' said Alice.

She was aware of the women's eyes on her as she walked away. At the top of the yard, Alice glanced back, expecting to see them still watching, but the women had gone. A cold frisson of fear made her shiver. There was a small consolation in knowing such doughty women were nearby, though she had a suspicion that she would find doors firmly closed to her, should trouble be encountered.

Turning the corner, she entered a lane containing a row of mean little terraced houses facing a high and untidily mortared brick wall that made Alice think of loosened teeth. She walked towards the dead end slowly, twice checking over her shoulder. The number of Polly Bramall's house was stencilled on the jamb of the door at the end of the row. Alice rapped her knuckles on the wooden planking.

The window beside the door was shuttered and thickly looped with spider thread. It had evidently been a while since it had been opened. Alice was congratulating herself on this observation, and beginning to suspect – with a relief she did not want to acknowledge – that this had been a wasted journey, when the front door on the other side of the shutter opened. A young girl who could not be more than seven or eight years old, wearing nothing but a loose smock over the knobbly bones of her bare shoulders, stuck her head out.

'In 'ere,' she hissed, reaching out for Alice's sleeve.

Alice batted her hand away. She was more rattled than she cared to admit. 'I'm looking for Mrs Bramall.'

'Aye, she's in 'ere, 'avin' some grub. Best be quick a'fore—'

The girl yelped as she was yanked back and a woman took her place. She came into the passage, pulling the door most of the way closed behind her, and looked Alice up and down. 'What's tha want wi' our Poll?'

Alice fixed a friendly smile to her face. 'My name is Alice Leigh. I'm an agent for the House of Help.'

The woman snorted derisively. 'Oh aye, that 'ouse. Tha's one of them do-gooders that does nowt but cause ructions.' She sniffed and rubbed her nose. There was an angry sore next to her mouth that Alice tried not to stare at. 'Tha knows the first thing Alfie did when he got out? Kicked the lass from 'ere to kingdom come, because o' thee.'

Alice glanced over her shoulder again, an involuntary movement that made her cross with herself. She had become infected by the oppressiveness of this lane that was immune to the sunlight. 'Polly left a week ago, before we were able to find her alternative accommodation.' She spoke in the firmest tone she could muster. 'If she has returned here, may I speak with her, please?'

The woman folded her arms. 'Aye, she's back, an' so is he, more's the pity. She came round this morning, after he'd buggered off, sharpish-like as soon as he'd gone, beggin' a cup o' tea. Poor lass reckons she's had nowt to eat for two days.'

The door widened an inch, the girl's head appearing, level with her mother's waist. 'I've given her some bread an' drippin',' she said.

'Get in, go on.' The woman turned back to Alice. 'She reckons he won't let 'er have owt 'til she starts earnin' her keep – on her back.' She paused, and Alice nodded to show she understood the woman's meaning. 'I've fed 'er, a' course, but she can't stay. I don't want him tearin' my place up, or me. I've bairns to look after.'

'Then she should return with me now,' said Alice, her voice breaking on the final word, when she had meant to sound authoritative. Her throat was dry as dust. 'Tell Mr Bramall you saw me fetch her away, if you like, Mrs...?'

'I'm not givin' thee my name. Wait 'ere.' She pushed the door open. 'Poll! Come out, love. Got somebody wants a word wi' thee.'

Alice tapped a foot nervously, unable to resist another glance down the passage. She ought to have asked where

Mr Bramall was and how long he was likely to remain absent. It occurred to her he might have been one of the men waiting outside the Orange Branch for the pub to open. She hoped that was the case.

The woman who emerged from the house was around Alice's age, but there the similarities ended. Polly was a full head and shoulders shorter than Alice, with a thin frame bordering on frailty. Her complexion was pale, a pallor accentuated by the curtains of long dark hair that hung over her shoulders. She was wearing the plain blue skirt and blouse she'd been given by the House, now crumpled and stained. The faint smile she gave Alice contained a weak measure of the derision her neighbour had displayed. These people had no faith in Alice or the institution she represented. How could she persuade them otherwise?

'Has tha come for this?' said Polly, plucking at the material of the blouse. She chewed on her lip. 'He's wantin' to sell this rig-out before it gets any muckier.'

'The dress was donated to you,' said Alice. 'You must keep it.'

Polly shrugged. 'Fancy clothes're wasted on this place, anyhow. He's already took the boots tha gave me.'

'You misunderstand,' said Alice. 'That's not why I'm here.' Her eyes fell to the clogs Polly was wearing.

'I give her them,' said the next-door neighbour. 'He's chucked everythin' out that he couldn't sell. Now he's after sellin' her.'

'I'm sorry,' Alice stammered. 'I don't understand. Why did you come back here? I hoped you'd accept our help.'

Polly didn't answer. She was looking over Alice's shoulder, her eyes widening in fright.

'I thought I told thee to keep theesen inside?'

It was a man's voice. The words were spoken lightly, even humorously, although the underlying menace was clear. Alice turned slowly, her heart in her mouth, her mind scrambling to come up with placatory words, and finding none. The man she faced was tall, with a shock of untidy dark hair, narrow eyes and a sulky set to his generous mouth. Alice blinked, for an instant convinced she was looking into the face of her beloved cousin Isaac, so strong was the resemblance, but Isaac wouldn't hurt a flea.

She stuck out her hand.

'Is it Mr Bramall?' Emboldened by the steadiness of her voice, she added, 'I'm Miss Leigh. I came to see how Polly was getting along.'

Alfie Bramall ignored her hand. 'An' what business is it o' thine?'

The idea of repeating the neighbour's complaint – 'Why, I'm a do-gooder!' – brought a bubble of hysterical laughter to Alice's throat. She coughed, and glanced at Polly, who stood frozen in place, her gaze fastened on her husband. The woman from the neighbouring house gave an almost imperceptible shake of her head. A warning.

Alice smiled. 'I befriended your wife when she needed help.'

'Help wi' what?'

All trace of humour had gone from his voice. He took hold of Polly's arm, digging his fingers into the bare skin beneath the rolled-up sleeves of her blouse. 'Tell 'em how tha dislocated that shoulder, an' how I would've taken thee to the infirmary if tha'd not run off.' He shook her. 'Go on.'

Polly spoke in a whisper. 'I fell downstairs, an' got confused,' she said. She looked into Alice's eyes for a moment before her gaze slid away.

He shook her arm again. 'And?'

'Alfie's right. He would've looked after me. He allus has done.' Her voice had dropped to a whisper. 'I should never have gone to that house o' thine. It were a mistake.'

The man gave a satisfied nod. Maintaining his grip on Polly's arm, pulling her along with him, he advanced on Alice, forcing her to take a step back. 'Off tha trots, now. I wun't show tha face again, if I were thee.'

Alice tried to see past him, desperately trying to think of a way of reminding Polly about her time at the house. Had she forgotten their conversation about finding a new life for her? They had sat, Alice, Polly, the warden and her deputy, before the warmth of the kitchen range, sipping tea. Polly had been assured she was safe and sound. What had possessed her to run back to this man?

'Mrs Bramall. Polly,' said Alice. 'Would you come with me, now, back to the house?'

Polly's mouth dropped open. She looked aghast.

Alfie Bramall laughed. 'Tha's got a brass neck on thee. Good job I've a sense o' humour.'

Alice ignored him. 'Polly, remember what we talked about?'

'No.' Polly shook her head vigorously. 'I'm best off 'ere.'

'Too right,' said Alfie Bramall.

Alice clasped her hands together. 'Can I just say one thing, Polly? You know where we are.'

'Aye, an' I know, an' all.' Alfie leaned down so his face was close to hers, blotting everything else out. 'Paradise

Square, in't it? House full o' women at number one. Oh aye, I've clocked it.'

Alice dipped her head, nauseated by the staleness of the man's breath. Again, he shook Polly's arm. 'But let's see what the wife thinks, eh? Owt to say, love? Poll?'

'No.'

'An' that's because what I say goes?'

'Aye.'

'Let this lass hear thee say it.'

'All right, Alfie. What you say goes.'

'Well, then.' He stepped back and Alice let out the breath she was holding. 'Sorry tha's wasted tha mornin', me dear.' He turned away, dismissing her. 'Now, Poll, what were tha doin', runnin' next door?'

Alice realised that at some point the neighbour had retreated into her house and closed the door. Tears of frustration rose in her eyes as she walked away. She had, in her naivety, imagined she would return to the house arm in arm with Polly. This was intended to have been her first real triumph as a volunteer agent for the House of Help, a signal to the warden, and to her mother, of her capabilities.

All she had done was make matters worse.

—

He was a lone figure standing at the foot of Pond Lane, leaning against the damp brick façade of the lead factory, a cigarette dangling from his fingertips, his cap pulled low over his brow. Alice's stomach dropped. She had gone too far, and now Alfie Bramall had come to get her. She watched him take a deep drag on the thin tube of tobacco, stub the cigarette out on the wall and let it fall to the ground. She was on the verge of turning on her heel and marching back to the House of Help, when he lifted his gaze, saw her, and grinned. It was Isaac.

Alice ran to him and embraced him, so overwhelmed was she with relief.

'Woah, steady on.' Isaac held her at arm's length, a concerned frown on his face. 'What's up wi' thee?'

'Nothing.' She laughed, shakily. 'I'm just glad to see you.'

'Well, that's allus good to hear.' He took off his cap and raked his fingers through his hair. 'Where've you been, then?'

Alice pouted. 'Trying to help a woman escape from her brute of a husband.'

'Any good?'

'No. I failed.' She tucked her hand into the crook of his arm. 'Don't you dare say anything to mother, Isaac Hinchcliffe. You know what she's like.'

Alice had walked from the Crofts back to the House of Help, collected her cape and bonnet, and briefed the warden. Hetty Barlow had refrained from comment, although Alice saw admonishment in the warden's eyes. *I told you so. What did you expect?* Miss Barlow was preoccupied with her forthcoming nuptials and, in Alice's view, had been unnecessarily dismissive of Polly's plight. Or perhaps Alice was being unfair. She couldn't bend everybody to her will, as her mother frequently pointed out.

'My lips are sealed,' said Isaac.

'Is she at home?'

'Would I have been waitin' on the street corner if she was?'

Alice frowned. 'Why aren't you at work?'

'Tha sounds like Silas.' His voice was tight.

'I'm sorry, I don't mean to.'

Isaac lengthened his stride and gave Alice a furious look. 'Me father's put me wi' the rollers an' I can't be doin' wi' it. I'm twenty-six, not some wet behind the ears lad.'

'Slow down,' said Alice. '*I* didn't put you with the rollers.'

Isaac ducked his head and grinned at her. 'Come for tea. Save me from their naggin'.'

'All right.'

They had reached the small and well-kept terraced house on the slope of Pond Street that Alice shared with her mother. 'I'd better leave a note,' she said.

Isaac followed her inside. 'Aunt Louisa's invited, if she's not workin'.'

Louisa Leigh had recently inherited a half-share in the hansom cab business she managed. In congratulating her, Alice had not been able to resist making the point that her mother managed her life without a man telling her what she should do. Of course, this set the two of them at loggerheads again. They were both entrenched in their positions, Louisa determined on a good marriage for her daughter, and Alice equally determined to find her own path, armed with the expensive education her mother had paid for in the hopes of securing an eligible bachelor. Then, Alice supposed, she must pretend all her married life that she was not as clever as her husband.

She found pencil and paper and left a note on the kitchen table while Isaac looked on. Alice peered over her shoulder at him. 'What are you smiling about?'

He shrugged. 'Nowt. Seein' you is allus a tonic.'

Isaac's adoptive parents, Silas and Harriet Hinchcliffe, owned a property in a wealthier suburb an omnibus ride across the town. They travelled there in companionable silence, sitting across from each other in the cramped interior of the lower deck. The two of them shared a secretive smile when, after a particularly sharp jolt, the portly man beside Alice began to loudly bemoan the state of the roads these days. The matronly woman sitting next to Isaac passed the time of day with him, commenting on the unusually changeable weather, Isaac nodding politely, the toe of his shoe tapping out a secret code against the toe of Alice's boot.

Later, she would remember the journey as a calm interlude before the storm.

Chapter 2

'Oh, look, he's walking, the little love!'

In the vestibule of the Hinchcliffe residence, Alice discarded her bonnet, dropped to her haunches and held out her arms. 'Teddy, can you come to me?'

Isaac looked on as the infant toddled determinedly towards Alice, socks puddling around his ankles, softly dimpled knees emerging from the hem of his night-shirt. He'd almost reached Alice's outstretched arms when he lost his footing on the polished wood surface, dropping onto his bottom, his mouth making an O of surprise. Alice scooped him into her arms.

Isaac laughed. 'They're like tiny drunkards, aren't they? Wobblin' all over the place.'

Taking Alice's elbow to help her up, he indulged in the fantasy, just for a moment, that they were a young married couple and this their child, their own child, not adopted, as Teddy was, as Isaac had been, all those years ago.

Alice rocked the baby against her shoulder. 'Poor Teddy, poor thing. Where is your mama?'

She moved through a shaft of sunlight that made a golden halo of her hair and intensified the cornflower blue of her eyes. Isaac cleared his throat. 'Tha's a natural,' he said.

'Oh no,' said Alice. 'You're not trying to marry me off, as well? My mother keeps a list of eligible suitors.'

Isaac grimaced. He doubted his name was on Aunt Louisa's list.

'Oh, don't feel too sorry for me,' said Alice. 'We've struck a bargain. Whenever she schemes it, I must endure a contrived meeting with a suitable young man. In return, I'm allowed to leave off the sewing and piano playing to volunteer at the House of Help, and pursue a project – well, it feels like more of a calling – I haven't yet told you about.'

What if he told her he had a suitor in mind, standing before her, to see how she would react, what her eyes might tell him. He could always make a joke of it if he saw horror in them, or confusion. Occasionally he wished they had not been raised alongside each other, that they could meet as the adults they now were. Then she might see him in a different light.

'Aren't you going to ask me what it is?' said Alice.

Isaac frowned. He hadn't been listening. Luckily, at that moment his father appeared.

'I turn me back for one second,' said Silas Hinchcliffe, 'an' the little varmint's escaped again. 'Ow do, Alice. I didn't hear you pair come in. Is your mother comin' for tea?'

'She's working, I'm afraid,' said Alice. 'I left her a note, though.'

'Somebody's got to keep thee in them fine clothes,' said Silas. He winked at her and turned to Isaac, tapping his arm lightly with a closed fist. 'Listen, son…' Then he seemed to check himself, and folded his lips.

'What?' said Isaac. His father only ever looked this discomforted when his wife was giving him a telling off.

Alice looked from Silas to Isaac and back. 'What's the matter, Uncle Silas?'

Silas gestured towards the closed door of the front parlour. 'Tha'd best go in. She'll have 'eard us an' – well, come an' see for theesen.'

A handful of worst-case scenarios flashed through Isaac's mind. He'd got a girl from Love Lane in trouble and she'd come calling. The landlord from the Blue Pig was pressing charges, although Isaac had paid for the damage done, and in any event he hadn't started the brawl. His father was removing him from the job on the rolling mill that Isaac had no aptitude for, although, surely, that humiliation would be meted out at the factory, not at home, and most certainly not, he hoped, in front of Alice.

Isaac followed Silas into the room, Alice bringing up the rear. His mother was sitting on the settee beside a handsome-looking woman Isaac placed in her late middle-age. A bulky and battered leather valise squatted by the woman's foot. A feeling he could not name washed over him. All he knew was that he was suddenly rooted to the spot, too afraid to complete the thought, the terrible suspicion, in his mind. A roaring in his ears muffled Alice's greeting to his mother.

'How are you, Aunt Harriet?' said Alice.

'This one is keeping me on my toes now he's found his feet.' Harriet took the child from Alice with a smile. Teddy slithered from her grip onto the rug and rolled the corner of it over himself like a blanket. 'But I'm all the better for seeing you, dear,' Harriet said.

The look she gave Isaac was filled with anxiety. 'You have a visitor, love.'

The stranger smiled, drawing his name out, her tone playful. 'Isaac. Don't you recognise me?'

He hadn't even the strength to shake his head, although he would only be denying what he already knew. The woman's face was freckled by the sun, like a field worker, her hair grey as steel under the wide-brimmed burgundy felt hat she wore. The skin around her brown eyes crinkled as she rose to her feet and held out her arms. 'Look at how tall you've gotten.'

Then he was in her arms, his nose clogged by the musky scent of her, horribly aware of his hands dangling by his sides. He was frozen, incapable of returning her embrace. He squeezed his eyes closed, as if that would make her disappear, or him. He wanted to walk out but wasn't even capable of that. When she stepped back – 'Let me look at you!' – and held him at arm's length, the air between them was too thick to breathe. Isaac looked sideways, towards the others. Why weren't they helping him?

Alice's face was set in an expression of polite enquiry. His parents were watching him carefully, Harriet smiling tentatively, Silas sombre.

The woman laughed and released him. She stroked his jawline. 'He does remember me,' she said, directing the comment towards his mother, 'even after all these years.' She smiled at Alice. 'And you're our Louisa's girl, aren't you? You're the spit of her. I'm Ginny.'

He could still feel the imprint of her fingers on his skin. The woman's next words fell like a boulder into his gut.

'I'm Isaac's mother.'

–

He was dumbfounded. The whole lot of them were behaving as if two decades of abandonment could be forgotten, wiped from the slate. Looking around the dining table, Isaac wondered at the ease with which his parents and Alice were conversing with this woman who called herself his mother. It was as if an elaborate joke was being played on him. He wished it was. But everyone continued in their assigned roles. Silas dished up baked cod and mint potatoes while Harriet explained that the baby, whom she had named Edward, although he'd been Teddy since birth, had been adopted from a poor young woman who had given birth while resident at the House of Help for Friendless Girls.

Isaac visualised himself upending the table and watching everything on it crash to the floor, putting an end to the charade.

'Well, you did a grand job looking after Isaac,' said Ginny. 'He's a fine young man.'

They all looked at Isaac, who stared at his plate.

Alice rescued him. 'Teddy coming to live with Aunt Harriet and Uncle Silas is how I first heard of the House of Help,' she said, 'and learned about all that the exceptional ladies who run the place do, helping fallen women and those not yet fallen, as well as orphans and women who simply need a temporary shelter. I volunteer there. It's very rewarding.'

Ginny chewed and swallowed the piece of fish she had speared on her fork and waved the implement in the air. 'Oh, Alice, I know all about being in that pit of despondency. Imagine being a young widow with a baby, cast out onto the street.' She looked at the fork in her hand. 'Driven out on the point of a pitchfork.'

Silas scoffed. 'I've 'eard it all now.' He explained to Alice: 'She were married to my older brother an' left me parents' farm after he died, left of her own free will to come here with this little chap.' He smiled at Isaac.

'Nobody chucked thee out. Oh Ginny, I'm rememberin' what you're like, now.'

Ginny glared at him then glanced at the others around the table and laughed. 'It's only a slight exaggeration, Silas, to say I was driven out. Why would I wait on your folks hand an' foot, and have no claim on the land wi' Peter dead and gone? A widow with a boy and no prospects?' She turned to Alice, lowering her voice conspiratorially. 'No. I'm glad I found Joe. We landed on our feet, all right. Gold mining, don't you know.'

'Gold mining?' said Alice, wonder in her voice. 'Joe is a gold miner?'

'Well, not as such,' said Ginny. She ignored Silas's snort of derision, keeping her gaze fixed on Alice. 'Me an' Joe ran a saloon bar in South Pass City.'

'South Pass City,' echoed Alice. 'It sounds so romantic.'

'Well, I don't know about that.' Ginny shook her head. 'Anyhow, all the miners came to us. We had a rum life. But the daft sod gambled it all away. Never did have much of a brain, that one.'

'Where is Joseph now?' said Harriet.

Ginny tilted her head, as if she was trying to remember where she had mislaid the man she had taken off to America with, leaving her five-year-old son to be raised by his uncle and aunt. Isaac, despite himself, wanted to hear the answer.

'I've no idea, love,' she said. 'I'd been savin' the dollars and dimes, on the quiet. Joe had got people after him, bad men, so I had no choice but to get away.' She raised her hands in a gesture of surrender. 'A long journey, a dangerous journey, but here I am.'

'Oh, my goodness,' said Harriet. 'That sounds quite frightening.'

'I don't regret any of it,' said Ginny. 'I saw a bit o' the world and learned a lot. Never say no to an adventure, that's my philosophy.'

Was this how she justified abandoning her son? Isaac watched Alice cut a potato into small pieces and feed them to Teddy, who sat on Silas's lap. She was rapt, hanging on this woman's every word.

'I would love to travel,' said Alice, wistfully, 'but I don't think my mother would allow it.'

'Why, you don't need her permission, or anybody else's,' said Ginny.

'Where *is* your mother?' said Harriet.

'Working,' said Alice.

Ginny cocked her head. 'What's our Louisa up to, these days? I remember her bein' in the doldrums.' She laughed, a little cruelly. 'I remember her workin' then an' all, day an' night. There has to be some respite from the daily grind.'

'Aunt Louisa's been a good mother to Alice,' said Isaac. 'Raising her alone, an' now trying to secure her future. She won't thank thee for advising her daughter to go runnin' off, away from her family, just because tha did.'

His cheeks reddened in the silence that followed. Alice reached across the table to touch his arm but he moved away. She sat back and sighed.

'Here's something to shock you all,' she said. 'I went into Jervis Court today.'

Isaac frowned, though he was glad of the change of subject. 'You din't tell me that's where you'd been.'

'What has tha mother told thee about gaddin' about in these places?' said Silas. 'This is what comes of not havin' a father to keep thee in check.'

Alice tilted her head, her smile impish. 'You do a well enough job, Uncle Silas.'

'What were you doing there?' said Harriet.

'I went to make a welfare check, on a woman who'd left the house before we could help her,' said Alice. 'Her husband is a rogue.' A shadow passed over her face, then she caught Isaac's eye and laughed. 'Do you know, he reminded me of you – in build and looks, I have to say, not temperament.'

'Then he must be a very handsome rogue,' said Ginny, putting her hand over his and squeezing his fingers. Isaac waited for her to relinquish her grip so that he could move his hands off the table, out of harm's way. He was a child of five again, tongue-tied and out of his depth.

Silas hadn't been fooled by Alice's laughter. 'So you met this man, this husband? Did he say owt to you?'

'No,' said Alice. She bent to kiss the top of Teddy's head, her cheeks colouring.

'Sure o' that?' muttered Isaac, but he was interrupted by Ginny, saving Alice from replying.

'I met my rogue here in town,' Ginny declared, and began to tell the tale of coming to Sheffield, widowed, little Isaac in tow, and meeting the love of her life. Here, Silas snorted again.

'Joseph Crookes,' he said. 'Crook by name and nature.'

'I was in love,' Ginny told Alice, who seemed to Isaac to be content to swallow whole everything this woman told her. 'And I knew Silas would look after the boy.'

The boy.

Silas clapped his hands together. 'Don't thank me. Harriet 'ere deserves all the credit, eh lad?' Isaac tried to muster a smile for his mother, for Harriet. Silas continued.

'Ginny weren't around for long. Took up wi' Joe an' hitched up her skirt an' off she flew.'

Harriet made disapproving sounds, but Ginny was laughing. 'Silas, you are terrible. As I said, Alice, I was in love and we do silly things, don't we, when we're in love? Do you have a beau?'

'A beau?' Alice shook her head. 'I have no desire to enlarge my menagerie of pets.'

'Alice's phrase du jour,' said Harriet. She smiled indulgently.

'I'm quoting an independent woman,' said Alice. 'A woman happy to remain a spinster.'

'Well, the spinster's missin' out,' said Ginny. Her laughter tinkled around the room like broken glass.

Isaac could bear it no longer. He gave in to the cold fury uncoiling in his belly. 'So tha's come back because tha's nowhere else to go, and here we all sit, pretendin' we're at some big family reunion?'

'Isaac!' Alice glared at him.

'Not at the table,' said Harriet, mildly.

'Oh, I'd be just the same.' Ginny leaned her shoulder against his in a grotesque display of affection that made him want to choke. 'Like mother like son, eh? Fiery souls.'

Isaac jerked away and scraped back his chair.

'Please don't get up,' said Harriet. 'I know you're upset, love, but we should remain civilised.'

Ginny seemed unperturbed. She reached across and patted his thigh. 'Stay a minute, will you? I've something you need to see.'

'Isaac,' said Alice, as Ginny left the room. The look of concern on Alice's face only stoked his anger. 'I know you've had a shock but there's no need to be rude.'

He gestured towards the door Ginny had left hanging open and said, a little too vehemently, hoping she might hear him, 'I've already got a mother, an' a father.'

He couldn't bear to look at his parents and could not say why. He was filled with a miserable sense of shame, and could not fathom that either.

'We've always told you the truth and we adopted you as our own, just as we have Teddy.' Harriet's voice wavered. She had never been able to bear children of her own. She'd had to settle for him.

'Tha's bein' childish,' said Silas. 'Be a man.'

Isaac looked away, shaking his head. Ridiculously, he was on the verge of tears. He was no more in control of his emotions than Teddy.

Ginny returned to a room heavy with the weight of unsaid words, humming a tune under her breath, seemingly oblivious to the tension in the air that whined in Isaac's ears. She leaned over his shoulder and placed a small half-circle of metal on the table by his plate. The fragment glinted silver in the light of the table candles.

'D'you remember this?' she said, her breath in his ear making the hairs on the back of his neck stand up.

Isaac leaned away. 'No,' he said, but picked up the piece of metal and feigned an examination of it, throwing a puzzled look at his mother, at Harriet, when she gasped in recognition.

'Yes, Harriet,' said Ginny. She sounded satisfied. 'This is my half of the silver dollar.' She sat down beside him. 'Do you still have yours?'

Isaac frowned and carefully set the half-coin on the table. 'I don't know what tha's on about.'

Ginny leaned forward, appealing to him with the same brown eyes he saw in the mirror. 'I sent the other piece to you, all the way from America, and I wrote that one day we would put the two halves together, to make a whole again. I made that promise to you, Isaac. To you.'

'That's a lovely gesture,' said Alice.

Isaac glared at her but Alice's eyes rested on the mutilated coin as if she was gazing on the world's greatest treasure hoard.

Ginny gave Harriet a sharp look. 'He did get the letter and the coin?'

Harriet nodded. 'Of course,' she murmured. 'We made sure to explain the sentiment behind it.'

'Well, then, where's your half?' said Ginny, to him.

'I must've lost it,' he said. He tried out a laugh. 'It were a long time ago, weren't it?'

'I suppose so.' Ginny leaned back in her chair, her mouth downturned. 'It doesn't matter, though I kept hold of my half all these years.'

There was a burning pain in Isaac's chest, like a hot coal. There was, after all, no satisfaction to be gained from hurting his mother, even if his callousness was as a mote of dust was to the moon, compared to hers. Now he could add guilt to the tumult of emotions he was trying so hard to conceal.

'Do you have accommodation in town?' said Harriet. She continued briskly when Ginny shook her head. 'Then you must stay with us, of course.'

After tea, the whisky bottle was produced and a toast made by Harriet to Ginny's unexpected but welcome return. Isaac forced the liquid down his throat. The woman who came to clean and occasionally cook for the Hinchcliffes had finished for the day so Ginny went with Alice to fetch towels and sheets and make up the bed in the spare room. Harriet excused herself to settle the baby, leaving Silas and Isaac to stew in one of their awkward silences.

Silas broke it. 'She's not a bad lass,' he said. 'Misguided, p'raps, when she were younger. She's come back because o' thee, tha knows.'

'Or because she's down on her luck,' said Isaac. He put on a show of yawning and stretching. 'I don't care, one way or t'other,' he said. 'I'm takin' Alice home and might as well stay on their settee tonight, all right?'

Silas nodded. 'Make sure tha doesn't skip off work tomorra, looks bad on me.'

'Aye, all reight, all reight.'

'Am just sayin', lad.'

–

Isaac scooped a handful of coins from the pot on the mantlepiece in his room and stuffed them into the pocket of his waistcoat. He would go to the pub after delivering Alice safely home, to try and drown his agitation in a few jars of ale. He had a key for Aunt Louisa's cottage but there were other settees – other beds – at his disposal. Pulling open the drawer of his bedside table, he took out a pack of cards and put them in the inside pocket of his jacket, being careful not to crush the loose cigarettes he'd stowed there. He closed the drawer and stood for a moment, unmoving. Finally, he drew the drawer open again, slowly, and, after another moment's hesitation, put his hand inside. With the tips of his fingers, Isaac found the scratchy wood on the joint at the very back where the paper lining was ripped. He glanced over his shoulder as his fingers closed over the fragment of metal hidden there.

His half.

'Isaac, what are you doing?'

He snatched his hand away and slammed closed the drawer.

It was Alice, calling from the foot of the stairs.

'Hold yer horses,' he shouted back, his voice hoarse. He sat on the edge of his bed. There was no number for the times he had lain here in the depths of the night, the sharp-edged talisman clutched in his small fist, praying for his mother to return. There must have come a day when that wish was made a final time, and then the dream abandoned.

She had deserted his prayers then. Isaac passed his hand over his eyes and told himself that none of it mattered, and that abandoned little boy no longer existed.

Chapter 3

He would be fifteen months old now, already walking, she imagined, and bravely uttering his first words. He would be calling another woman *Mama*, and finding his consolation in her arms.

Leaning against the hansom cab's cushioned back-rest, Hope tore her gaze away from the young woman steering a baby carriage along the pavement. She looked up instead, through the trapdoor in the roof, at a clear blue sky bisected by the driver's reins. Sometimes – most often when she saw a mother and child together – her sorrow swept over her like a wave and left her floundering. The rest of the time she counted her blessings, and they were many, considering the circumstances that had brought her to the House of Help.

Today, for example, was Thursday, her favourite day of the working week. She would be remaining late into the evening, teaching the night class for residents who wanted to improve their reading and writing. These classes were open to outsiders too, to townspeople who paid a fee that went into the thirsty coffers of the house. Raising funds and seeking donations of furniture and clothes was a Sisyphean task. Hope's role as deputy warden was unpaid, which helped matters. Her wealthy parents, when they failed to persuade her to leave a place that had first given her succour and then a job, provided Hope with a generous stipend, so horrified were they of seeing their daughter demeaned by a waged job.

Her father, in his letters, continued to express his desire for her to return home and assume her rightful name, the name he had bestowed upon her. She had proved her point, he asserted, and must now be assimilated back into polite society and find a suitable husband. Hope, named so by the good people of the House when she fetched up on their doorstep, had her qualms, her nagging doubts that she kept concealed, but there was one thing she knew for certain: there was no going back. Emma Hyde, and all that had happened to that unfortunate creature, was gone.

Her father might be more forceful in his demands, were it not for the fact she was now living permanently at Tylecote, the mansion of acquaintances of his on the outskirts of town, and travelling daily to Paradise Square. He would not have her live at the house, amongst women he denounced as *fallen* and *thieving*. For her part, Hope would prefer to stay with the women and the girls she had made it her life's mission to help, but decided this was a concession worth making.

Her mother, in her letters, was less forthright and a hundred times more hurtful. Her darling Emma was brave – braver than her mother could ever be – to remain in a town that contained the child she had given up, with people who were cognisant of her disgrace, change of name or not. Hope kept the circumstances of her child's conception in a padlocked box at the back of her mind. Even if she was able to confide in her parents about the trauma she'd endured, they would continue to view a pregnancy out of wedlock as a disgrace she had brought upon the family. Being taken by force was no excuse.

It didn't bear thinking about. So she counted her blessings instead.

The cab pulled up on the cobbles of Paradise Square and Hope passed a handful of shillings through the hatch to the driver and climbed down, reaching back inside for her basket.

'Ten o'clock, then?' he said. 'It'll not be me, but Arthur's a steady hand.'

'Yes,' said Hope. 'He's driven me before. Thank you.'

Clara was on her hands and knees, scrubbing the front step, a bucket of suds by her side. She sat back and shaded her eyes. 'Tha knows what, Hope, having the sun shinin' down makes this half the work. What's tha got for us today then?'

'A treat from the garden.' Hope lifted the lid of the basket and moved aside the muslin. The interior was crammed with large ripe strawberries, packed around a stoppered earthenware jug. 'From the hothouse,' she said, 'and fresh cream to go with them.'

'I'd best have a taste,' said Clara, wiping her hands on her apron and taking a strawberry. She bit into it and spoke around the mouthful. 'Tha knows, for quality control.'

'Take another,' said Hope. 'They won't last two minutes in this place.'

In the kitchen, two of the residents of the house were making ready for the arrival of Cook, who would prepare the hot midday meal and sort out something for tea. She ruled the kitchen with an iron fist, and only those residents tasked with helping her were allowed over the threshold outside mealtimes. Otherwise, the house would be out of food in no time. While the older resident, a nineteen-year-old rescued from a charge of vagrancy, tended the range, the younger girl, barely turned thirteen and returned from an unsuccessful domestic placing, was rubbing a cloth on the tabletop, creating an ever-widening circle of flour from what had probably been only a minor spill. The warden, sitting at her usual small table in the corner of the room, caught Hope's eye, nodded at the table and rolled her eyes.

'Did you bring more o' them cakes?' the girl said to Hope.

Hope shook her head. The previous day she had brought three paper bags filled with apple muffins. Now empty, the bags lay flattened and folded on the bureau, to be used for some other purpose. *Waste not, want not* was one of the mottoes of the house.

'They all went, I see,' she said.

'Have you brought owt, though?' The girl was eyeing the basket.

'Yes. Strawberries, to have at teatime. And cream. Good morning, Miss Barlow.'

Hope had never used the warden's given name, having come to the house as a girl in need – in dire need, fearing for her life – and by now *Hetty* would feel too strange on her tongue. Miss Barlow had protected her, had given her the courage to begin afresh, and helped Hope find her calling. All the riches in the world could not persuade her to leave this place. Certainly, her father could not, and nor could Angus, not that he would.

To hide the blush that rose in her cheeks at the thought of a man she had considered a good friend until only the day before, Hope turned her back on the warden and lifted the kettle from the range.

'Rosie is leaving us today and needs to go wi' a good recommendation,' said Miss Barlow. 'As for you pair, that'll do. Thank you.'

'But this damnable flour...' said the young girl.

'I'll clean it up,' said Hope, quickly. 'Go on now.'

'And if I hear language like that again,' said Miss Barlow, 'you'll be out on your ear, so think on.'

The two residents wished Hope a good morning as they left the room. They clattered upstairs, all the way up to the attic dorm they shared, their laughter floating down.

Miss Barlow tapped a pencil against her chin. 'Do we say Rosie's mended her ways?'

'Is her new employer aware of all the facts?'

'No,' said Miss Barlow. 'So I'd say nowt about it. If there's one thing she deserves it's a fresh start with a clean reputation.'

Rosie was sixteen years old, a workhouse runaway caught stealing food from the kitchen of the Victoria Hotel. She was going to a position in a nearby town, where she would be trained inhouse as a maid of all work. Hope glanced at the clock on the wall. One of today's tasks would be to walk the girl to the railway station for the midday train to Chesterfield. Once Rosie was earning a wage, she would be gently encouraged to reimburse the house for the new set of clothes with which she had been provided, and only once she could afford to do so. Some ex-residents were generous to the house, others were never heard from again. Amelia, housekeeper and Miss Barlow's daughter, denounced those who disappeared without a backward glance as ungrateful. Hope knew better. A fresh start sometimes meant obliterating what had gone before. Or trying to, at least.

Miss Barlow scribbled on the notepaper then held it before her eyes, arm outstretched. 'Sensible, willing to learn, hard worker,' she muttered. 'I keep putting it off but I don't think I can do wi'out reading spectacles. Then I'll have completed my journey into old age.'

Hope laughed. 'You're barely forty.'

'Said from the lower slopes of the hill I'm already over,' said Miss Barlow. She gave Hope a shrewd look. 'What's up?'

The question caught Hope off guard. 'What do you mean?'

'I can see there's summat on your mind.'

'Well, there is. It's Angus.' She put a hand over her mouth.

Miss Barlow raised an eyebrow. 'You're supposed to stopper your mouth before you let the cat out o' the bag, not after. He's proposed, has he?'

'What makes you say that?'

'Am I wrong?'

'Wrong about what?'

Amelia stood in the open doorway, her hands on her hips. 'Wrong about what?' she repeated. 'Summat else I'm the last to know about?'

Defeated, Hope collapsed into a chair. 'I shouldn't say. I haven't had time to consider my reply, and we have your wedding to look forward to, Miss Barlow. This can wait.'

'Don't worry about me,' said Miss Barlow. 'I'm hardly the blushin' young bride-to-be, am I? The more there is to celebrate, the better.'

'Is this Angus?' Amelia leaned against the kitchen bureau and folded her arms. 'Has he asked thee to marry him?' She snorted. 'Don't look at me like that. He set his sights on you a long time ago. I predicted it, as I recall.'

Hope opened her mouth to respond, but Amelia carried on. 'Here am I, doomed to spend the rest of my days keepin' this place in order, an' you,' she pointed at her mother, 'are getting wed to a rich widower in a few weeks, an' you' – turning the accusing finger on Hope – 'have the grandson of the bleedin' town crier goin' down on one knee.'

Miss Barlow laughed. 'Angus's grandfather is an alderman.'

Amelia shrugged. 'Town crier, alderman or suchlike. Makes no odds. There's nowt on the horizon for me, as per, except to walk my own mother down the aisle.'

Miss Barlow muttered under her breath. 'Who else would I ask?'

'Why, nobody,' said Amelia. 'I want to do it!'

Miss Barlow raised her voice to match Amelia's. 'Then what are you complainin' about?'

Hope looked from one to the other. 'Ladies, please. Angus hasn't asked me to marry him. We've merely started a conversation.'

'What does *that* mean?' said Amelia.

Hope blushed. 'Angus has asked me whether I might look upon him as more than a friend.'

'That's just the way your lot talk,' said Amelia. 'Round an' round the 'ouses. That's as near as makes no odds to an outright proposal.'

It had been, of course, and, she had realised subsequently, contrived by the people she was staying with, who were aware her parents would approve of the match and evidently felt able to act on Angus's behalf. He had been invited for an early supper and afterwards asked Hope to sit with him on a bench in the garden in the golden light of the fading day. Her hosts were curiously absent.

'How long,' Angus had asked, 'have we been friends?'

Hope had frowned. She had been picking the petals, one by one, from an oxeye daisy he'd plucked from the ground and presented to her. 'Two years? Nearly all the time I've been here. Why?'

He had leaned forward, clasping his hands between his knees. 'Then I can confide in you that I have fallen in love, that I have been falling in love, throughout all this time.'

Hope heard only that he had fallen in love, his subsequent words drowned out by that declaration. She stared at the back of his head, the half-shorn daisy dropping forgotten from her hand. He had met someone. She supposed that was inevitable, but she could not breathe, so unexpectedly crushed was she. Then Angus had turned to look at her, a mischievous smile playing at the corners of his mouth. 'Hope. Lovely Hope. Do you think you could ever consider me as more than merely a friend? Could you love me in return?'

'Look at her!' Amelia's words pierced Hope's reverie. 'She's miles away. I suppose I'll go.'

'I'm sorry,' said Hope. 'Go where?'

Miss Barlow smiled. 'There's somebody at the door, love. I asked you whether you'd go and see who it is while I finish this note, but Amelia can, just as easily.'

Amelia left the room, muttering about being everybody's dogsbody. The sound of the door knocker being slammed against the plate continued to echo through the house. Hope and the warden exchanged looks.

'Somebody's not lettin' up,' said Miss Barlow, rising from her chair.

The two women hurried out of the kitchen after Amelia, down the dimly lit hall. Clara poked her head out of the front parlour, eyebrows raised, and at that moment the banging stopped.

Amelia stood, her hand wrapped around the brass knob of the mortice lock, hesitating to open the door. Hope knew what she was thinking. Women in need rarely made so much noise when they turned up on the doorstep, while police officers and railway station porters delivering waifs and strays to the house were generally sensitive to the need not to alarm the inhabitants. This was more likely to be an impatient deliveryman, although they tended to come to the back of the house, or somebody with a grievance. The house had recently dealt with irate parents who, once their daughter had been found a job, turned up to demand she hand her wages over, even though they had thrown her onto the street. Miss Barlow had sent them packing.

Clara came into the hallway, wielding a broom, her jaw set.

'Clara, don't be daft,' said Miss Barlow. She nodded to Amelia, who pulled open the door.

There was nobody there.

'Well,' said Amelia.

Hope went to the threshold and looked around the square. The driver of a cab was waiting for two gentlemen in tailcoats and toppers to embark. He flicked the reins and the vehicle moved away, revealing the bright pinks and yellows of the flower cart in its regular spot, and pedestrians criss-crossing the square. A group of uniformed boys were making a racket outside the private school. A door opened, which acted to subdue them immediately, and they filed inside. Hope opened her mouth to reassure the others that high-spirited youths were no doubt to blame, playing the eternal game of knock and run, but the words died on her lips. A broad-shouldered man, bare-headed in dirt-streaked trousers and jerkin, was peering through the window of their front parlour, shielding his eyes with one muscular forearm. He held a hammer in his other hand.

The man straightened up, and saw her.

Hope stepped back and closed the door and turned the key in the lock in one swift motion, her heart beating fast. She stumbled backwards, colliding with Amelia, as another fusillade of knocks reverberated through the house.

'He's got a hammer,' she stammered.

'We do have some jobs need doin' round the house,' said Miss Barlow.

Their nervous laughter was cut short by another round of blows.

'He'd better not make a mess o' that door,' said Clara. 'It's only just been repainted an' the new lock put on.'

'He won't bust through that,' said Amelia.

'Fetch 'er out!' The yell made them all jump. 'Fetch 'er out now or tha'll know about it! I can hear thee in there cluckin' like hens!'

Miss Barlow drew a deep breath and yelled back. 'It's the police we'll be fetchin'!' She turned to Clara and lowered her voice. 'Will you go?'

'Aye.'

Clara rested the broom against the wall and turned on her heel.

'Go with her,' said Miss Barlow to Amelia.

Clara and Amelia hurried towards the back of the house to exit through the backyard into the gennel and set off towards the nearest police station in Castle Green. The station was less than half a mile away but the route through town would be busy. The women would hopefully encounter a bobby en route.

Hope rested her hand against the doorframe and called out as steadily as she could: 'Who are you looking for?'

'I'll tell yer who I'm lookin' for.' He kicked the door. 'Me wife, Polly Bramall. I know yer in there, Poll, hidin' behind the skirts o' these interferin' bitches. Tha's gone too far this time.'

'I'm sorry, Mr Bramall,' said Hope. 'Polly isn't here. She did seek our help, but she left and hasn't returned.'

'Don't gi' me that. Nowhere else for her to run. Are you the bitch that came nosin' round?'

Miss Barlow mouthed the word, *Alice*. 'Mr Bramall,' she called, 'the lass who came to see you was worried about Polly's welfare, an' it looks like with good cause. We've sent for the police.'

Hope flinched when a door slammed somewhere above her head. She went to the foot of the stairs, ready to warn anybody who attempted to descend to return to their dorm and remain there. When the man spoke again, his tone was conciliatory.

'Look, I only want to see 'er, make sure she's all right. Polly, love. Come on. Let me in.'

'How long has she been missing?' said Miss Barlow.

'Since yesterday evenin'. I'm reight worried.' His voice roughened. 'Oh, 'ey up. Here she comes. Best let us in now, eh? Wouldn't want—'

Hope clapped her hand over her mouth when his voice was drowned out by a shriek. It was a woman's terrified cry. Miss Barlow didn't hesitate. She turned the key in the lock and threw open the door.

The woman was shoved over the threshold, her bonnet askew and blonde hair falling over her face. He came in behind her.

It was Alice. Hope reached for her but he jerked her back against his body, as easily as if she was a ragdoll. Alice gasped when his arm went across her throat. She attempted to kick him in the shin with the heel of her boot and tugged at the arm restraining her. He tightened his grip and roared in her ear, 'BE STILL.'

'Alice, do as he says,' said Miss Barlow.

Hope was astonished to hear her speak so calmly. She would take her lead from the warden. 'We haven't been lying to you,' she said, keeping her eyes fixed on the man's face, horribly aware of the hammer he was gently swinging back and forth. 'Polly isn't here.'

'But the police will be,' said Miss Barlow, making a point of glancing behind him at the door that stood wide open. 'Any minute now.'

Hope saw the uncertainty in his eyes. 'Then where is she?' he said, moving further into the hallway, dragging Alice along with him. 'Tell me where she is an' I'll leave thee in peace.'

'We told you, we don't know,' said Miss Barlow. 'Please let Miss Leigh go.'

His lip curled. 'Tha can 'av her.'

Alice stumbled as he thrust her away and, once again, Hope reached out for her, keeping her gaze fastened on the man. Instead of accepting Hope's embrace, Alice turned on him. 'How dare you come here, frightening women? You're no better than a wild animal!'

He ignored her and strode to the foot of the stairs. 'Who's up there, then? What if I go an' take a look? You hidin' up there, Polly?'

'You're a bully and a coward,' Alice continued. 'You should be locked up.'

'Hush, Alice,' said Miss Barlow. 'If I were you, Mr Bramall, I'd scarper. You go up there an' you'll be trapped, won't you, once the police come? Leave now and we'll say no more about it.'

'Disgusting animal,' said Alice. 'No wonder Polly—'

Hope talked over her. 'Mr Bramall, your wife is not here. We did try to help her, that's true. She decided to return home to you. You should take your leave now.'

Whether it was her words or the warden's – certainly, Alice wasn't helping the situation – the man paused, his foot on the first tread of the staircase. 'Polly! Get down 'ere!'

Nobody moved. Alice, thankfully, had subsided. She was pressing at her throat with shaking fingers.

'You're facing arrest for assault against an agent of the house,' said Hope.

'It's time you went,' said Miss Barlow.

The women shrank back against the wall as he stalked to the door. He glared at Alice. 'Tha'd do well to stop puttin' ideas in people's minds or tha'll get what's comin' to thee.'

Alice followed him to the threshold. 'I'm not afraid of you,' she called after him.

He threw his parting shot over his shoulder as he trotted away. 'I'll be back to torch this place an' all you women in it, an' the wife an' all. Tell her that from me.'

And he was gone.

Tears welled in Hope's eyes. 'My goodness,' she said, but could not continue.

Alice, white-faced, turned to the warden. '*Has* Polly returned?'

Miss Barlow put a reassuring hand on Hope's shoulder. 'He'll be picked up by the police, don't you worry, either of you.'

'But where is she?' said Alice.

Hugging her elbows, Hope took a deep breath. 'We must tell the police that he threatened us, threatened the house,' she said. Alice was glaring at her. 'What is it?'

'What about Polly?'

'No, she's not returned, Alice, despite your efforts,' said Miss Barlow. 'You know there's only so much we can do.'

Alice threw up her hands.

'She's gone to a neighbour, perhaps,' said Hope gently, 'or a family member.'

'The neighbour I saw was afraid of him,' said Alice. 'And Polly has no family. She told us that, when she first came here – when she first came here wanting help!' She stalked back to the door. Her shoulders sagged. 'Here they come.'

Hope came up alongside Alice. The local beat constable was hurrying up the square, flanked by Amelia and Clara. 'It will be all right,' said Hope. Empty words were all she had to offer. She couldn't shake from her mind the fury on the man's face, or the angry words he had spat out. If Polly had found the courage to leave, Hope prayed her husband would never find her.

Chapter 4

The redbrick façade was unadorned, presenting an unfashionably mundane face to the world. But appearances could be deceptive, Alice knew. The Gower Street library contained worlds.

Isaac had taken the books from her arms on Alice's front doorstep and commenced to tease her about them as the two friends strolled into town. It was a warm and humid Saturday afternoon and Alice had the dull ache across her forehead that meant a storm was coming. Her mother had insisted she wear the new fur-edged capelet that had cost Louisa seven shillings. 'Just give it an airing,' she'd said.

Alice had rolled her eyes. 'I'm only running an errand,' she gestured to Isaac, 'with him in tow.'

'*Him?*' said Isaac. 'I suppose it's not worth lookin' fine for me.'

Alice wasn't sure whether this was a serious complaint or whether Isaac was teasing her. It was probably the latter but she took the capelet from her mother's hands. 'I don't see how a visit to the library is a special occasion.'

Louisa had smiled. 'Who's to say you won't meet a fine young gentleman there, one that loves books as much as thee?'

'She's *going* wi' a fine young gentleman,' said Isaac. 'Tho' I can't say I love books like Alice does.'

On the corner of Gower Street, he hopped off the pavement so he could get ahead of her, walking backwards and brandishing one of the books. Alice grimaced sympathetically at a man who was forced to dodge out of Isaac's path but was disinclined to scold him. She was enjoying his sunny mood. It was a welcome change from Isaac's moroseness of late, which had to do with the return of his mother.

'This one,' he said, 'what's it about then?'

'It's about the dangers of playing God,' said Alice. She bit her lip. It had been several days since Polly Bramall's husband had shown up at the House of Help. According to Miss Barlow, who was being kept up to date on developments by the police, Polly had not returned home and Mr Bramall was languishing in a cell awaiting a magistrates' court appearance on charges of threatening behaviour and assault. He had a criminal record and jail was on the cards. Alice could be grateful for that small mercy, although it did nothing to assuage the guilt she felt, even as she told herself that the person truly at fault was the poor woman's husband. Had she made Polly's situation worse by meddling? Alice had tried to talk to Isaac about it – had even confided in him about being manhandled, a detail she would keep from her mother – but all Isaac had said was that he'd hunt down Alfie Bramall himself and see how brave he was squaring up to a man instead of a bunch of weak women. He hadn't understood why Alice took umbrage at this.

'Playin' God, eh?' Isaac raised his hands into claws and growled. 'I thought tha said it were about a monster bein' brought to life?'

Alice laughed. 'I did. You do listen to me, after all. You ought to borrow it, provided there's no waiting list.'

'Hmm. Bit too far-fetched for me.' He fell back into step alongside her. 'An' this one. A ghost wandering the moors, was it? Did it not scare you, readin' it?'

'I don't scare that easily.' Alice smiled. After finishing the novel, she had slid into bed and pulled the sheets over her head, convinced if she peeked out a ghoul would be waiting in the corner of the room, emerging from the blackness of another realm to claim her. 'Isaac, you should exercise your imagination more.'

'I told thee,' he said, 'I can't be doin' wi' made-up stuff. Men like facts, not fiction. Women are...' he seemed to search for the word '... softer.'

Alice rolled her eyes and yanked open the door to the library.

'I should've opened that for thee,' said Isaac.

He followed Alice to the long walnut counter in the borrowers' lobby and deposited the books on the polished surface.

'I'm capable of opening a door, Isaac,' she said, catching the eye of one of the clerks.

The young man came forward with alacrity, slipping ahead of another clerk making a beeline for her, and smiled warmly over the top of his halfmoon spectacles. He had a short, tufted beard on his chin that always brought to her mind a goat.

'Miss Leigh,' he said. 'Marvellous to see you again.'

Alice couldn't see how this remark warranted the scowl Isaac threw his way.

'I'm goin' upstairs to the news room,' Isaac said, setting off towards the staircase, 'to see what marvellous things are happenin' in the real world.'

The newspaper room was a male domain, while the smaller room beside it was reserved for women and tended to be stocked with magazines and recipe books. Alice had, once, ventured into the news room, wrinkling her nose at the fug that hung in the air, but soon retreated under the open glares of the occupants. 'I might just as well have entered a public urinal,' she had told Isaac. She enjoyed making him guffaw with laughter.

A third member of staff entered through a door from the stacks, so that she now faced three young men behind the counter, all smiling at her. 'Shall I fetch out the list, Miss Leigh, for your perusal?' said Mr Billy Goat.

Alice offered her widest, most sincere smile. 'I won't be borrowing from the lending library today,' she said. 'I'd like to look at some reference books on a particular topic, if I may? Anything you have, anything at all, locally and nationally, that can be brought to the ladies' reading room? And I'd like to take notes, if you could furnish me with writing materials?'

Mr Goat raised his eyebrows. 'I shall see what I can do, Miss Leigh. And the topic?'

Alice lifted her chin. 'The female suffrage movement.'

—

She nodded absently when Isaac found her surrounded by textbooks and pamphlets and announced he was going down to the Corner Pin for a pint of porter and would return at six o'clock, when the library closed.

She had been in the act of writing down the address of a local women's suffrage committee that seemed to meet only sporadically, but put down her pen after Isaac's interruption, sat back and sighed. There were some small victories to cheer, a few crumbs amongst precious little else. Women were now permitted to own property in their own name, while almost a decade ago women who lived on the Isle of Man – she had to refer to an atlas to see where that was – were granted suffrage. In 1882, just before Alice turned fifteen years of age, Josephine Butler had come to Sheffield to rally support for the cause. There was an ongoing and seemingly active campaign to build support for suffrage amongst working women, but it was in Manchester. Taking herself off to that town to lend her support would test her mother's patience a little too far.

Mr Goat strolled towards her. He was the sort of fellow her mother might add to her list of suitors, with his starched collar and pocket watch. Louisa would ask him what he earned and he would talk earnestly about the increasing popularity of libraries and how one day he would have his own to run. Alice frowned. That wasn't an altogether unattractive prospect.

'Have you found what you're looking for, Miss Leigh?'

She shook her head. 'Plenty of talk of female enfranchisement in committees run by men. Failed attempt after failed attempt to make it lawful for women to vote, obviously all made by male politicians for there are no females in power. There's no real impetus for change, no passion. Where's the *action*?'

The clerk nodded sympathetically. 'They do say the pen is mightier than the sword.'

'And I say actions speak louder than words. And why must progress be so painfully slow?'

'Miss Leigh, patience is a virtue.'

'Does that make impatience a sin?' She folded her arms, combatively. She was enjoying this conversation. 'Am I a sinner, sir, for asking for equality?'

'Hmm.' He stroked his tufty beard. 'Do you know our kingdom's first female political association was created in

47

this very town many years ago, by women who had been involved in the Chartist movement?'

'I've been reading about it.' Alice smiled. 'You're a supporter of the cause?'

He spread his hands as if to say *of course*.

'Many men,' said Alice, 'in fact, I would say the vast majority of men, aren't.'

'Would that include your companion?'

Alice narrowed her eyes, uncomfortable on two fronts. Firstly, that there was an implied criticism of Isaac in his question, and secondly, that the clerk was really asking something else entirely. She supposed it was her own fault, for brazenly engaging in conversation. She got to her feet and gestured to the document-strewn desk.

'Thank you for your assistance today.'

The clerk looked crestfallen but quickly recovered himself. 'I hope to see you again soon, Miss Leigh.'

Alice waited on the doorstep of the library for Isaac to return from the Corner Pin, fielding an enquiry from another clerk about her wellbeing by telling him her companion was on his way. The clerk reminded her the library was due to close and withdrew. Perhaps Isaac had met acquaintances and lost track of time. The public house he had gone to straddled the junction of Gower Street and Carlisle Street and was one of two dozen pubs and beer houses in a half mile radius serving thirsty steelworkers coming off shift from the giant works of Bessemer's, Cammell's, Atlas and the rest, including Hinchcliffe & Son, where Isaac remained unhappily employed under the weight of *& Son*. Alice had yet to discover a firm's name emblazoned on one of the towering buildings with the epithet *& Daughter*. The very idea would make Isaac laugh. She would have to remember to mention it to him, to watch his face light up at her expense. He'd been what her mother would call a *mardy arse* ever since Ginny had returned.

Now, *she* was an outspoken sort. Alice must rally her to the cause, enlist her help in creating a new, vibrant group. The local women's suffrage committee had been active once but seemed to have lost momentum in recent years. It had been created in 1864, the same year as the Great Sheffield Flood. For as long as she could remember, Alice had been regaled with tales about the Dale Dyke Dam burst by her mother, whose life was almost claimed by the deluge, and by her aunt and uncle, who were also swept up in the disaster. Aunt Harriet had lost a cousin, aged only six, and Alice, born three years later, had been named for that poor little girl. Any women's group that Alice created would not be a talking shop. Then what would it be? How might she lobby for change? Through the direct action she had spoken of to the library clerk?

Her train of thought was interrupted by the sight of Isaac rounding the corner. They raised a hand to each other in salute at the same moment, her involuntary smile of delight matched by the grin on Isaac's face. Above his head, the sky was the colour of slate. A flash of lightning was followed a few seconds later by a distant rumble of thunder, sounding in her ears like suppressed rage.

They hurried through streets that had been sun-dappled and were now in shadow, as if a cloak had been thrown over the world. Alice felt the first fat drops of rain on the hood of her cape and took Isaac's hand, quickening her pace.

'So you see,' she said, 'we need to do more, to demonstrate the strength of feeling. Something that will attract attention, perhaps even garner a newspaper headline.'

'We?' said Isaac, pulling her back towards him. 'In case you haven't noticed, I'm a man.' He bent to say these words in her ear as a cart clattered past noisily and she smelled the beer on his breath, the stale smoke on his clothes; manly odours that stirred a nameless emotion in her gut. Sometimes she forgot they were no longer children.

'Well, not you, obviously. The whole world already revolves around you.' She lifted her chin defiantly when Isaac laughed. 'I shall create a stir. Wait and see. I shall enlist Ginny. She's very worldly.'

The mention of his mother's name brought that familiar scowl to Isaac's face, and his mood changed in an instant. He increased the length of his stride so that Alice had to trot to keep up with him. She let go of his hand.

'Isaac, wait.'

He rounded on her. 'Why's tha so impressed by that woman? And why'd you want to act like a man?'

'I don't!'

'I suppose you'll be wearin' tailcoats an' a top hat next.'

'Lend me your britches,' Alice said, 'and I'll give you this dress to wear.'

Isaac's mouth twitched. Alice put her hands on her hips.

'Now?' He made a show of looking around. 'That'll create a stir.'

They stood smiling at each other in the middle of the rain-speckled pavement. Surely the downpour was only moments away. Alice tore her gaze from the generous curve of his lips. 'And then you *will* be part of my campaign. We'll be in it together.'

'Alice, I'll do owt you ask o' me' – he took her hand as the heavens opened – 'except to dress up like a woman. Come on, or we'll be drowned rats.'

Isaac left her on her doorstep, turning up his collar and explaining he had somewhere important to be, before hurrying away without explanation. Alice was sorry to see him go but, on entering the house and hearing voices from the front room, she decided it was probably a blessing. Ginny was sitting on the settee, sipping from one of the decorative sherry glasses that Alice had only ever seen behind the glass of the display cabinet. Ginny must have brought the sherry. Her mother didn't touch alcohol and never had, as far as Alice knew. Louisa sat in her chair by the side of the hearth, drinking tea. She had a pained expression on her face but mustered a smile for her daughter.

'You've not brought any books back, love.'

'Not today, no.' Alice turned to Ginny. 'I decided to do some research instead, into the female suffrage movement. You inspired me, Ginny, with your stories of the women of Wyoming.'

'Ginny, is it?' said her mother, raising an eyebrow.

'Oh, Louisa,' said Ginny. 'Don't fret. We've never stood on ceremony, have we? And Mrs Hinchcliffe is such a mouthful.'

Louisa gave her a speculative look. 'So you never married Joseph Crookes.'

Ginny swallowed her sherry. 'I was just getting to that part of the story. Alice, fetch the bottle from the kitchen, would you? It's on the dresser. Are you sure you won't take a drink?'

The second question was directed at Louisa, who merely shook her head.

Alice eyed the teapot. 'Is there any left?'

'Aye,' said Louisa. 'It's just brewed. Where's Isaac? I thought he were stayin' for tea.'

Alice glanced at Ginny. 'He had something to do. He was very mysterious about it, too. I'm sure he would have shown his face, Ginny, if he'd known you were here.'

Ginny shook her head. 'That's kind o' you to say, but I think it's the opposite. He's avoiding me. I must say it's hurtful.'

'Well,' said Louisa, 'it's a shock for the poor lad. How long has it been, and then you turn up out of the blue an' expect to pick up where you left off?'

'Mother!' said Alice.

'Not quite where I left off,' said Ginny, with a sly smile that Alice couldn't interpret. 'We've both come a long way, Lou, haven't we?' She reached out to clutch Alice's hand. 'I can see Isaac thinks the world of you, my lovely. Put in a good word for me? I am his mother, after all.'

'He'll come around,' said Alice. 'I'm sure of it.' Sure of no such thing, she made the excuse of going to the window to escape Ginny's grasp. Rain lashed against the pane. 'Listen to that.'

'It'll clear the air,' said Louisa.

Ginny tapped a fingernail against her empty glass.

'Oh!' said Alice. She showed them the damp hem of her dress. 'I'll be back in two shakes and will fetch your drink.'

She changed into a housedress and closed the window of her bedroom that she'd earlier lifted a couple of inches. The weather changed quicker than Isaac's moods. The boards beneath the window were speckled with rain but, she decided, not enough to need mopping. Running downstairs to the murmur of conversation from the front room, Alice went into the kitchen, took a cup from the cupboard above the sink and the milk from the cold shelf in the pantry. Hooking the cup handle around her thumb, she picked up the sherry bottle and, hands full, returned to the front room. Ginny was relating her tale, Alice's mother regarding her with a sceptical expression on her face, which Alice considered to be unfair. She was probably jealous of the other woman's adventures, having never herself ventured beyond the town boundary.

Alice replenished Ginny's glass and perched on the arm of the settee, swiftly becoming engrossed again in a story she'd already heard at the Hinchcliffes.

Her mother shook her head when Ginny got to the part about Joe losing everything in a game of cards. 'That sounds about right,' Louisa said, a grim tone to her voice. It was the only comment she made for the duration of the tale. Alice wondered what the relationship was between the two older women. Perhaps this was something she could ask Ginny about, ideally when they were alone, and learn something about her mother's past, and perhaps even about the identity of her father. With no specific memory to call on, Alice was nevertheless certain she must, as a child, have pressed her mother on the subject, and over time come to the realisation there would be no answers forthcoming, and it would be better if she stopped asking.

What little information she had gleaned came from her aunt and uncle, and generally through eavesdropping on their conversations. Louisa had been engaged once, or almost, but rejected her suitor. Alice had the impression that this suitor wasn't her father, although she couldn't say why. Louisa had made a good life for herself and her daughter, and Alice should be grateful. That was what

Uncle Silas told her whenever she tried to push at the closed door of the past. Closed, and locked.

Isaac was no help. He'd been five when Alice was born and said he had only a hazy recollection of a baby keeping him awake with her constant grizzling. Alice already knew that, after her birth, her mother had stayed with the Hinchcliffes for a little while before she found the cottage to rent. What might her mother say now, if Alice asked her outright who her father was? She didn't dare, that was the truth of it.

A silence had fallen. Alice rushed to fill it. 'Ginny,' she said. 'I thought you might be able to help me with the cause of female suffrage, as you've come from a place where women can vote and you must know a little about it.'

'Female what?' said Ginny.

'Suffrage,' said Louisa, heavily. 'The right to vote. Alice has been non-stop about it since your return. I think you must've put ideas in her head.'

'They were already there!' said Alice, affronted.

'Suffrage,' said Ginny. 'I've not heard that word before.' She shook her head. 'I never voted. I don't think it would've been allowed, bein' a foreigner. I've never been interested in politics, anyway.'

'But all women should have the same right as the women of Wyoming,' said Alice. She liked the sound of that. *The women of Wyoming.* 'And we don't even have to travel so far to find enlightenment. There's an island not two hundred miles from here that has granted female suffrage. Women can vote in elections!'

She sighed in exasperation at the blank look on her mother's face.

'The place is called the Isle of Man, Mother. It sits in the middle of the Irish Sea.'

'Never heard of it,' said Louisa.

'Well, all right,' said Alice. Neither had she but admitting her ignorance felt like conceding a point. 'But do you know, I discovered today that there was a rally here, in Sheffield, organised by Josephine Butler. She spoke at Cutlers' Hall and was the only woman on the platform, and the whole thing chaired by a man, which is typical isn't it?' She paused to breathe. 'But that's not the point, not really. Mrs Butler said we should wage war on the laws that curtail women's freedom, wage war to the death.'

'I've never heard of her, either,' said Louisa faintly.

Ginny laughed. 'Is this what happens when you over-educate girls, Louisa?'

Alice decided she'd ignore *that* remark and ploughed on. 'But weren't you aware at the time, Mother? I read that she created quite a stir. I thought you might have attended the rally.'

'I expect I were busy raisin' a bairn,' said Louisa, 'an' workin' all the hours God sends.'

Alice shook her head impatiently. 'Did you know that it was only earlier this decade that the age of consent was raised from thirteen to sixteen? Can you imagine? Mrs Butler played a role in that change, and she campaigns for female suffrage and she is a friend to fallen women. Prostitutes!'

Ginny laughed and cut her eyes at Louisa. ''Ey up.'

'Alice!' her mother said, although she was staring at Ginny. 'I din't raise you to be vulgar. I think this conversation's over.'

Ginny stood up, a little unsteadily. 'Nature calls,' she said.

After she had left the room, Louisa turned to Alice. 'Listen, love. I know Ginny of old. She likes to spin a yarn and she likes to stir the pot.'

Alice frowned. 'What do you mean?'

'Don't be so trustin', that's all. Mischief follows that one round. An' who's to say she ever even lived in this Wyoming place? Joe Crookes is real enough, or was. I wouldn't set much store by owt else she tells you.'

'You sound like Uncle Silas.'

'Aye, well, he knows her of old, an' all. Just be careful, that's all I'm sayin'.'

'All right.'

When Ginny returned, she winked at Alice. 'My ears have been burning.'

'Oh no,' said Alice. 'I was just telling Mother that I think Josephine Butler might be interested in the work being done by the House of Help. I shall put that in my letter to her. I'm going to write to her.'

'Surely she's an old lady now?' said Ginny.

'Not that old. I'll get her advice, on how to proceed.'

'Wi' what?' said Louisa.

Had her mother been listening to a word she'd said, or was she so preoccupied with Ginny's doings? Alice gathered all her patience. 'Female suffrage. I need to know what I should do. When I join the women's suffrage committee, or create my own group, I must come armed with ideas.'

Ginny held out her glass for more sherry, looking at Louisa, who sat stoney-faced while Alice poured. 'Lou, I ran a saloon bar. I've a high tolerance and I hope that you, of all people, aren't sitting in judgement. Will you take a drink, Alice?'

She might have, were it not for her mother's obvious discomfort. 'No, thank you,' she said.

'I do have a word of advice for you,' said Ginny, 'speaking woman to woman.'

'Yes?' Alice was flattered. Ginny didn't look upon her and see a child as her mother did. Ginny took her concerns seriously.

'We women have other means to bend the will of a man to ours,' said Ginny. 'There's no need to be shrill. A lovely looking lass like you can have any man wrapped round your little finger in no time.'

Alice hid her disappointment behind a polite smile. She would not waste her breath trying to explain to Ginny how she had missed the point. She recalled her conversation with the library clerk. Men were complacent, and why wouldn't they be? The world was set up in their favour. The fight for equality could only be waged by women. Why not her?

Chapter 5

His father had steel in his blood.

Isaac had been told the tale many times, how Silas had, as a youth, run away from his parents' farm, over the hills and far away to the fabled heart of the kingdom's steel industry. How he had almost lost his life in the Dale Dyke Dam burst, and how it had been his good fortune that the disaster brought him into Harriet's orbit. How, from lowly apprentice to steel factory owner, Silas had realised his ambition and now employed a workforce of two hundred men manufacturing armour plate and gun barrels.

'Instruments o' war made by Hinchcliffe & Son,' said Isaac, 'an' the demand grows an' grows. Me father's in his element an' that element is iron.'

'I take it you're the son, then.'

Isaac disentangled himself from the crumpled sheets, stood and flexed his shoulders. 'Aye, though that's stretchin' the truth. I'm his brother's lad. He died an' me mother ran off an' Silas adopted me when I were a little lad.'

'So, you fell on your feet.'

Isaac's eyes roved over the naked form of the young woman in the bed. Her skin was burnished by the glow from the lamp beside the bed, her full lips parted in a half-smile as she watched him observing her. She was perfect, like a painting. All he knew about Dolly, apart from her name – and even that might not be her real name – was that she was new to the house in Love Lane, and new to the world's oldest profession. She was freshly complexioned with an air of innocence about her despite the acts the two of them had been engaged in the past hour.

'How old are you?' he said.

'Nineteen.' She pulled up the sheet to cover her nakedness. 'Why d'you want to know? Are you a policeman?'

Isaac scoffed. 'No.'

He went to the window and lifted the net, yawning and scratching his belly as he peered outside. Lights glowed fuzzily behind half a dozen windows in the houses across the street, workers already rousing themselves for the early shift or returning to their beds from a night's labour. Alice would be sleeping soundly in her bed, dreaming an innocent's dreams, an idealist who was ignorant of the ways of the world. God love her for trying to make a difference. A thought occurred to him. 'Dolly, has tha ever heard o' the House of Help?'

'Another question.'

He turned to her, letting the net fall. 'They help lasses. A friend o' mine's involved. I could ask her to take thee there.'

'What for?'

'Well, they'd get thee a job, a proper job, in service or summat. Tha'd not have to' – he paused, aware of the incongruity of the situation, and of his nakedness – 'do this.'

She pouted. 'An' there I went thinkin' you liked what I do.'

'Aye.' Isaac laughed, embarrassed. 'I don't know what I'm on about, love.'

Dolly turned her back on him, her long dark hair fanning across the pillow. 'I picked the lesser o' two evils, coming here.'

'Oh aye?' He told himself to stop thinking about Alice. She didn't belong in this room, prompting him to make daft suggestions. Dolly was a grown woman, and not his responsibility. 'What was the other one?'

'Not telling, constable. You'd best get dressed, love, or Ma will be knockin' on the door.'

Isaac sighed. 'Reight enough.'

He pulled on his trousers, shirt and waistcoat and retrieved his cap, hesitating at the door. 'I'll maybe see thee again, Dolly.'

She didn't reply and Isaac saw from the slight rise and fall of her shoulder under the thin sheet that she had fallen asleep. Her scent clung to him as he quietly let himself out.

Daybreak caught up with him as he walked towards the banks of the Don, the mild air filled with the shouts of deliverymen, the rumble of the wheels of barrows, carts and carriages and the rhythmic clop and canter of horses' hooves. He was making his way through a familiar forest, where brick chimneys were the towering trees, releasing columns of smoke to rise and scatter, their burning scent filling his nostrils. Crossing the Don at Lady's Bridge, he continued along the flat stretch of the Wicker, passing under the wide arches of the railway viaduct and on towards the dense copse of factories beyond Savile Street. His path brought him within spitting distance of the Gower Street library.

Warmth coiled from the pit of Isaac's stomach when he thought about Alice, along with a desperate yearning that he knew no other woman would ever satisfy. Strolling to that library, Alice on his arm, he had known what a fine-looking pair they made and challenged with his eyes every passing man who dared to glance her way, and there were many who did. This, and the recollection of her excited chatter over some women's rights twaddle, made him smile as he trotted across Occupation Road. Women's rights. Well, Alice had always had her passing fads and this was only the latest. Her passionate nature was one of the many things he loved about her. When, he wondered, hopping into the gutter to allow a woman pushing a pram to have the pavement, would he work up the nerve to tell her how he felt? It had better be before Alice was pushing a pram of her own, married to another man when Isaac knew he and she were meant to be together.

He had kissed her on the lips, once, on the day she turned twenty. They had been messing about, chucking bits of birthday cake at each other, after all the others had gone to bed. They'd drunk too much beer and the two of them were giddy, like little kids again, chasing each other around the kitchen table, until Isaac slipped and Alice reached out to save him from falling, pulling him towards her, their faces inches apart. Buttercream was smeared across her chin and he wiped it off with his thumb and, without really intending to, kissed her. Her mouth tasted sweet and her lips were soft. The heat of a furnace blast filled his chest. She was kissing him back. But when they broke apart Alice's eyes had widened in what he assumed was shock. Isaac had lost his nerve, had laughed it off, and she had joined in, with what he took for relief. A birthday kiss, nothing more.

They were not related but had called each other cousin all their lives. How was he ever to cross that chasm, to make the leap to lover? He might land safely in her arms, or she might reject him, laugh, even, in the face of his confession. She would assure him their friendship would continue but his dreams would be burned to slag. He would be forced to carry within him forever the furnace blast heat of that single shared kiss.

Isaac strode along the deserted pavement in front of the tall iron gates of the main entrance to Hinchcliffe & Son. The day shift workers were already inside. He was late. He let himself in through the side entrance, trotted across a yard busy with men loading and unloading carts and barrows, and into the office where the time cards were kept. From there, he opened a door that led into a narrow corridor with whitewashed stone walls, the deafening roar and grind of the factory floor beyond the entryway at the end of the passage filling his ears. His gut contracted when he saw his father conferring with one of the foremen at the far end of the corridor. Silas looked up and gestured for Isaac to join him, then finished his conversation with the foreman. The man gave Isaac a brisk nod and disappeared down the steps that led to the factory floor.

'Where's tha bin?' Silas said, when Isaac reached him. He was frowning impatiently but it was the wounded look in his eyes that penetrated Isaac's disregard and pricked at his conscience.

'Got waylaid,' he mumbled.

Silas shook his head. 'Tha's let me down again, lad. Tha's let me down again.'

—

Isaac had been absent from the previous three Hinchcliffe Sunday dinners but Alice had prevailed on him so here he was, slouched at one end of the kitchen table. He was slightly the worse for wear after sinking three pints of ale in the hostelry his feet had walked him into on his way home from playing rounders. He'd joined a team of lads from work in an informal contest with another firm. They played on a piece of land beside the public baths and Isaac might not have bothered with it, but it gave him the excuse of being out of the house and away from Ginny's constant mithering.

Silas sat facing him at the other end of the table and the women – Alice, his mother, Louisa and Ginny – were fighting for elbow room down the sides. Isaac couldn't understand why the family never ate Sunday dinner around the much larger mahogany table in the dining room, where his parents infrequently entertained fancy guests.

The back door stood wide open, serving merely to exchange the warm air outside for the warm air of the kitchen, as far as he could tell. Teddy had been put down for his afternoon nap in a bassinet on the doorstep and was already fast on, undisturbed by the birdsong and the sounds of the town beyond. Sarah Hodgetts, the woman employed to cook and clean for the Hinchcliffes, had dished up roast chicken, potatoes, asparagus, peas and creamed spinach and left for the day. Harriet had made an apple cobbler and custard for pudding.

Alice gave Isaac a satisfied smile that said *Aren't you glad to be here?* He wrinkled his nose in reply. Silas told him that the two men would be rolling up their sleeves when it came time to wash the pots. 'We'll gi' the women a rest, for once,' he said, and set about separating the chicken's legs and wings from its body.

Isaac grunted in reply.

'I've got an announcement,' said Alice, her eyes spark-ling. 'I'm organising a meeting to encourage women to fight for the vote.'

'Good for you!' said Ginny.

The gratitude on Alice's face made his gut churn. Her admiration of Ginny was not becoming any easier to bear.

Louisa rolled her eyes. 'Can we 'av a rest from it for one minute?'

Harriet laughed. 'I'll come to your meeting, Alice.'

'Thank you,' said Alice. 'Uncle Silas, will you come too?'

'Looks like I'll be overseein' a job that day,' said Silas. 'We're installin' new arc lights in the factory or I would come, a'course.'

'How do you know,' said Alice crossly, 'that you can't come to my meeting when I haven't even given you the date of it?'

This made everyone laugh, even, eventually, Alice.

'Who's installin' the lights?' said Isaac, as casually as he could.

Silas shrugged. 'We've had a couple o' quotes. Why?'

'I just think it's about time, that's all. Gas lighting'll be obsolete before tha knows it. On the streets an' in the home.'

'I'm not sure about this electric lighting,' said Harriet. 'It seems dangerous.'

'Well, Ma, it's coming,' said Isaac. 'Two million pounds is gettin' spent on a new network in London. There are streets down there already lit up like Christmas. An' there's a local company makin' no end of applications to the council to put in systems.' He caught the speculative look Silas was giving him. 'Have you heard o' them, the Shef-field Telephone Exchange an' Electric Light Company?'

Silas nodded. 'Aye, I have.'

'Speaking of electric light,' said Alice, 'why don't you tell Ginny about that football game Uncle Silas took you to? D'you remember? I was so jealous.'

'Football matches aren't for women, let alone young lasses,' said Silas.

'Don't set her off again,' wailed Louisa.

Earlier, Alice had begged Isaac to be kind to Ginny. Now, she looked at him pleadingly. Isaac's heart began to pound. Alice might just have, unwittingly, handed him the means to deliver his news. He would do it here and now, in front of all his family. Someone might come to his defence, and pigs might fly.

'Aye, I'll never forget it,' he said. 'John Tasker—'

'It were a sight for sore eyes,' interrupted Silas.

Ginny made disapproving noises. 'Let the boy tell the story.'

Isaac ignored her, addressing himself to Silas. 'It were John Tasker started up this electric light company, tha knows. Last year, he set up floodlights so as the men could work on the new isolation hospital at Lodge Moor round the clock.'

'For the smallpox outbreak,' said Harriet. 'I remember it.'

'Aye, an' he's also lit a colliery with these arc lamps tha's talkin' about installin'. Each one has the light of three thousand candles.'

'I'm sure I don't want to hear about smallpox or miners,' said Ginny. 'What about this football game, then?'

Harriet smiled. 'He went on about it for weeks afterwards, him and his father both.'

Isaac smiled back at her, although an anticipatory guilt over what he was about to do swirled in his gut. 'Aye, them lights outshone the moon and turned night into noon.'

'Very poetic,' said Ginny.

Isaac finally addressed her directly. 'The light's shinin' on that pitch were that bright the players had to shade their eyes.' He looked at his father. 'Remember?'

Silas smiled and nodded in agreement.

'Aye, a proper spectacle,' said Isaac. 'Then they got on wi' the game as if it were nowt.' He tapped the table with his fingertips. 'Blues won two nil, an' all.'

'I remember the roads around Bramall Lane bein' besieged,' said Louisa. 'Must've been twenty thousand there.'

'Seems like it was a big deal,' said Ginny.

'It was,' said Isaac. 'Tasker built wooden stages ten yards tall in each corner o' the ground. He had a portable steam engine behind each goal that were drivin' dynamo machines, one for each light, see?'

'An' there's me thinkin' tha were just enjoying the spectacle,' said Silas. 'Tha seems to know a lot about it all o' a sudden, and this John Tasker. Hero of thine?'

Isaac took a deep breath. 'The science is there.' He measured out beats of distance along the table with one cupped hand. 'It's gone from a toy to a luxury to replacing gas. Don't tha think that's grand?'

'Aye, a'course I do, son. I'm all for progress.'

His heart was thumping. 'I'm reight glad Alice asked about that game.' She beamed at him. He smiled weakly back. 'It's all blowing up now they've found a way to run electric supplies over greater distances.' He paused. 'Tasker was only tellin' me this the other day.'

'Oh aye?' said Silas. 'Was he, now. The other day, you say.'

Isaac nodded. His tongue felt thick in his mouth.

Silas had been looking at Isaac through narrowed eyes but now he smiled and nodded. 'I suppose it's like makin' steel,' he said. 'Allus experimentin' an' testing an' refining. Gettin' it just so. It's good to be inquisitive. Has tha been in our lab, lately? Maybe lab work would suit thee.'

Isaac didn't know how to respond to this but fortunately his father kept talking. 'A young lad like yersen will see many transformations in all sorts o' things over the comin' years, that's for certain.'

'Cabs running on motor spirit instead of horse power,' said Louisa. Everybody stared at her. 'Just summat I'm hearin' about. I like to stay abreast.'

Isaac's heart was now beating so hard he was surprised the kitchen wasn't filled with the sound of it. The moment to speak was passing by but the words were backed up in his throat, choking him.

He cleared his throat.

'I'm goin' to work for him, for Tasker.'

Isaac gulped as everyone around the table switched their attention from Louisa to him.

'He's offered me a job.' He held his father's gaze. 'An' I've taken him up on it.'

He flinched when Harriet dropped her cutlery onto her plate with a clatter. Silas leaned forward and stared at him, his face reddening, and even though he had never raised his hand against him, for a moment Isaac thought his father would come around the table and strike him. Surprisingly, he found he wanted to laugh in Silas's face, so overwhelming was the unexpected wave of exhilaration that swept up from his toes to engulf his whole body. This was what freedom felt like. He clamped his jaw tight.

But it was Silas who laughed. 'Don't be daft,' he said. 'What about the job tha's already got? Hinchcliffe & Son. That's thee, that second part, in case tha'd forgot.'

'I've not forgot,' said Isaac. He jerked his thumb towards the bassinet near the back door. 'You've another son now, waitin' to be cast in iron. As for me, I'm startin' at Tasker's.'

'When?' said Harriet.

Isaac found her eyes harder to meet. 'Tomorra.' He glanced at Alice who had folded her lips together as though she might burst into tears. 'Tomorra,' he repeated. 'It's settled.'

Harriet and Silas were looking at each other. Aunt Louisa was shaking her head. Like Isaac, Ginny was examining the others' faces and had a broad smile on her own.

'You never said anything,' said Alice.

'I couldn't, 'til it were certain – 'til I were, and I am,' said Isaac. 'It's a small concern now but business'll grow an' grow. There's money to be made. A lot o' money, Ma. This is good news for me.'

'Don't I keep saying?' said Ginny. 'Like mother, like son. Isaac's striking out on his own to seek his fortune.' She nodded sagely. 'I'm so proud of you.'

Isaac bristled. 'This has nowt to do wi' thee.'

'There's no need for that,' said his mother, Harriet.

'I think there is.' Anger flooded through his body. 'Silly woman wi' her put-on airs an' graces. Soon got her feet under the table, didn't she? Soon got her hooks into you lot.'

'Pack it in, Isaac,' said Aunt Louisa.

68

'I'm not a little lad to be told what—'

'QUIET.'

The roar came from Silas.

Teddy began to wail. Harriet pushed back her chair, glared at Silas and hurried over to console the baby, lifting him into her arms and turning to face Isaac, her cheeks flushed. Isaac folded his arms.

'Tha can't blame me for wakin' him,' he said.

'No,' said Harriet, 'it seems you're blameless in every way. Pure as snow and just as cold.' She pulled the bassinet over the threshold and, muttering about the whole town knowing their business, kicked closed the back door with a cry of pain. 'How can you do this to your father?'

Harriet stumbled back to her chair. She'd slammed the door shut with her bad foot. Isaac had expected Silas's fury. His mother's anger, so rarely displayed, was harder to bear.

'I'm sorry, Ma, but like I said, he can train Teddy up, can't he?' he said, pushing back his chair. Silas had his head in his hands. 'I'm not thine to order about.' He turned on Ginny. 'I'm not thine, neither, an' I've no interest in what tha's got to say, now or ever. Tha landed here like a... like a cuckoo in the nest. An' now I'm gettin' out of it. Tha's pushed me out.'

Ginny burst into tears. Alice glared at him and crouched beside Ginny's chair to comfort her.

'Look,' said Louisa. 'Sit down. Finish your dinner and then you have a chat wi' your father, in private, where this should have been kept in the first place. Come on, lad.'

'No.' Isaac gripped the back of his chair and pushed it under the table. 'I'd best be off.'

Silas finally raised his head. 'If tha goes now,' he said slowly, as if measuring the weight of every word, 'after springin' this on us wi'out a care in the world, tha's gone for good. We don't mean owt to you, do we?'

The two men locked eyes. 'It's not like that,' said Isaac.

'Did you know about this, Alice?' said Harriet.

'No!'

'Did anybody hear what I said?' said Louisa. 'Both o' you need to calm down before owt more gets said.'

'I think enough's been said already,' said Ginny, sniffling into a handkerchief. 'This is all so upsetting.'

Louisa snorted. 'You're not the centre o' this drama, love.'

Isaac tore his gaze from his father's accusing eyes. 'I'll go, then,' he said, turning away from the table, 'an' I'll not be back. Don't worry theesen about that.'

His whole body burned with the injustice of it. Silas had backed him into a corner. If Isaac stayed now, he would be defeated, persuaded of the folly of leaving the family firm, and would return to Hinchcliffe's tomorrow with his tail between his legs. Word would get round the factory, and he'd be treated with barely concealed contempt by the other men.

'Isaac, please don't go,' said Harriet.

Alice got to her feet as if she would run to him. Isaac put out his hand to stay her. He stalked to the back door and walked out, leaving the door gaping.

His father hadn't uttered another word.

Chapter 6

'Here she is,' said Amelia, as Hope entered the front parlour to find the warden and housekeeper sitting shoulder to shoulder on the chaise longue, examining a notebook on Miss Barlow's lap. 'D'you want to invite your Mr Deveraux? The lovely Angus?'

Miss Barlow was chewing the end of a pencil. She looked up at Hope, one eyebrow raised.

'Invite him where?' said Hope.

'To the wedding, a' course!' said Amelia. 'We're drawing up the list for the church service and the wedding breakfast. It'll not be a fancy affair, like I'm sure yours will be. No white gown, no orange blossom and lace veil, God forbid. Hetty's too old, plus there's me to take account of, and Bertie's done it all before.'

'What a cheek,' said Miss Barlow. 'Carry on like this an' you won't get an invite.'

Hope sat on the piano stool and smoothed out her skirt. 'White and orange are for purity,' she said, 'so that counts me out, too, I'm afraid.'

'Oh, dear,' said Miss Barlow. 'Sorry, Hope. She's like a bull in a china shop, isn't she?'

'Oh aye,' said Amelia. 'I forgot.' She laughed. 'Sorry, love. What's the face for?'

Hope sighed. 'Pay no attention to me. I'm out of sorts.'

Angus had pressed her to return his declaration of love. What was preventing her from giving herself to him? He knew about her past and accepted it. Why couldn't she? And round and round she went, like a child's spinning top, wobbling with uncertainty. Was she to take a sledge-hammer to the comforting walls of the new life she had built, and allow this man – admittedly, this man she loved – inside? The prospect was terrifying.

Hope mustered a smile for Amelia. 'So, tell me who'll be coming.'

'Your beau, I hope,' said Amelia, 'so as we can all drool over him.'

'Amelia!' said Miss Barlow.

Hope laughed. 'He is very handsome,' she said, and blushed.

'I'll have him if you won't,' said Amelia. 'Have you given him your answer yet? Poor fella.'

'Read me your list,' said Hope.

Miss Barlow cleared her throat. 'I'm inviting all those women and girls who are resident on the afternoon of September the thirteenth, plus the trustees, and agents, and Bertrand's daughter, Flora – as well as two from his gentlemen's club, and his secretary, the vicar and...'

'Decrepit old men,' said Amelia. She waggled her eyebrows. 'How old's this vicar?'

'I can't imagine you as a vicar's wife,' said Hope, already cheered by Amelia's ebullience.

'The vicar *and* his wife are invited,' said Miss Barlow, 'and one or two of our biggest benefactors, and...' She tapped her chin with the pencil. 'That's about it.'

'I told her, this is her wedding breakfast,' said Amelia, 'not a fundraiser for the house.'

Hope laughed. 'These are all people who have become friends, over time. We are a family, here in this house, are we not?'

Miss Barlow nodded. 'An' I don't want a lot of fuss,' she said. 'We'll be married in Bertrand's parish church and I'll decorate this room with flowers for the wedding breakfast afterwards. We'll have cold cuts and cake.'

'And wine,' said Amelia. 'Let's at least break one house rule.'

'Aye, all right, and wine,' said Miss Barlow. 'I'll order in some bottles. Enough for a glass each.'

'Might need more than one,' said Amelia. 'Can you believe she's picked Friday the thirteenth, Hope? What d'you think o' that?'

'I'm not superstitious,' said Hope. She held up crossed fingers, making Amelia splutter with laughter.

'Come to think of it,' said Miss Barlow, 'we should be asking for donations to the house, instead o' wedding gifts. It's not like I need a trousseau.'

'What about poor old Bertie?' said Amelia with cheek. 'He's not got two farthings to rub together, has he?'

Bertrand Wallace, treasurer to the House of Help, was a wealthy widower and Miss Barlow would be moving to live in his house, while remaining warden. She'd retain her office that was situated off her existing quarters on the ground floor, across from the main parlour, and Amelia would take her bedroom, permanently freeing up a dorm bed. It meant Amelia would be answering knocks on the door in the middle of the night. She'd told Hope this was a small price to pay for having a bedroom to herself at last. The trustees had been talking about a move to bigger premises in the square, lamenting the lack of space here

73

at number one, but Miss Barlow said bellyaching about it was the furthest they ever seemed to get.

Clara stuck her head into the room. 'Here you all are,' she said. 'Room for a little 'un?'

She ushered Alice in. 'How do, Hope. Two more for tea, I take it? There's four lasses gettin' under my feet in the kitchen, Miss Barlow. Does it take that many to make potted meat sandwiches?'

'Gives the young ones summat to do,' said the warden.

'I can stay,' said Alice. 'A cab is collecting me at eight o'clock.'

'I could also stay,' said Hope. 'If your mother can arrange for me to be delivered back to Ranmoor before it gets dark? My hosts become anxious if I'm out very late.'

Alice nodded happily. She brandished a scroll of paper. 'Ladies, I have something to show you,' and dropped to her knees to unfurl it, nudging Amelia along the chaise longue and holding it flat on the faded material.

'My goodness,' said Hope.

Alice smiled. 'Do you like it? Once I've included the venue and the date and time, I'm taking this to the printers. I hope you'll display one in the window. And I'll advertise in the local *Telegraph* or *Independent*.' She see-sawed her hand. 'Which do you think would be best? Perhaps I should advertise in both.'

The poster was edged in red with *WOMEN'S SUFFRAGE* printed boldly across the top. Under this, the words *A public discussion every female should attend.*

'Every female?' said Amelia. 'Where're you holding this meeting? Hyde Park cricket ground?'

'I don't know yet,' said Alice. 'Look, I've left a space here. I know I might attract only a handful of people, perhaps up to a hundred?'

'Lay on cake,' said Amelia. 'People will turn up for cake. You should add that in.'

At the bottom of the poster, Alice had inscribed *Votes for Women. For the future of all our daughters.*

'Can't argue with the sentiment,' said Miss Barlow. 'What does your mother say?'

'That she'll pay for it,' said Alice. 'The printing costs, the advertising costs and the venue. Within reason.'

'That's exceptionally kind of her,' said Hope.

'I suppose it is.' Alice sighed. 'She's going along with this in the hopes I'll fail miserably and tire of the whole business, and then I can marry Jemima's son and start producing grandchildren.'

'Who's Jemima?' said Amelia. 'And who's her son?'

Alice rolled up the poster and retied the ribbon around it. 'Jemima Greaves. She ran the hansom cab business and, when she died, she left half to my mother and this son of hers inherited the other half. Mother thinks he's a good prospect. Keeps it all under one roof, I suppose.'

'Have you met him?' said Hope.

'A few times, in the yard.' Alice shrugged. 'I am not looking for a husband at the present moment.'

'I am,' said Amelia. 'Tell me more about him. Unless the reason you're not interested is because he looks like a toad. Is he covered in boils?'

'No, he's passably handsome, and he makes me laugh, but I'm not going to marry him,' said Alice.

Amelia poked herself in the chest with one finger and gave Alice a meaningful look.

'All right,' said Alice. 'I'll introduce you.'

The evening meal was finished and the kitchen tidied up. Hope sat at the piano in the front parlour, gently playing for the half a dozen residents in the room. Amelia had her head bent over a pile of mending. Sitting close by the piano, Alice had been reading a book by the light of the evening sun streaming through the window, but was now deep in conversation with Miss Barlow, who had declared she had paperwork to finish but was waylaid by Alice and now perched on the arm of her chair. Those residents with a ten- or twelve-hour working day ahead of them had already retired to bed, and the younger girls were in the kitchen, playing Parcheesi. They would be instructed to go to bed at nine o'clock.

Hope moved her fingers over the keys and tuned in idly to the conversation between the warden and Alice.

'And with Isaac so troubled I'm glad Aunt Harriet has the baby to keep her busy,' Alice was saying.

'How is Teddy getting on?' said Miss Barlow. 'He must be walking and talking by now.'

'Oh, he's a darling little lad. And he absolutely loves her like she's his own mother,' said Alice. 'He'll never know any different, will he? I remember he was such a tiny scrap when they brought him home from here.'

Hope was aware of the warden's sidelong glance in her direction. Her fingers faltered on the keyboard. Was that an expression of concern on Miss Barlow's face? Alice had begun volunteering at the house around the time Hope gave up her baby but remained unaware of her history. Alice could not be blamed for the piercing sorrow or the memories her remark had provoked. Hope had been lucky she wasn't thrown out of the House when her condition became impossible to hide. Instead, her disgrace had led her to her calling. She wondered what had become of Teddy's mother.

'You ought to pay the Hinchcliffe family a visit,' Alice was now saying, 'see how Teddy has settled into his new life. After all, you helped bring it all about. He's already walking, and babbling away, mama this and dada that.'

This time, Miss Barlow looked directly at Hope with alarm in her eyes. Hope closed the lid of the piano as the warden got to her feet.

'I'll think on it,' said Miss Barlow, 'but now paperwork calls, and I've a book I aim to finish tonight. Amelia? Can you lock up, love, after Alice and Hope have gone?'

Amelia nodded without looking up from her needle-work.

'Don't forget your poster,' said Miss Barlow to Alice. She gestured towards the residents. 'Why don't you tell these ladies about it?'

Alice's eyes lit up. 'Yes, I must!'

'Goodnight, Hope.'

So the warden wasn't going to explain to her the reason for her alarm. A suspicion began to form in Hope's mind. She dismissed it immediately. It couldn't be.

'Goodnight, Miss Barlow,' she said.

As the time to leave approached, Hope stood by the window, waiting for the cab to appear and listening to Alice implore the women to join her campaign. 'Did you know,' she declared, 'that women get paid half what men do, even if they're doing the same job?' One of the women muttered that was the way of the world and nothing would change it. They all had more pressing concerns than the injustices of inequality.

Dusk was falling. Either that, or the darkness on the rim of sky above the square's roofs and chimneys signalled another impending thunderstorm. A shudder ran through Hope's body. She couldn't shake from her thoughts that look – might it even have been fear? – on the warden's face. Alice's relatives had adopted a baby, a boy. A boy who was now speaking his first words. The family was called Hinchcliffe. And what had been the mother's name? Hope rubbed her forehead. Harriet. That was it. Harriet Hinchcliffe.

She had not seen the couple who came to the House of Help in the days following the birth of her illegitimate child, only heard their voices through the door. She had signed her rights away on the promise of a better life for him, and for her. Hope recalled wondering, the last time she held her newborn in her arms, whether she would forget him, over time, whether the fierce love she had felt towards him on the day she gave him up would diminish, fade and die. She had been foolish to imagine so.

Hope turned to Alice and pasted on a smile. 'Our cab is here.'

–

They lived in opposite directions. The driver scratched his head and said he would first deliver Alice home to Pond Street, that destination being a lot closer, then travel out to Ranmoor. He might pick up a passing fare to bring back to town, if he was lucky. Hope could wait at the house, if she liked, save herself a leg of the journey.

'No,' she said. 'If you don't mind, I'll accompany Alice.'

'I don't mind at all, love,' the driver said cheerfully. 'It's up to thee.'

The two women climbed into the cab.

'As sharp as you like, an' hang on tight,' the driver said, climbing onto his box. 'Storm's comin', an' I don't fancy bein' caught out in it, not one bit.'

'Goodness me,' said Hope.

Alice tucked her arm into Hope's. 'He's such a worry-wort. Don't pay him any attention. Next time, we'll duet on the piano,' she said.

'Do you play?'

'Oh yes, my mother made sure to give me a good education, as befitting the wife of a young professional gentleman.' Alice laughed. 'She wants me married off but doesn't believe in leading by example.'

'And the Hinchcliffes,' said Hope. 'Who are they? If you don't mind my asking.' She clung to the strap hanging from the wall of the cab as it lurched forward. 'I couldn't help overhear you talking about them to Miss Barlow.'

'Silas and Harriet Hinchcliffe, my uncle and aunt,' said Alice. 'They're not really relatives of mine but they have been friends with my mother since before I was born. They adopted Isaac twenty years ago when his mother disappeared.' She hesitated. 'She's back now. It's a difficult situation. Anyway, they adopted Teddy in the spring of last year. I think that Harriet must have been unable to bear children.'

'Goodness,' murmured Hope.

'I haven't spoken out of turn,' said Alice. 'They don't mind people knowing that their children are adopted. They love them as their own.'

'No, no. I'm happy for them, and for the children. You are very close?'

'We are,' said Alice. She smiled. 'Isaac is a dear friend, the dearest.'

Hope tightened her grip on the strap as they rounded a bend in the road. The driver hadn't been exaggerating when he'd hinted they'd be travelling at a fair lick. She clenched her teeth against a nausea she wasn't sure was from the ride or the conversation.

'Think the wheel left the road there,' said Alice, laughing.

Hope smiled weakly. 'Your aunt and uncle,' she said, a few moments later. 'Do they live near you?'

'They're across the town,' said Alice, 'in one of the newer houses in Wellington Street. Uncle Silas likes to be near work, or they would have moved further out, somewhere a bit greener, though Isaac would have hated it.' She laughed. 'I can't imagine him among the cows and sheep. Though his grandparents were farmers.'

Hope nodded absently as Alice continued to tell her about the woes of her cousin Isaac, whose mother had shown up out of the blue. Her thoughts swooped and fluttered, afraid to settle. What could she do, after all? She regretted having overhead the conversation, having actively *listened in*. Nothing good ever came of snooping.

After Alice had said her farewells and accepted Hope's insistence on paying the full fare, she asked the driver whether a detour to Wellington Street would take them too far off the planned route. No, he replied. It was on the way, give or take.

'Can you drive along the street, please?' said Hope. 'I won't require you to stop at all. Just please let me know when we're there.'

He accepted this with a shrug.

Some time passed before a knock on the roof hatch told her they had reached Wellington Street. The cab slowed but did not stop. In the gloom, Hope made out a Methodist chapel, the brick façade and iron gates of some kind of manufactory, a grocer's shop and a public house with a sign swinging beneath a lamp. The wind was getting up. The cab passed the pub before she could make out the name of it. They passed a row of terraced cottages and, at the end of the road, several detached houses set back, three storeys in height, windows glowing. Was her son inside one of these dwellings, being cradled to sleep? She craned her neck to keep the street in view as the cab turned a corner. A sudden flash threw the buildings into stark focus, then was gone, leaving the street darker than before.

The threatened storm had begun.

Chapter 7

'How is Mary Shaw, the girl I brought in yesterday?'

Alice was sharing a pot of tea at the kitchen table with Clara, who had finished work for the day but exclaimed that if she didn't get off her feet for five minutes she'd be walking home on stumps.

'That quiet lass?' said Clara. 'Sozzled?'

'That's the one.'

Alice had collected the girl from the police court where Mary Shaw had been brought for being intoxicated on the street. The girl had given her age as fourteen and agreed to go with Alice readily enough. The address she had supplied to the police was a lodging house on Love Lane. Mary Shaw reckoned that was where she'd always lived.

'She's gone,' said Clara. 'Went first thing.'

Alice put down her cup, dismayed. 'That was quick. She didn't run off, did she?'

'No, no. Sent to a refuge in Chesterfield to steer her away from the direction she were headed in. This place is full to busting, anyhow.'

'Nothing new there,' said Alice. 'I would have liked to have wished her well.'

Clara eased her feet back into her boots, gritting her teeth. 'Amelia's on the warpath.'

Alice sighed. 'So I gather.'

Much to Amelia's dismay, a decision had been made to partition the warden's quarters once Miss Barlow had moved out. The intention was to create an additional room that would accommodate two beds and a chest of drawers. Amelia would sleep in the remaining space, adjacent to the office. 'An' smaller than it!' she had complained. 'Wi' Hetty trampling backwards an' forwards, an' all. At this rate, she'll be climbin' over my bed to get to work.'

It shocked Alice that Amelia called her mother by her given name. If Alice tried that with Louisa she'd get clouted about the ear.

Clara finished her tea, flattened her hands on the tabletop and pushed herself to her feet with a groan. 'Time I were off. I'll see thee tomorra. No rest for the wicked, eh?'

Alice wrinkled her nose. This was one of her mother's favourite expressions. Alice couldn't imagine Louisa Leigh ever having been wicked, despite the mysterious circumstances surrounding her own parentage. But it was true her mother never seemed to rest. If she wasn't working on the cab business then she was working on Alice, who ought to be married or at least engaged by now and whose reluctance to sacrifice her freedom was a daily affront to her mother. Louisa had always kept a small circle of close friends, comprising Jemima Greaves before she passed, Silas and Harriet Hinchcliffe, and Daniel Housley, who worked as company secretary for Hinchcliffe & Son and was a frequent guest at the Hinchcliffe household. Aunt Harriet had assured Alice that Daniel was a confirmed bachelor but she had seen the way he looked at her mother when he thought himself unobserved. Could

Daniel Housley be her father? She'd often wondered. He was kind to her, no more, in his diffident way.

Voices drifted in from the backyard, Clara's and a man speaking in apologetic tones. Then Clara stepped back into the kitchen, Constable Goodlad on her heels. The constable looked taken aback when he saw Alice sitting at the table.

'I've told him,' said Clara, 'that the warden's out an' Hope's gone for the day. But he's summat to say.'

Constable Goodlad looked chagrined. 'I can return in the morning.'

Clara threw up her hands. 'Make yer mind up.'

'What is it?' said Alice.

He turned to her, his expression now unreadable. 'I'm here regarding a former resident.'

'We've had a lot o' them,' said Clara, in a milder tone. She was, Alice could tell, becoming intrigued.

'I should come back tomorrow, to speak to the warden directly,' said the constable. Clara raised her eyes to the ceiling. 'There'll be an inquest, you see, that a witness from this house might be required to attend, bearing in mind recent, ah, events that occurred here.'

Unease stirred in Alice's gut. An inquest meant a death. 'Won't you sit down?' she said.

'I prefer to stand, if you don't mind.'

Alice and Clara exchanged glances as the constable removed his police helmet and pressed it against his chest. He glanced at Alice then directed his words at Clara.

'Please pass along to Miss Barlow that I'm very sorry to inform you all that the body of a young woman has been discovered on the riverbank down by Halfpenny Bridge,' he said. 'It was... she was in the reeds. The old tollkeeper found her.' He paused. 'He'd gone down to fish.'

Clara shook her head. 'An' hooked a drowned woman. Poor fella. An' poor woman.'

Now Alice knew why the constable was so uncomfortable. An image sprang unbidden into her mind of long black hair tangled in roots and rushes, of white limbs floating and of a hollow-cheeked face emerging from the depths, a face she knew, black accusatory eyes turned on her, a smell of the swamp. Heat swept through her body and was just as suddenly replaced by an icy cold. She shivered, and whispered: 'No.'

The constable nodded. 'I'm afraid so.'

'He killed her,' said Alice, 'and came here pretending she'd run off, to give himself an alibi.' Another shudder wracked her body. She clenched her fists. 'Or she went back to him, yes, thinking... well, I'm not certain what she was thinking, but there was nobody to protect her.' Her voice rose. 'He'll hang for this.'

'No.' Constable Goodlad spoke gently. 'No, Miss Leigh. I'm sorry to say it was self-murder.'

The words were a punch to the gut. Alice put her hand over her mouth, nauseated.

'Oh, my goodness,' said Clara. 'We are talkin' about Polly Bramall, aren't we? Just to be clear.'

'Yes, didn't I state her name? I'm sorry. Mrs Alfred Bramall.' The officer replaced his hat and backed towards the door. 'I'll return in the morning to speak to the warden, if you could pass the message along. I'm very sorry.'

Alice finally found her voice. 'No,' she said, before he could leave. 'No, the man's a brute. I've encountered him twice now and each time he made threats. I know what he's like, what he's capable of doing.' She thrust out her chin. 'You're wrong. Polly didn't... She wouldn't... She was so young. My age.'

Constable Goodlad stopped on the threshold. He dropped his head before looking up at Alice, his eyes filled with compassion. 'On the night she disappeared,' he said, 'we had a report from a member of the public who reckoned he'd seen a woman jump from the bridge at Newhall, a dark-haired woman wearing only a – excuse me, ladies – wearing only a thin shift. He said he thought at first he'd seen a ghost. A search was made and nothing found.' The constable paused. 'Initially, we had reason to doubt the reliability of the witness.'

'Drunk, was he?' said Clara.

'He may have imbibed some alcohol,' said the constable.

Alice wanted to laugh at his pompous tone, or cry. She fought the rising sense of horror that constricted her gut. She recognised now what she had seen in the woman's eyes when Polly had dared to glance in Alice's direction during the confrontation with her husband in the Crofts. Alice had thought it fear. There had been fear, of course there had, and derision aimed at Alice, for being so foolish as to believe she could help, but not in that instant. There had been something else in Polly's eyes, something worse than fear, worse than terror. It had been hopelessness.

Still, Alice shook her head. 'Polly wouldn't do that.' Then a thought occurred, a chink of light in the dark. 'How do you know the woman found is Polly? How do you know you're not mistaken?'

'Miss Leigh,' said the constable. 'There's no doubt as to her identity. Her husband has confirmed it. I am very sorry.'

She went back to the house the next morning, after a sleepless night, hoping to find the warden at home. Clara let her in, with a sigh. 'Is that summat else for me to look after? I'd only kill it.'

Alice put the plant pot she was carrying on the floor inside the door and brushed crumbs of soil from the bodice of her dress. The bright green leaves of the parlour palm reached as high as her hip.

'It's heavier than you'd think,' she said, 'but no, it's not for this house. Is Miss Barlow in?'

'Office,' said Clara. 'All morning, she reckons. She were grumblin' about paperwork. He's already been back, that bobby. She knows all about it.'

Alice tapped on the door of the warden's quarters and, without waiting for a reply, marched inside. The door to the office was open and Miss Barlow was standing at the window, holding swatches of material up to the light. The warden started guiltily, then smiled.

'I didn't hear you knock, love.' Alice had never seen her look bashful before. 'I'm choosing the colour for my wedding dress, though I reckon I've run out o' time to sew it. I've allus got my russet to fall back on.'

'I like the blue,' said Alice. 'Although russet will suit the season.'

'Let's just hope September will be more settled, weatherwise,' said Miss Barlow.

Alice clasped her hands together. 'You heard about Polly.'

'Aye. I am sorry, love. The constable's been back with a little bit more information than he gave you and Clara yesterday.'

'What information?' Alice dared to hope. 'Has the husband been arrested?'

Miss Barlow put the swatches on her desk. 'Let's go and sit down. I'd put the kettle on but I've women in the kitchen helping Cook make dinner, and we don't want all and sundry putting in their tuppence-worth.'

They went to the parlour, where Miss Barlow pushed open a window. 'Stuffy,' she said by way of explanation. She sat on the chaise longue and patted the seat beside her. Alice sat down heavily, with a sigh. 'Listen,' said the warden. 'Everything the constable told you yesterday is the truth.'

Injustice burned in Alice's chest. She'd been practising her argument all night and was determined to have her say. 'Even if she was the instrument of her own demise,' she said, 'it's murder. He drove her to it and he should hang. Any jury would convict him.'

The sympathetic look on the warden's face was unbearable. 'She's gone, Alice. I am very sorry.'

'That's what the constable said,' said Alice. 'When are people going to stop being *sorry* and *do* something. Why is it always the women that suffer? We're at the mercy of men in the home and in the world because we don't have a voice.'

She got up and marched to the window and back again, unable to remain still. 'We don't have any power at all. We're victims. Polly knew it. She knew there was no hope. I saw it in her eyes. Nobody helped her.'

'Sit down,' said Miss Barlow. 'You're wearin' a hole in the carpet.'

Alice sat and put her head in her hands. The warden patted her shoulder. 'We tried to help her,' she said. 'We did our best. That's what you should remember.

Alice, there's more to tell.' Alice looked up, her vision blurred with tears. 'That husband of Polly's,' continued Miss Barlow, 'the police have warned me that he might be gunning for the house, and for you, from the things he's saying. He'll calm down, and I'm sure he's not a complete fool, but have a care. You mustn't attend the inquest. None of us will go. We'll hand in a statement explaining our involvement with Polly, all right?'

'I'm not afraid of him,' said Alice. 'If I ever come across him, he'll be getting a piece of my mind.'

'What would be the point, love? I've told you this before, we did what we could for Polly Bramall. You can lead a horse to water.'

'I know that,' said Alice.

'All right.' Miss Barlow glanced at the closed door of the parlour. 'I'm glad you've called by. There's summat else I need to talk to you about.' She bit her lip and gazed out of the window. 'It's a delicate situation.'

'Go on,' said Alice. The warden evidently wanted to occupy her with house business, to take her mind off the tragedy.

'We had a girl here, a young girl, around your age, who had been…' the warden paused, 'mistreated, and the result was that she was carrying a child. She wanted to stay at the house but that would have been impossible, with a baby on the way. She agreed to give him up for adoption. That baby is Teddy, your cousin.'

Alice frowned. 'I know Teddy was born here. It's how I heard about this house and came to volunteer.'

'Yes. I could never have anticipated that,' said Miss Barlow. She laughed shakily. 'Have you heard the saying, it's too close to home? It's certainly an unfortunate set of circumstances.'

'Why unfortunate?' said Alice.

'Alice, you were talking to me about Teddy the other day. Do you remember? Hope was playing the piano. It was the night of that storm.'

'Yes, I remember. I brought my poster to show you. Hope shared my cab home.'

Miss Barlow closed her eyes briefly then looked at Alice. 'Hope doesn't know.'

'Doesn't know what?' said Alice impatiently.

'Hope doesn't know,' said the warden, 'that Teddy is her child.'

–

Outside, the air was stifling. Alice's head began to ache. A passing gentleman lifted his hat and smiled his amusement at the wreath of leaves around her face. There was no easy way to carry the palm, but she would manage it, without help, thank you very much, sir. The details of Hope's story whirled in her mind. How terrible it must have been, to give away her baby, to not know where he was, when all the while Miss Barlow and the trustees of the House knew and could never tell. And now Alice, too, was sharing that burden.

She crossed the dusty cobbles towards the dwellings at the foot of the square. Several women in light cotton headscarves were standing outside the butcher's shop, baskets on their hips, nattering away. This was Alice's ideal audience. If only she had printed her posters, she might hand them out. She resolved to carry copies around with her for this eventuality. Progress had been made. The venue was set. Her mother had assured her that an upstairs room in the vestry hall at number fifty-four

Cemetery Road in Sharrow would suffice. A cab driver would deliver Alice and remain parked on the street until her meeting was completed.

It was a terrifying prospect, but she would go through with it for Polly's sake, and for Hope's.

'How will it work?' Louisa had asked. 'I mean, what will you be talkin' about?'

'It's a call to arms,' said Alice, grandly, to cover the fact she hadn't really thought that far ahead.

'Well, good for thee, though I can't see how one woman alone can make a difference. It's a man's world, love, and I can't see it changin'.'

Her mother's scepticism only strengthened Alice's resolve. She shifted the weight of the palm in her arms and bade the women good morning. Were they each content with their lot? She had assumed that all women would, in general terms, be in favour of more equality. Then she had come across, during her research at the library, a cutting from a local newspaper decrying female enfranchisement, a letter to the editor warning in strident tones that the vote would have a degrading effect on women's minds, and that Adam must rule over Eve. That it was written by a woman was the most disheartening element. Alice had tried to shrug it off, but it felt like an attack on her person. Isaac found it amusing and said it was probably written by a man, the aim being to keep women in their place. But what if that place led them to ruin?

In the world of her devising, Hope would keep her baby, and Polly Bramall her life.

Chapter 8

The room above the butcher's shop came sparsely furnished with a meagre fireplace, a table and two folding chairs with slung seats. The bed, wardrobe and washstand were concealed behind a heavy wool curtain that divided the room in half, bisecting the window that overlooked Paradise Square. This meant guests such as Alice would not have to gaze upon his unmade bed or the piece of battered tin he used for an ashtray, that was all but invisible under a pile of cigarette ends.

Isaac opened bottles of ginger beer and they each unfolded a chair and sat contemplating the potted palm on the table between them. The glossy leaves only made its surroundings seem even more drab.

'Not to be ungrateful or owt,' said Isaac, 'but I've not really got room for it. An' I don't think it'll thrive, neither. Sorry, lass.'

'It's not from me,' said Alice. 'It's from your mother.'

'Which one?'

Alice pulled a face. 'Aunt Harriet says these are easy to look after,' she said. 'Do what you like with it but I'm not carrying it back, not in this heat.' She took a swig of ginger beer, straight from the bottle. Isaac was relieved she hadn't asked for a glass. He had only one, a pint glass he'd liberated from the Q in the Corner, and that had rolled under his bed days ago.

Isaac wanted to ask what possessed his mother to send a potted palm. An olive branch would be more appropriate. Although, he reminded himself, it was he who had walked out on his family, not the other way around. 'How is she?' he asked.

Alice shrugged. 'She misses you.'

'And what does Silas say?'

'Nowt,' said Alice. 'I'm sure he regrets what he did say, though.' She frowned. 'When did you stop calling him Father?'

Isaac drummed his hands on the table. 'Silas is his name, in't it? An' he's not my father.'

Alice shook her head in her usual brisk dismissal of anything he said that she had decided she would not tolerate. He watched the blonde curls resettle around her face, his gaze roaming her face, flitting away from her delicate mouth that was pretty, even when downturned. Did she ever think about that kiss they had shared?

'I've enough on with Amelia referring to her mother as Hetty,' said Alice. 'Is this a modern trend that has passed me by? Isaac, are you listening to me?'

Isaac flapped a hand. 'It's too hot to get cross, love. Is the other one still about?'

'Yes,' said Alice. 'I can understand you not calling her mother, but she does have a name, too.' She leaned forward, pushing some palm fronds to the side so she could narrow her eyes at him, giving him the curious feeling of being hunted down.

'What?' he said.

'I wish you'd stop acting like an overgrown infant and accept Ginny into your heart. Give her a chance, as your parents have.'

'I've not got the energy,' he said. 'Nor the inclination.'

Alice leaned back in her chair and cast her eyes to the ceiling as if she'd find more sense up there. A crack ran the length of the yellowed surface, disappearing behind the room-dividing curtain. Smaller lines radiated from it, creating tiny islands of plaster on the verge of crumbling away. He'd not seen the shoddiness of the room when he'd taken it, such was the abruptness of his departure, nor had he noticed the lack of plates and cutlery in a so-called furnished place. Sheffield's famous knives and forks were distributed worldwide but appeared to be a scarcity in rented accommodation within the town itself. Now he viewed his accommodation through Alice's eyes and found it wanting.

She was studying him again. Isaac shrugged.

'You've always been a terrible sulker,' she said.

'An' you've always been a bossy little madam.'

'I prefer assertive,' said Alice. 'I should know better than to try to persuade you to do anything, even if – no, *especially* if – it is in your own interests.'

But she returned his smile. Nobody knew him better than Alice.

'I've been preoccupied, with my campaign,' she said. 'I'm sorry for that. I wish you would reconcile with your parents.'

'A man o' five-and-twenty shouldn't be livin' with his parents,' he said, 'nor faffin' about wi' one apprenticeship after another in his father's firm.' He held up a hand to forestall any argument and swallowed the dregs of his ginger beer. 'Ready to go, then?'

Isaac shrugged on his jacket and followed Alice down the narrow set of stairs concealed behind a door on the shop floor of the butcher's. He offered his arm when they reached the street and Alice took it. The sun was shining, he was drumming up business for his new employer and he was in Alice's company. They were arm in arm and there would be no better time to ask. Now was the moment. He squeezed her fingers.

'Aunt Louisa found thee a suitable match yet?'

Alice laughed. 'No. Such a thing doesn't exist.'

He slowed his pace until they were being overtaken by other pedestrians on the crowded pavement, one of whom muttered something about supplying them with a bench to sit on. He would tell her that such a suitor did exist, that he walked alongside her, now. He imagined her mouth dropping open in surprise then curving into a smile as he hastily reminded her they weren't blood relatives, but that their bond went deep as the Don – no, that river was filthy, a cesspit. He shook his head, exasperated with himself. Their bond went deep as the sea that neither of them had ever seen. He would take her there one day, to the coast, to Cleethorpes or Scarborough. If she could only look at their shared love in a different light, she would see the rightness of it. She would look at him in confused wonder. He'd tell her he could wait. Alice would laugh at this. All right, fair enough, he wasn't the patient sort, but if she needed time to consider his request to court her, he would give it, gladly.

He stopped and turned to her.

'What is it?' said Alice.

Isaac took a breath and held it, waiting for the rattle of a passing wagon to subside.

Alice peered into his face. 'You look very serious.'

And the words would not come.

'It's nowt.' He shook his head. 'I were miles away, thinkin' on summat. It's to do with work.' He looked up when a shadow fell across the street. 'Looks like rain. Come on.'

It had been a silly idea, declaring his love on the pavement surrounded by strangers. He would wait until the next time she came to visit, so they might be alone, and he could kiss her. He would wait until he had found better lodgings. He might even make more of an effort with Ginny, and show Alice how magnanimous he could be.

On Church Street, they strolled past a rank of hansom cabs on the road outside the iron railings of St Peter's, Isaac paying more attention to them than he might otherwise. He already knew that the drivers who rented cabs and horses belonging to Greaves & Sons plied their trade both here and at the exit to the railway station, these being the busiest for passing hire. Greaves's yard was equidistant between the two locations and a hive of noisy activity when Isaac and Alice turned the corner onto the cobbles. Cabs were being cleaned of mud and dust, lamps polished, horses exchanged and drivers coming and going from the food shack. The scene was as familiar as the wallpaper at home – though he told himself to stop thinking of it as home – but Isaac looked about him with a fresh perspective as they skirted horse dung and hay to reach the rickety staircase to the office above the stable blocks. He had delivered a new account for the Exchange and Electric Light Company and, in the moment that he entered the headquarters of Greaves & Son, Isaac was certain nothing could dislodge the elated grin from his face.

A man was standing beside the desk that Aunt Louisa sat at. He sported a trim salt-and-pepper beard, a blue waistcoat and a collar starched to within an inch of its life. His hand when Isaac shook it was firm but his skin was soft. No yardman or driver, then.

'This is my business partner, Barnaby Greaves,' said Louisa, 'and this, Barnaby, is the man bringin' the latest wonders o' the world to our door. What's our number again, Isaac?'

'Three oh oh,' he said. This must be the Greaves son Alice had spoken about. Isaac gave her a sidelong look. She had been mocking her mother's production of another suitor but the smile she now gave Barnaby Greaves extinguished Isaac's good mood like a candle snuffer meeting a flame.

'Pleased to meet you,' said Barnaby Greaves. 'And lovely to see you again, Alice. I gather we're signing the contract today.'

'Aye,' said Isaac, 'an' we'll have the telephone wire installed in the next few weeks. Three oh oh.' He was repeating himself like a doddery old fool. It unnerved him to see Alice in such proximity to a man her mother saw as a suitor, as if at any moment a vicar would spring out of the cupboard and marry them. 'I mean to say,' said Isaac, 'your customers'll be able to summon a cab any time durin' the day, and all through the night an' all.'

'We're interviewin' telephone call operators,' said Louisa, 'though I'll be on hand to help too, a' course.'

'You already do too much,' said Alice.

'My sentiments exactly,' said Barnaby Greaves. 'Won't this availability to all create more work for us to do? Is this really the cure-all you suggest?'

A punch would cure the man of the smug look on his face. Isaac wanted to lift him by the starched collar of his shirt and tell him about the fifty thousand messages telephoned through the exchange in the first week of August alone.

'Like Isaac says, it will transform the world,' said Alice. 'The fire brigade has a direct wire number now, via the police, and I hear the quicker response has checked no end of outbreaks from becoming much worse, from disaster in some cases.'

Isaac gave her a grateful look. 'Aye, that's true.'

'Can't stop progress,' said Aunt Louisa. 'We're gettin' electric wires at the same time, aren't we, love?'

Isaac nodded.

'Although, thinkin' on it,' Louisa said, 'there was a workman last week installin' electric lights at a jeweller's – the one in the high street, I forget the name, do you know, Alice?' Alice shook her head and Louisa continued. 'He nearly died… Kilner's, that's the name of the place.'

'He fell off a ladder,' said Isaac. 'As men have been doin' since ladders were invented.'

During this exchange, Alice had gone to the window to look down on the yard.

Louisa caught Isaac's eye. 'I don't know if she told you, but our girl's had some bad news. One of the women from that house, found in the river.'

'Polly Bramall,' said Alice, without turning. 'Took her own life, thanks to that brute of a husband.'

Barnaby Greaves went to her side, straightening the cuffs of his shirt in a fussy manner that set Isaac's teeth on edge. 'I'm very sorry to learn that,' he said.

Alice smiled up at him. 'Thank you,' she said.

What could she possibly see in him? Isaac reminded himself that Alice was resisting her mother's attempts to marry her off, but now, he saw with dismay, Louisa was regarding the couple with a small, satisfied smile on her face. And they made a handsome couple too, framed by the light streaming in through the window.

Isaac clapped his hands. 'Reight,' he said. 'Shall we get on wi' it, then?'

After they had completed the paperwork, Aunt Louisa brought out a bottle of spirits and three tumblers. She wouldn't have any – Isaac had never seen her touch a drop of liquor – but insisted the others should make a toast to progress. Isaac and Barnaby locked eyes to knock back their tot of whisky. Alice swallowed hers just as quickly as the men but began to cough. Before Isaac could react, Barnaby had taken her hands and was peering into her face, a concerned expression on his face. The laughter died on Isaac's lips.

'She'll be reight,' he said gruffly.

'It's not really a suitable drink for a young lady,' said Barnaby.

This time, Isaac did laugh. 'Don't poke the bear,' he said. 'This one reckons to be the equal o' any man.'

For a moment, Alice looked like she might take offence but instead she slapped Isaac's arm and he duly pretended she had done him a serious injury. Barnaby looked on, bemused.

'Now, now, children,' said Louisa.

'Cousins,' said Alice, affectionately.

'Kissing cousins,' said Isaac.

The words were out before he'd even completed the thought. Raising a hand to clap over his mouth, he checked himself, continuing the movement to run his fingers through his hair, forcing a laugh that was more like a sigh. Aunt Louisa gave him a speculative look but Alice appeared not to have even heard him speak. She had pulled Barnaby Greaves to one side and the pair were conversing in low murmurs. When she turned to Isaac, the man stood at her shoulder, a broad smile on his face. A grin of triumph.

'I'd be very happy to come for tea with you next Tuesday,' said Barnaby Greaves to Louisa. She raised an eyebrow. 'Alice has just invited me.' He held up his manicured hands. 'I promise we won't be talking business.'

—

Isaac pounded down the stairs, stamping his rage on every step. She had declared she would not tether herself to a man, yet here she was having her head turned by a weakling in a fancy waistcoat. Women were fickle and not to be trusted. Alice, Ginny and Dolly, and all. His face frozen in a polite grimace, Isaac had made his excuses and left. Crossing the yard, he turned and glanced up to see Alice standing at the window. She smiled and raised a hand in farewell and Isaac nodded brusquely and strode away, pulling up his collar as fat drops of rain began to fall.

What a miserable summer this was turning out to be.

Chapter 9

Hope rapped on the door to the porter's lodge and mustered a reassuring smile for the girl who stood beside her. Behind the tall iron gates a gravel drive disappeared into the fog, a road to nowhere. She suppressed a shudder.

The door opened and they were ushered inside. The girl immediately dropped onto a chair at the back of the room, complaining of tired feet. The sight of her thin white fingers resting on a belly swollen tight against the threadbare dress she wore was too much for Hope. She turned away and swallowed the lump in her throat, desperate to collect herself so that she could explain the situation to the uniformed man who had admitted them. It would not help anybody if she broke down in tears. The composure she prided herself on seemed to have deserted her. Finally, Hope glanced across at the girl, who was staring into the middle distance, seemingly oblivious to her surroundings. She knew all too well what was to come. It had been explained to her.

The Fir Vale workhouse was north of the river, two omnibus rides away from the house in Paradise Square where the girl had spent the night, having been ejected by her parents when her condition could no longer be disguised. It was Amelia who had suggested over breakfast – and out of the girl's earshot, thankfully – that they take a cab across the town, but this had been vetoed by Miss

Barlow. 'Nobody,' she had said, 'turns up at those gates in a hansom cab. It would be cruel.'

Amelia hadn't understood, but Hope did.

They had waited in the kitchen for the girl to return from the water closet. 'If I was her,' said Amelia, 'I'd go an' hide under the bed, except she wouldn't fit.' Miss Barlow had hushed her and begun to tell Hope about the workhouse. Built eight years ago to suit its purpose, it had a school, a hospital, a separate asylum building – 'For the feeble-minded,' Cook had interjected – and a garden and a bakery producing hundreds of loaves a day. The girl would be given work to do and a meat dinner, or at least a good portion of hash, every day of the week, with porridge and bread for breakfast and tea.

'Best tell her to pick out the beetles from her food,' said Cook. 'Best warn her about—' Hope never got to hear the rest. The warden had silenced Cook with a look.

Now, Hope went back to the girl and sat beside her.

'Someone will be along to collect you.'

The girl looked at her. 'Will you come?'

Hope was caught off-guard. 'To visit, you mean? I'm not sure that's permitted. But you must come to see us, when you get back on your feet.' She tried to sound encouraging. 'Yes, come and visit and tell me how you're getting on. This won't be forever, you know. It's a temporary, ah, circumstance.'

The girl shook her head. 'I meant now. To come inside wi' me.' She put her hand on the side of her belly and flinched. 'It dun't matter.'

Hope looked away, blinded by tears, groping for the girl's hand, finding the bones of her fingers.

'It's all reight.' The girl extracted her hand. 'I've taken up enough of tha time.'

On the long gravel drive, Hope twisted her hands into the borrowed shawl the girl had handed back and watched her walk slowly towards the workhouse with a nurse from the lying-in ward. The fog was dispersing, the high clock tower now visible, positioned centrally between three-storey blocks, as if waiting to fall on the small figures walking towards it.

The girl didn't look back.

–

Hope sat on a bench in Paradise Square, the shawl in her lap, her fingers moving restlessly over the frayed tassels as if they were prayer beads. Families were not permitted in the workhouse. Husbands were separated from wives, children from parents and babies from mothers. Hope had been spared the workhouse but her arms were empty. Marriage to Angus, any children he might give her, would not fill the void in her heart.

An old woman, bent under the weight of a heavy shawl and large black bonnet, sat beside Hope and tipped crumbs from a paper bag onto the cobbles. Pigeons swooped down to jerk and strut around their feet. The woman nodded happily and seemed about to speak so Hope got up, smiling vaguely, and walked away, her steps hasty, although she had nowhere to go but back to the house. She stopped near the edge of the square, over-come with weariness at the thought of conversing with a new arrival needing comfort, or listening to Miss Barlow fret about the wedding that was three weeks hence, or enduring Amelia's teasing. It was getting to the point where Hope would give Angus an answer just to shut Amelia up.

She had been rude to the old woman. It would have cost her nothing to pass the time of day with the old soul. Hope decided that she would walk until her temper was restored. Let her feet carry her where they might. She draped the shawl around her back and over her arms, pushing away the faint idea that she might later cover her head to disguise her identity, and continued to fiddle with the wool fringe as she walked along. Her mother's voice followed her. *Stop fiddling, it's unladylike. And where are you going, alone?*

Hush, mother.

Like flowers, crowds bloomed in the sunshine. Always the busiest part of the town, Coles Corner at the junction of Fargate and Church Street was thronged with colourfully dressed ladies and smiling gentlemen, and Hope, her body damp with the heat of the day, was glad to keep her mind occupied in navigating the pavement and roads. She passed the shopfronts of Fargate, following the incline to Barker's Pool, a square without sides and the highest point of the centre of town. Angus had told her Balm Green was the old name, still used by some, as this was where lemon balm was once cultivated. If she had a sachet of the leaves, it might combat the stench coming from the gentlemen's urinal that squatted in the middle of the thoroughfare. Hope hurried on. Outside the music hall, people were queuing in small groups, chatting or sunning themselves or greeting passers-by while they waited to buy tickets to the latest show. Hope had gone there with Miss Barlow and Mr Wallace to an afternoon organ recital. She had smiled to see the two of them surreptitiously holding hands, their fingers interlaced in the gap between their seats, and smiled now at the memory of it.

It was only when she turned onto Carver Street that she could admit to herself where her feet were leading her. Hope's heart began to pound as she rounded the corner to arrive on Wellington Street. Without pausing, or she might have lost her nerve, she stepped inside the grocer's shop and was enveloped in the jarring aromas of spices and pickles, roasted coffee and human bodies. Several customers were queuing to be served. She would have to wait her turn while the grocer and his boy fetched and carried, rang up purchases and filled baskets and cloth bags with paper-wrapped parcels. Waves of anxiety tugged at her gut. This was madness, she should leave, hurry back to the house. No, she must go on, having come this far. A woman joined the queue behind her and was greeted by the woman ahead of Hope. She stood awkwardly between them as they chatted about the weather, a new grandchild and the price of flour. And now she was at the head of the queue, standing at the counter before the grocer who raised his eyebrow expectantly.

'Can you tell me, sir,' said Hope, 'if you know, that is, which house on this street is occupied by the Hinchcliffe family?' She tried for a polite smile, but her cheeks trembled with the effort of maintaining it. 'I'm hoping to speak with Mrs Silas Hinchcliffe.'

The man frowned. 'I'm not sure I...'

He was interrupted by a harried-looking woman two places behind Hope, holding a baby in her arms while a child clung to her skirt. 'She's at number fifty-seven,' she said. 'Are you buyin' owt? Look sharp if not.'

Hope mumbled her thanks. Back on the street, she walked past the manufactory she had seen at nighttime from her seat in the cab, and the same row of brick terraced houses before she came to a plot of open land strewn with rubble and weeds and, beyond that, the larger detached properties. She stopped outside number fifty-seven, then crossed over the road to stand opposite the dwelling. Again, she told herself she ought to return to the house. The foundations of her suspicion lay in that startled look given her by Miss Barlow, a flimsy reason to continue. But there was more. The child was the right age, the right sex. He had come from the house. Hope closed her eyes. She had signed the paperwork releasing him.

The prisms of lustre vases in the downstairs bay window of the house fractured the sunlight into shards. How might she reach between those daggers of light to knock on the door? Her child resided in this house, or not. Either eventuality might shatter her heart. She tried to recall Alice's exact words to Miss Barlow. *He'll never know any different. You helped bring it about.* Her mother's lament came to her, too. *How can you remain in a town that contains the child you gave up?*

Hope re-crossed the road and stood before the black painted door. There was a knocker and, to the left above the lock, a striking instrument for a bell. Her stomach shrinking in fear, Hope lifted the small brass lever and let it fall. She could hear the bell ring on the other side of the door and, after a few moments, the sound of approaching steps. She inhaled sharply and stumbled back. What had possessed her? She was acting like the kind of person Amelia would call a barmpot. There was still time to conceal her face behind the shawl, to hurry away. Her identity had never been revealed to her child's new parents, Miss Barlow had sworn this to her. Likewise, she had never been given theirs.

The door opened, and she remained rooted to the spot.

'How do,' said the woman on the threshold. She was holding a boy on her hip, a fat-cheeked little creature with a blond mop of hair the exact same shade as Hope's. He held a lump of cheese in his fist and was regarding Hope through narrowed eyes, as if she might steal it from him.

Miraculously, she found her voice. 'Good day. Am I speaking to Mrs Silas Hinchcliffe?'

'Nope.' The woman tipped her head to the side and looked Hope up and down. 'I'm Ginny Hinchcliffe, her sister-in-law who's been left holding the baby, as per usual. Is there a message?' She shifted the boy to her other hip. Hope tried not to stare at him. 'He's a bruiser, this one. They're at the bank, the pair o' them, growin' their empire. Come on in.'

To Hope's astonishment the woman simply turned and walked away without waiting for a response. Hope looked down the street. She might leave, still, but now she had seen the child it was impossible not to follow the woman inside. She hurried down a walnut-panelled corridor and into a sitting room made cosy with velvet cushions and throws and candelabra everywhere Hope looked. A blue Jasperware vase stood in the veined marble fireplace. Sheet music rested above the exposed keys of an upright piano of lacquered walnut. The lustre she had seen from across the road sat on a round mahogany table. Hope had thought the size of the house modest considering Teddy's adoptive father owned a steel works but the furnishings were decidedly not.

The woman pointed to an armchair beside a table holding a crystal bowl of walnuts and Hope obediently sat. The surface of the lace cloth was pocked with broken nutshells. She put the boy down – he steadied himself by placing a chubby hand on Hope's knee, melting her heart

– and picked up the nutcracker from the rug and placed it on top of the bowl. 'What have I told you about playin' with this, Teddy?' she said, giving Hope a chagrined look. 'I remember this from when my Isaac was a babe. You need eyes in the back of your head.'

Hope watched Teddy stagger towards a wooden rocking horse in the middle of the room. She put her hand on her knee where he had touched it.

'Sorry,' said Ginny Hinchcliffe. 'Did he cover you in crumbs?'

'No, no.' She gulped. 'That's quite all right.'

Ginny tilted her head to the side again. The scrutiny brought colour to Hope's cheeks.

'So, what can I do for you?'

'I'm actually in search of Mrs Hinchcliffe's niece, Alice Leigh. Do you know Alice?'

'Course I do. Lovely lass.' Ginny shook her head. 'She has some silly ideas in her head, though. A good-looking girl like her should be interested in one thing and one thing only.'

'What's that?' said Hope, faintly. The boy was yanking at the horsehair mane.

'Behave, Teddy,' said Ginny. 'We've company. Finding a husband to keep her in clover, a'course.'

Teddy poked at the rocking horse's large green glass eye with a stubby finger and stumbled back towards Hope. She caught his hands in hers and examined his face, the snub nose, the dimpled cheeks and large blue eyes. Weren't all babies blue-eyed? Hadn't she heard that somewhere? It didn't mean anything. She shouldn't try to find signs that didn't exist.

'I'll rock you,' she said gently. 'May I?'

'Be my guest,' said Ginny. 'D'you want a cup of tea?'

'No,' Hope said over her shoulder as she carried Teddy to the rocking horse and sat him on it. 'Thank you, but I won't keep you.' She tried for a light-hearted tone. 'I imagine our paths crossed and Alice is at the house now, looking for me. This is one of the addresses she gave, should we ever need her. I'm deputy warden there.'

'A young girl like you?'

Hope smiled politely.

She held Teddy around his firm little middle and rocked the horse back and forth, facing away from Ginny Hinchcliffe so that the woman would not see the yearning written across her face.

—

Hope stiffened when she heard voices from outside the room. She had accepted a cup of tea after all and had been content to be regaled by Ginny's adventures on distant shores while Teddy chased a spinning top about the room.

'Finally,' said Ginny, rolling her eyes. 'They do take advantage of me, I have to say.'

A middle-aged couple entered the room, the woman handsomely attired, her hair dressed in a neat chignon beneath a hat that was not the fashion but suited her red hair and high cheekbones. She smiled enquiringly, but kindly, at Hope. The man Hope presumed to be Mr Hinchcliffe was, she could tell straightaway, of rougher stock, as attractive as his wife but in a wilder way. His hair was unkempt, his hands those of a working man. Teddy launched himself at the man, who swept him up into his arms. ''Ey up, lad. Been charmin' the ladies?'

Alice came into the room, her eyes widening when she saw Hope. She laughed lightly. 'This is a surprise. What brings you here?'

'A friend o' thine?' said the man.

Introductions were made and they engaged in small talk about the weather. Yes, it was exceptionally warm today, but the summer had been unseasonably affected by thunder and lightning storms. Alice talked about the autumn wedding of the warden of the House of Help, now two weeks away. Mr and Mrs Hinchcliffe agreed that there was a special quality in love found later in life, although they had found theirs in their youth, and they smiled affectionately at each other. Hope liked them at once.

Ginny declared she was going upstairs to lay on her bed. 'That child has exhausted me.'

After she had gone, Hope began to tell the Hinchcliffes that Teddy was a fine young boy, and obviously well loved, but her eyes filled with tears and she trailed off. She feared she was on the point of breaking down entirely in front of these strangers, who were now looking at her with concerned expressions. Alice saved her this indignity.

'Shall we walk back to the house together?' she said. 'I need to speak with Amelia. Do you know, I think I've found the perfect beau for her.'

Mrs Hinchcliffe laughed. 'You and your machinations.'

'I don't know this Amelia lass,' said Mr Hinchcliffe, 'but I already feel sorry for her.'

Outside, Hope focused on putting one foot in front of the other while Alice chattered away about her forthcoming meeting. 'You'll come, won't you?'

'Of course,' Hope murmured.

Eventually, Alice asked the question she had been dreading. 'You never really explained, I'm wondering how you came to be at my aunt and uncle's house today?'

Hope could not use the same excuse she'd given Ginny. Alice had never listed the Wellington Street address as a place she might be contacted, and Hope had not come up with a reason for seeking Alice out. If she answered Alice's question with a question of her own, and paid particular attention to Alice's response, perhaps the truth might be revealed. She thought about the dimples in Teddy's cheeks, dimples like her own, and set her jaw.

'If you knew something,' said Hope, 'about Teddy's parentage, who his real mother is, say, would you reveal it to me? I know he is adopted, from the house. I overheard you talking about it with Miss Barlow.'

Alice laughed, an artless sound as far as Hope could tell. 'What on earth do you mean?' she said. She looked away from Hope's gaze, down the street. 'Let's cross here, shall we, while it's quiet.'

On the other side of the road, Hope stopped and faced Alice. 'I'm sorry, I should make myself clear. I gave up a child. He would be Teddy's age now, or thereabouts.'

'Oh,' said Alice. 'I'm so sorry. I wasn't aware.' She fanned her face with her hand. 'This heat…'

'I apologise if I am making you feel uncomfortable.' Hope shook her head when Alice began to protest. 'But I would value your advice.'

Alice cast her eyes around as if she would rather Hope take advice from the pavement shoeshiner who was sitting on his box nearby, waiting for trade. 'Oh?' she said.

'Your aunt and uncle adopted Teddy from the house, is that correct?' asked Hope.

'Yes,' said Alice. She looked miserable.

'I think he might be—' Hope gulped and flattened her hand against the base of her throat, fearful of the words that clamoured to be spoken. 'Alice, I think Teddy might be my son.'

The dam broke on the tumult of emotions she had struggled to keep at bay. Blinded by tears, Hope was barely aware of Alice taking her hand and leading her towards the entrance of a nearby alleyway, away from the busy pavement and curious stares of passers-by. A few steps into the shadowed passage, Hope leaned back against the damp brick and wiped her face with her fingers, as a child would. The two women looked helplessly at one another.

Finally, Alice reached out to pat Hope's arm, tentatively. 'At the very time a handkerchief is needed, I don't have one to offer.'

Hope shook her head and took a deep breath and then regretted it. The air was rotten. She turned her head towards the main street, where, incomprehensibly, everyday life went on. 'I shouldn't have spoken.'

'But you did,' said Alice, gently. 'Why do you believe Teddy is your son?'

Hope's throat closed. A deep sense of shame prevented her from telling Alice she had eavesdropped on her conversation with the warden.

'Perhaps,' continued Alice, 'you ought to speak to Miss Barlow.'

Overwhelmed by the concern on Alice's face and the kindness in her eyes, Hope instinctively embraced her. She felt Alice's hesitation before her arms went around Hope. The reason for Alice's reticence was clear. She must find Hope wanting, now she knew the truth about her, that Hope was the mother to an illegitimate child, and that she had given that child up.

But there was nothing but sympathy in Alice's eyes when she pulled away to examine Hope's face.

'Don't despair,' said Alice. 'My mother always says it'll all come out in the wash.'

Hope searched her eyes. 'Will it?'

'Well, I don't know.' Alice pulled a face, making Hope laugh despite herself. 'It's another one of her many sayings. Don't pay me any mind.' She gently tucked a loose strand of hair behind Hope's ear. 'Listen, Hope, don't pay owt I say any mind.'

Chapter 10

Polly Bramall was buried in a common grave, unmarked. From the dock, her husband claimed she had shamed him and he was not sure he could, in all good conscience, attend the inquest. The magistrate replied that he would do Mr Bramall the favour of removing that dilemma and sentenced him to three weeks' incarceration for threatening behaviour. This information was relayed to Alice by the warden, who in turn had it from Constable Goodlad.

Only in death had Polly Bramall escaped her husband's clutches.

'I'm told he still carries a grievance against us, against this house,' said Miss Barlow, closing the house ledger and replacing it in her desk drawer. 'So have a care. He'll be out before we know it.'

Alice had been leaning on the doorframe. She straightened and crossed her arms. 'He's got a brass neck,' she said fiercely. 'He drove her to—'

Miss Barlow held up a hand to silence her. 'All I'm sayin', love, is stay out of his path.'

'He'd best stay out of mine.'

Alice had come to seek out the warden while waiting for Amelia to change out of her housekeeper's uniform. Alice had been seated at the kitchen table scribbling notes that would form the basis of her speech on female enfranchisement and quickly became absorbed in the task.

Posters were now on display at the venue, as well as in the front room windows of family, friends and acquaintances, and a paid advertisement placed in one of the local newspapers. She had written to Mr Mundella, the local member of parliament, inviting him to attend, and received a thank you note but, frustratingly, no response to her request in the negative or affirmative. Letters had been posted to the aldermen of the town and their wives, and she had also written to the first woman to win a seat on the School Board seven years earlier, a formidable woman who now chaired it. Ms Sarah Ruth Wilson regretfully could not attend but promised to spread the word, and suggested Alice target the working women of the town. Alice duly stood outside factories when the whistles blew and pressed her leaflets into the hands of women coming off shift.

None of these workers stopped to enquire further and she saw several women ball up the paper and drop it onto the pavement without even affording it a glance. Afterwards, Alice had salvaged what she could.

'You were grubbin' about in the gutter?' said Isaac, incredulously, when she told him this. 'Makin' a fool o' yersen wi' this daft crusade?'

Alice had been furious with him, the angriest she'd been since they were children and he would trip her or steal a beloved toy or ruin a game he happened to be losing.

He evidently mistook her stony silence for acquiescence, for he continued his argument. 'Why are you even botherin' with all this? Nowt'll come of it, this fad o' thine. Grow up, Alice. For once, do as your mother tells you an' make her happy.'

Alice had reminded him he wasn't the most dutiful son in the world, and he'd snapped that his problem was he had mothers to spare. As was usual of late, they had parted on bad terms.

Scribbling away at the kitchen table, she had forgotten she had something of import to tell Miss Barlow. Now, standing on the threshold of the warden's quarters, she glanced over her shoulder, anticipating Amelia's return at any moment, and wrung her hands.

'What's up?' said Miss Barlow.

Alice blurted out the words. 'Hope knows Teddy is her son.' The warden's eyes widened as Alice hurried on. 'At least, she thinks he is. She's not certain. She turned up at my aunt and uncle's house.'

'Oh dear.' Miss Barlow put a hand to her mouth. 'Was anything said?'

'No.' Alice glanced down the hallway then back at the warden. 'Fortunately, I was with them, with Aunt Harriet and Uncle Silas. We returned together and Hope was already there, playing on the carpet.'

Miss Barlow raised an eyebrow. 'On the carpet?'

'With a spinning top. With Teddy.'

'All right. Go on.'

'I took her away as fast as I could, and she asked me whether he could be her child. So she must've been listening to us.' Alice took a breath, her chest tight with a gnawing sense of guilt. Poor Hope, forced to put two and two together from an overheard and careless conversation. 'I feel responsible.'

Miss Barlow sat back and pursed her lips. 'And what did you say, when she asked if Teddy was hers?'

'I only said that she should talk to you.'

'And when exactly was this?'

Alice bit her lip. 'A few days ago. I haven't had the opportunity to tell you before now.'

'And your aunt and uncle?'

'They have no idea, I'm certain of it.'

The door to the warden's quarters was flung open and Amelia marched in, elbows akimbo as she fiddled with the ribbon of the straw boater she wore. 'Can somebody help me wi' this? I can't get the bow right.'

Alice spoke in a rush. 'Hope told them she'd been looking for me regarding a house matter. She said I'd given my aunt and uncle's address as well as my own.'

' 'Ey up, another new hat?' said Miss Barlow. 'I'm sure all your income goes on hats, what d'you think, Alice?'

The warden's eyes told Alice that the subject of Hope was closed.

'I think it's lovely,' said Alice. 'Especially with the dress.'

Amelia had forsaken her regular black for a dove-grey jacket over a white blouse and dark blue skirt. Her thick, dark hair was tied back in a loose ponytail and her brown eyes sparkled. She looked perfect for the occasion Alice had contrived to arrange. Pushing the complexities of Hope's situation to the back of her mind, she helped Amelia with the ribbon of her bonnet.

'There.'

'Thank you. I was all fingers and thumbs.' Amelia turned to her mother. 'I'll be back by six o'clock. On Shank's pony or in one o' Greaves's cabs if the weather turns.'

Hetty Barlow looked pleased as punch. 'Enjoy yourself, love,' she said. 'Alice, give your mother my regards.'

'I will,' said Alice. And she would, later, after her little soiree, when her mother returned home from work.

She hurried back to the kitchen to scoop up the papers she'd been scribbling on and tucked them into her purse. There were seven days left in which to hone and refine and practise a passionate declamation. And only a week after that would come the wedding of the warden to the treasurer of the trustees. Alice intended to invite Isaac as her guest, however disgruntled with him she might be, and try to repair their friendship. And, in this moment, she had another design, involving Amelia. Her heart tripped with delight in these well-intentioned schemes.

'Come on,' she said to Amelia, 'let's make hay while the sun shines.'

They called into a bakery on Norfolk Street to collect the pastries that Alice had ordered the previous day then doubled back on themselves to Pond Street and the cottage Louisa Leigh rented. Inside, Alice had already prepared the sitting room, filling the grate with fresh flowers and straightening the furniture. She put out the cat and set the kettle on the stove to boil. When the knock on the door came at precisely three o'clock, Amelia put her hands to her face, her eyes wide, prompting a burst of laughter from Alice. Still, her own face was heated when she admitted the man who stood on the doorstep.

She led him into the sitting room, where Amelia was waiting.

'This is my friend Miss Amelia Barlow,' said Alice. 'Amelia, I'd like you to meet Mr Barnaby Greaves.'

–

'Let me borrow your hat,' said Alice.

Barnaby handed it over and she sprinkled folded bits of paper into it like confetti.

'Charades?' he said.

'Yes,' said Alice, 'and you go first, Amelia.'

Amelia's teacup clattered into its saucer. 'I'm not a good enough actor for this. You start us off, Alice.'

'I can't.' Alice couldn't keep the mischievous grin from her face. 'I know all the answers.'

'Aye,' Amelia replied with a smirk. 'All the answers to everything, eh?'

Barnaby laughed. 'I've heard Miss Leigh is somewhat opinionated.'

'How dare you!' said Alice in mock horror.

They were conspiring against her and she could not be more delighted. Earlier, relishing her role as chaperone, Alice had deliberately left her two guests alone, giving the excuse of preparing the tea tray, and taking her time about it, but returned to find them sitting in a palpably awkward silence. She'd hurried out again. A parlour game would break the ice. They were too few to play Pass the Slipper so she had hastily assembled a game of Charades.

And, look, already the ground was thawing.

'Give it here, then,' said Amelia, and took one of the scraps of paper from the hat. She got up from the seat Alice had placed her in beside Barnaby and unfolded the paper. She frowned.

'Is this a play, or a book?' she said. 'I can't make head nor tail of it.'

Barnaby laughed. 'If you have the answer and still can't work it out, there's no hope for me.'

Amelia held it up to the light. '"Women of—" what's this? I can't read the word "*something* thought were once—" another long word, hang on "were once denounced as witches and burnt at the stake."'

'Well,' said Barnaby, 'this isn't the light-hearted game I was anticipating.'

'Independent,' Alice blurted, a blush rising to her cheeks. 'Women of *independent* thought. I was jotting down ideas for what I'm planning to say at my meeting. Look on the other side! Oh, for goodness' sake.' She waited for their laughter to subside. 'Let's play on.'

'Ah, I know this,' said Amelia. She screwed up the paper and looked for somewhere to put it. Barnaby held out his hand. 'No peeking, Mr Greaves,' she said primly, dropping the scrap into his palm.

Alice watched him watching Amelia as she put her palms together as if in prayer then opened out her hands. She hid her smile of satisfaction.

'Book,' said Barnaby.

—

Barnaby had fetched up coal and lit a fire, and they were toasting crumpets when the rattle of the front door announced the arrival home of Alice's mother.

'Oh, she's early,' said Alice.

Amelia stopped scooping butter onto a knife, like a child caught in a naughty act, and Barnaby set down his plate and straightened his collar. Alice sighed. Their intimate afternoon tea party was over.

Louisa entered the room carrying a wicker basket, with another woman following behind her. Ginny bestowed smiles all round, her eyes coming to rest on Barnaby. Alice made the introductions.

'Well,' her mother said, 'are you stayin' for tea?' She lifted the basket. 'I've a pie just needs warmin' through. There's enough.'

Amelia shook her head. 'Thank you but I should be gettin' home.' She turned to Alice. 'I've had a lovely time, best time in ages.'

'Yes, Alice is the perfect host,' said Barnaby, 'and a credit to her mother.'

'Get away,' said Louisa, a broad smile on her face.

'He's a charmer,' said Ginny. 'Are you staying, Mr Greaves?'

'No, I'll leave you in peace,' he said.

Alice saw Amelia and Barnaby out then galloped back to the front room window and lifted the net in time to see them set off in opposite directions. He hadn't offered to walk her home? Or perhaps he had, and Amelia had refused. Crestfallen, she let the curtain drop.

'A handsome young man.' Ginny dropped onto the settee. 'I'm beat.'

'Mother's business partner,' said Alice. She straightened her shoulders and cut her eyes at her mother. '*A reight eligible young bachelor.*'

'You might well mock,' said Louisa. 'But I'm glad to see you've finally come to your senses.'

'Not me,' said Alice. 'I thought I'd introduce him to Amelia, see how they get on.'

Louisa rolled her eyes.

'And how did they get on?' said Ginny.

Alice see-sawed her hands. 'Seemingly well.'

Ginny laughed. 'Might require a bit more of your matchmaking, eh?'

'Is this the housekeeper from that place you practically live at?' asked Louisa, tetchily.

'Marry well and live in ease,' said Alice. 'It's only what you keep telling me.'

'Aye, you. Not half the town.' Louisa shook her head. 'I'll get tea goin'. Ginny, want to help?'

It struck Alice that her mother was always twitchy in the presence of Isaac's mother. She wondered, again, about their shared history.

'I'll keep Alice company,' said Ginny. 'I'm worn out.'

Louisa pressed her lips together and exited without another word.

'Your mother wants us all to work as hard as she does,' said Ginny.

'I beg your pardon?' Alice laughed. 'She doesn't want me to work at all.'

'Aye, well, she's got me learnin' this telephone business. Says I can have a job sittin' and waitin' for it to ring an' then I'm to organise a cab for some lord or lady.'

'It doesn't sound over-strenuous,' said Alice, 'compared to working in a saloon in a gold-mining town.'

Ginny smiled. 'Did I ever tell you about the time...' and she was off on one of her outlandish-sounding stories. Alice only half-listened to this latest tale, nodding politely from time to time, wanting to get onto her own agenda before her mother returned.

'Ginny,' she said, during a lull in the monologue. 'May I ask a favour? Will you join with me if I set up a women's group? Will you help me?'

'What, a sewing circle or the like?'

'No.' Alice laughed. 'A group that will fight for the rights of women.'

'You're not still going on about that, are you?' The woman sounded genuinely puzzled.

Alice was momentarily lost for words. 'Do you know,' she said finally, 'rebellious women were called witches not so long ago, and murdered by the state.'

'Hundreds o' years ago,' said Ginny. 'Times have changed.'

'Not enough for my liking. Look at Polly!'

Ginny looked bemused. 'Who's Polly?'

'She came asking for help, and we tried to give it. She's dead now, by her own hand, because she could see no escape.' Alice pressed a hand to her mouth. She refused to give in to tears. Swallowing the lump in her throat, she continued. 'And there's Hope's situation, too. What about her? Would you tell her that times have changed, that women are not still being mistreated?'

'Oh yes, Hope.' Ginny tapped her chin. 'She's the one from your women's house who turned up the other day. She was very taken with our Teddy. What injustice befell her, then?'

'A terrible injustice,' said Alice. 'She had a child out of wedlock, was forced to give him up and pines for her little boy every day.'

Ginny's eyes were sparkling with curiosity. 'She's a dark horse, isn't she? Can't judge a book by its cover, eh? What happened to him, her boy?'

Alice faltered. She was caught on the hook of Ginny's inquisitiveness. She ought never to have opened her mouth. 'He... ah, he was... um.' She set her jaw. 'He was adopted.'

Ginny's eyes narrowed. 'How old is he?'

'I'm not sure,' said Alice.

'You're not a very good liar. You know what I'm thinking, love. Her turning up like that. You should have seen her, mothering little Ted. In tears, she was. Thought I didn't see.' Ginny smiled, a cat who'd got the cream. 'You told me it was Teddy's adoption led you to that house, where Hope just happens to work. My, my. What a nerve, turning up like that. What will Silas and Harriet have to say about it?'

Alice gasped. 'Ginny, you mustn't interfere. *We* mustn't interfere. Promise me you won't say anything.'

Ginny tilted her head and widened her eyes in a parody of concern that made Alice's gut churn. 'But the woman's evidently out of control. I'm only thinking of Harriet. Here I am' – she spread her arms – 'returning out of the blue, although nobody could blame me for seeking out my son, and here's your friend Hope coming to claim the other lad. Poor Harriet.'

Alice pulled at the collar of her blouse as if that might prevent the heat from rising into her cheeks. This was all her doing. She had spoken carelessly, intent only on enlisting Ginny to the cause. Stupid, stupid.

Then Ginny laughed, a sharp bark that made Alice flinch. 'I'm only teasing. You know you're about as red as a tomato.'

'It's too warm in here,' said Alice. 'We should never have lit a fire on a day such as this. I don't know what we were thinking. Let's talk about my campaign.'

Ginny smiled craftily. 'It's funny, I remember now that you couldn't get her out of the house fast enough. Who else knows?' She nodded towards the door. 'Your mother in on it?'

'No! Listen to me. I misspoke.' Alice was embarrassed by her pleading tone but the idea of Ginny revealing the truth was too horrifying to contemplate. 'It's not our business. Please, Ginny. Can you keep this to yourself, for me?'

The smile dropped from Ginny's face. 'I suppose Hope can join me in the good-for-nothing club.' Her voice was bitter now. 'I abandoned my child, don't you know, to run off with a crook and have now come crawling back on my knees expectin' charity.'

Alice was shocked. 'Says who?'

Ginny shrugged. 'It's what you're all thinking, the whole lot of you.' She tilted her head towards the door. 'Your mother too, and she was no angel.'

'Well, I don't think that,' said Alice. 'I think you've got gumption.' She hesitated. 'What do you mean about my mother when you say that?'

Ginny gave her a speculative look. 'Tell you what, if you can persuade that son o' mine to come and see me, then I'll keep your little secret, cross my heart, and I'll even answer some of those questions I know you've got, about yourself, about your mother.'

Alice's heart jolted. 'And about my father? Did you know him?'

Ginny wagged her finger. 'Get Isaac to forgive me first. Cast a witch's spell on him. He thinks the world of you.'

'You don't know him very well if you think I've got any influence,' said Alice. 'He won't listen to me.'

Ginny's stony expression told her that she had better try. In the beat of silence that followed, Louisa shouted from the kitchen. 'Anybody comin' to eat this or shall I gi' it the cat?'

'Coming,' called Alice. She turned to Ginny, took in the arched eyebrows that posed a challenge Alice must accept, and the wounded eyes that touched her heart. 'All right, Ginny, I promise to try my best.'

Chapter 11

The two children sat together, shrouded in darkness on the top stair, eavesdropping on the adults below. Isaac had warned Alice that if anyone appeared they were to run, as silently as they could, back to their beds and pretend to be sleeping. This made her giggle and he'd had to summon all his patience to wait until she could be trusted to remain quiet before they crept down the darkened hall. Isaac might have attempted to persuade his little cousin to go back to her bed but knew she'd become narky and then, inevitably, he would be the one in trouble. Alice was half his age, a pesky little creature just turned five with a bottomless well of stupid questions.

But now, finally, his patience was being rewarded. Elbows propped on knees, Isaac cupped both ears, straining to hear with all his might over the ticking of the grandfather clock in the downstairs hall. They were talking about his real mother, the one that had run off. It had never been described to him in those terms, but he knew.

Amid the murmured conversation, Aunt Louisa's voice suddenly rang clear. 'And it's how many years since that letter? An' not a peep out o' her. She's not comin' back, I'm telling thee.'

'I say good riddance. I could see what were comin' as soon as she took up wi' Joseph Crookes.'

That was his father. Isaac leaned as far forward as he could without toppling down the stairs. He'd heard this lament before and knew his mother wouldn't stand for it.

'Please, Silas. Passing judgment on his mother won't help that poor mite upstairs. What if she does return, and Isaac's mind is full of poison?'

'He's not heard owt from me.'

'What are they on about?' said Alice in a whisper to wake the dead.

'Shush!'

Isaac clouted her on the arm, which was a mistake. Alice's mouth dropped open in dismay. Any moment now a screech like chalk down a blackboard would emerge from that tiny throat. Isaac put his finger to his lips, his face creased with fury, and pulled her to her feet. At the same time, the door to the sitting room snicked closed. The two children froze for a moment, staring wide-eyed at each other, then Isaac gestured for her to go to the bedroom she was staying in for the night with her mother. But despite all his efforts to shoo her away, Alice followed him into his room.

'You hit me,' she said, triumphantly, once they were inside and the door safely closed. 'Aunt Harriet'll tan your hide in the mornin'.'

'Only if tha snitches on me. If you do, I'll hit you again.'

Alice didn't deign to reply. She tugged open the top drawer of the bureau by his bed. 'Have you any spice?'

'No.'

'My mama gave you some fudge squares.'

'I ate 'em all up.'

Alice pouted. 'What were they talkin' about? Was it about Christmas? I want skates.'

Isaac sighed. 'No.' He flung himself onto the bed and lay prone. 'It was about me.'

'Oh.' Alice plonked herself beside him, pushing her weight against his hip. 'What about you?'

'Alice, get yersen off to bed.'

She shook her head. 'You can't make me.'

The family joke was that Alice was Isaac's shadow. It was true that he could never seem to shake her off. Why hadn't Louisa a boy he could teach to play football instead of this little squirrel poking her nose into everything?

'Tell me what they were sayin',' said Alice. She affected the lisp she knew worked wonders with adults. 'Please tell me. Please, Isaac.'

He rubbed his eyes. 'All right then. Your uncle Silas and aunt Harriet aren't my real parents. They took me in when my mother ran off, when I was little like you. She got in wi' thieves and killers.'

Alice's mouth dropped open again, this time in shock. 'Stop fibbing. It's a sin to tell a lie.'

'I'm not fibbin'.' He sat up with a groan. 'Look, I'll show you summat she gave me before she ran away. Then go to bed, all right?'

When he pressed his half of the silver coin into her palm, Alice scowled. 'It's broken, an' it's sharp.' She ran a chubby little finger along the edge. 'Ouch.'

Isaac took it from her, squeezing it in his fist. 'My real mother's got the matchin' piece.'

Alice was as wide-eyed as an owl. 'Did she bite it in half?'

'No, you daft apeth. It were done wi' a jeweller's saw. That's what Father reckons. It's an American coin.'

'American!' Alice whispered the word with awe. 'What does that mean?'

'Means nowt.'

'Where is she now, your mama?'

'Nobody knows.' He spoke flippantly, demonstrating to her that he was being a man about it. 'Aunt Louisa's right. She'll not be back. Father's right too, whatever Mother says.'

'Do you miss her?' Alice hugged her elbows. 'I'd cry if my mama went away. I'd never stop cryin'.'

Isaac shrugged. 'Can't miss somebody you don't remember.'

Alice examined his face. 'So you're not sad?'

'I'm not sad.'

She burst into sobs.

'What's up wi' thee now?' said Isaac.

'What if my mama goes away an' I forget all about her?' She jumped off the bed and ran to the door, reaching up to wrench it open, wailing her head off.

Isaac let her go. Later, as he lay in bed, the door opened and Harriet came in. He had hurriedly turned away and closed his eyes as soon as the doorknob began to turn but he knew his mother by her soft steps and the scent she wore. She whispered his name and when he didn't respond sat on the edge of his bed and stroked his shoulder, and told him that if he ever had any questions, about his mother or anything else, she would try her hardest to answer them.

Isaac kept still until she went away.

—

He was gazing out of the window of his room above the butcher's shop, smoking a cigarette and watching the world go by, when he saw her walk to a bench, sit on it and look straight at him.

Instinctively, Isaac stepped back. She couldn't have seen him for the glare on the pane but it was clear Alice had told her where he was lodging. Stubbing out the cigarette, he grabbed his jacket and cap and went down. He was prepared for a lecture but there was no denying the lift in his spirits the sight of her had given him. He approached unseen and squinted down at her, relishing the warmth of the sun on his neck and the brightness of the cobbles from a passing shower. The air was, briefly, fresh as new paint.

' 'Ey up.'

'Good morning.' The corners of Harriet's eyes crinkled with pleasure. 'It appears I've been reduced to stalking you.'

Chastened, Isaac sat beside her and nudged her shoulder. 'I were comin' to see thee, next Sunday or the one after. Work's been busy.'

He waited for her to tell him this was a poor excuse.

'Do you know,' said his mother, 'yesterday I had a sudden recollection of reading in the local newspaper the results of the Birmingham election. This would have been in April.'

Isaac scratched his head, wondering what this had to do with his failings as a son. 'Oh aye? A few month since, then?'

'Yes.'

Harriet leaned away to study his face. Whenever she did this, he felt as if all his deepest thoughts were written on his skin for her to read.

'It must have stuck in my mind,' she said, 'because of the droll way it was reported. The newspaper office had acquired one of these telephonic instruments and the result was received on the new instrument seven minutes before it arrived by telegraph and pneumatic tube, making telephony the clear winner.' She shook her head in wonderment. 'If anyone had told me that you'd end up working for the company supplying this new-fangled machinery I would never have believed them. I can see why it excites you.'

Isaac waited.

'But be that as it may, your father is disappointed.'

'Aye,' said Isaac. 'I worked that one out for mesen.'

'He hopes you will come back. He misses you.'

'Has he said as much?'

Harriet smiled. 'You're as stubborn as each other.'

'I suppose *she's* still at the house.'

'Ginny is, yes. I've managed to persuade your aunt Louisa to offer her a job.' She sighed. 'We'll see.' This was as close as his mother would come to suggesting that Ginny wouldn't last two minutes at Greaves's cab company. 'Your father didn't help, when I was appealing to Louisa.'

'What did he say?'

'He called Ginny a flibbertigibbet.'

Isaac laughed. 'I'm sure that's not news to Aunt Louisa. I'm goin' to see her now. First job o' the day. D'you want to come along? It's a hike, mind, for thee.'

His mother stood and Isaac took her arm. 'Let's take it slow, then,' she said.

Steering her through the busy streets of the town, he told her about his training as an engineer for the Telephone Exchange and Electric Light Company and about the projects being undertaken.

'Mother, you ought to get a device installed.'

'I wonder at the expense of it, for the return,' said Harriet.

'One day, every household will have its own personal telephone. Lines are goin' out to Baslow, next.'

Harriet smiled. 'I'm not acquainted with anyone in Baslow. But the idea of voices being transmitted through overhead wires does intrigue me. Isaac, will I be able to eavesdrop on private conversations as I walk along the street?'

He laughed. 'Soon, me an' thee will be able to natter to each other from miles apart as if we're in the same room.'

'It will save me when I want to speak to my son,' his mother said, 'from having to come and find you.'

When Isaac and Harriet entered Louisa's office above the yard, she was fiddling with the device that hung on the wall beside the window, her blonde hair like Alice's haloed against the bright pane. She looked over her shoulder at them. 'What d'you make o' this, then?'

Harriet went over and tapped gently on each of the two bells at the top of the rectangular wooden board. A round mouthpiece sat centrally below them, above it the maker's mark like a moustache. 'A face,' she said, 'startled because its long nose has drifted off to the side.'

Isaac lifted the speaker from its cradle. 'It's not connected,' he said, a question in his voice.

'No,' said Louisa, 'they're out there now, fixing summat or other. Tha's late.'

He grimaced. 'I would've been quicker but...'

'He kept my pace,' said Harriet.

Isaac kissed his mother on the forehead. 'I'd best go.'

He jogged downstairs, fully aware he would be one of their topics of conversation. Oh, to be a fly on the wall. Or not. Nothing good ever came from eavesdropping.

Isaac tolerated the telling off he got from the engineer he was apprenticed to, pulled his cap low and set to the tasks he was given, with none of the resentment he'd felt, wrongly or rightly, at Hinchcliffe & Son.

At dinnertime, he wiped his hands on a rag as he watched Louisa wave his mother off in a cab, declined the offer of a pork pie in the drivers' shack and followed his aunt indoors.

'No Barnaby Greaves today?' Isaac said, as casually as he could.

'Scarce as hen's teeth when I need him,' said Louisa, 'though he seems at Alice's beck and call.'

Isaac's stomach plunged. 'Would you see her wed to him?'

His aunt turned at the top of the stairs and looked down at him. 'Listen, lad. I don't want my girl workin' the way I did. I don't want her wi' a job an' bairns and a bloke to run round after, allus worryin' where her next shilling's comin' from an' worn out from cookin' and cleanin'. I've seen it enough times.' She gave him a long look before turning away. 'I'd never force owt on her. You should know that.'

Isaac followed her into the office and closed the door behind him. 'Can I have a word?' he said.

'Have as many as tha likes. I'm not chargin' thee for them.' Louisa unwrapped the shawl from around her shoulders then thought better of it. 'Is it me, or is there a proper nip in the air today?' She dug a shovel into the scuttle and tipped a few pieces of coal onto the kindling in the grate. 'Runnin' out,' she muttered.

'Don't you have a boy for that?' said Isaac.

'Aye. Here. Tha knows where the cellar is.' She gave him the scuttle and sat in the chair by the hearth.

If he went off on an errand to fetch coal, the chances were good he'd return to find someone in her office, demanding her time, or she would still be alone but he would find he'd lost his nerve.

'Can I have that word first?' asked Isaac. He stood before her, scuttle in hand.

Louisa gazed up at him, her eyebrows lifted in surprise. 'What's up, love?'

'Nowt.' He took a breath. 'I mean, it's past time I settled down, an' there's only one girl for me, allus has been the case, an' I want your blessin', if you can see your way to giving it.' He paused. 'I'm talkin' about Alice.'

'Aye, I've worked that out.' Louisa sat back and folded her arms. 'You're cousins.'

'We're not,' said Isaac, vehemently, and then, more calmly. 'We're not related by blood. Are we?' She shook her head. 'Then there's nowt in the road, unless Alice feels different, an' I won't know that 'til I ask her.'

'All reight then.' Louisa nodded. 'To be honest wi' thee, I already knew.' She laughed gently. 'You should see the look on your face. Remember last time you were in, an' you were callin' the pair o' you kissing cousins? It was written all over that face o' thine. Alice can't see the wood for the trees, though, eh? Isaac, you're a decent lad, but I can't speak for her.'

'Will you allow it?' said Isaac.

'What if she says no?'

'We'll carry on as before, won't we?'

Louisa didn't answer.

Isaac spread his hands. 'I'm bringin' in the business.'

'You are that, lad.'

'She'll want for nowt.'

Louisa nodded slowly.

'I've to get back to work,' said Isaac. 'Don't say owt, will you, Aunt Louisa?'

'A' course I won't. Only this, an' take note.' Louisa leaned forward and took his hand. 'Like I said, I want an easy life for my girl, though heaven knows she tests my patience. Wait, let me finish. Tha's chucked thee inheritance away for a dream. I've had it on good authority there's an upset o'er these private companies runnin' wires in all directions and one day soon it's all comin' under the control o' the Post Office. What will tha do then?'

Isaac shrugged. 'I've heard that, an' all. They'll still need engineers. But I tell thee what, Aunt Louisa, I'd go back to Hinchcliffe & Son wi' me tail betwixt me legs if Alice'll have me an' if that's what she wants.'

—

Tucking under his arm the packet of sausage meat the butcher had thrown to him with a whistle, like he was a dog – although it was gratis so he wasn't really in a position to complain – Isaac fished in his pocket for his key, glancing up when he caught movement out of the corner of his eye. His heart leapt for joy. Alice was sitting at the top of the stairs, adjusting the ribbon on the bonnet resting on her lap. He had her mother's blessing. It was past time he declared himself.

'That's all the important women in me life in one day,' he said. 'Mother, Aunt Louisa and now thee. Three Queens o' the land.'

Alice raised an eyebrow. 'Which am I?'

'Queen of hearts, a'course!'

He'd made her laugh. Climbing the stairs towards her, Isaac held out his dirt-grimed hands, palms up then palms down, for Alice to examine. 'Best get mesen washed if tha's bringin' me home for tea. Look at me, I'm loppy.'

'Doesn't bother me.' Alice held out her hand and he pulled her to her feet. 'You can come for tea, if you want, but I've something to give you first.' A line appeared between her brows. 'It's important.'

Isaac squeezed her hand. 'All reight.'

Inside, she sat at the little table. He was aware of her eyes on him as he had his wash at the sink. Blinded by soap, he reached out a hand for the towel, enjoying the feel of Alice's cool fingers brushing his when she passed it over. He rubbed at his face and his hair and imagined them together, living in this simple domesticity. When he opened his eyes, it would be to find his wife dishing up plates of stew, her apron stretched over a rounded belly. The smell of just-baked bread would fill the kitchen. There'd be a woman who came in to clean and a neighbour who'd take in their laundry. He would never complain if he found Alice with her head stuck in a book. He had it all worked out.

The grin on Isaac's face faded when he turned towards Alice and took in her anxious look and, in the same moment, saw what she had placed on the table. The towel dropped from his hands.

Alice didn't speak. Keeping her eyes on his face, she gently pushed the two halves of the silver dollar together, to make a whole.

Chapter 12

If she was discovered, Hope intended to say she was busy preparing for that evening's reading and writing class. She walked the length of the room, trailing her fingers along the spines of the donated books crammed on the makeshift shelf on the wall, a pinewood dado that would serve until a bookcase could be sourced at no cost to the house. She used her thumb to rub a mark from the slate board that stood on its easel in the corner of the room. There was a residue of chalk smeared across the surface that no amount of elbow grease could erase.

Hope dropped into her chair, leaning against the curved backrest, crossing her ankles with a sigh. Made of walnut with a plush green leather seat, this chair – donated by a wealthy patron – had casters for feet and was a favourite with the younger residents who launched themselves and each other across the room whenever they got the chance at it. Clara complained they were ruining the floor but Hope was content to tolerate these small rebellions. There would be few opportunities for horseplay once the girls were put into service.

She had wiped away the tears of many bewildered girls, and women older than she, who had landed on the doorstep. Hope didn't know all the answers, and often there were no adequate answers to be found, but she listened and had a knack for getting to the truth of a situation.

When Miss Barlow praised her to the skies, Hope quailed inside, for she knew she was an imposter who found it easier to focus on the plight of others than to examine her own life. She had changed her identity when she arrived at the house and although there were no secrets remaining, she was under no illusions. She was hiding, still.

Planting her feet on the ground, Hope rolled the chair gently backwards and forwards, a wry smile on her face recalling the emotions of her day. In this moment, she was literally in hiding, having already run the gauntlet of Amelia, of her courtship with Angus and then Alice. She needed ten minutes alone to breathe. To take it all in. Leaning back again with another sigh, her gaze followed the coalsmoke from half a dozen chimneys rising to meet a low ceiling of cloud. Rain was forecast. The summer had been unsettled, stiflingly hot one minute and thunderous the next, the season seemingly over before it had begun. Autumn had arrived with a brisk snap of its fingers. Maybe Mother Nature was to blame for the febrile mood that hung over the house.

Amelia had been the first to collar her, immediately after breakfast. Hope had answered the door to two workmen come to measure the warden's quarters ahead of making alterations to the room. It was a simple matter of installing a partition wall and the job would be completed, they said, in a jiffy. This had further enraged an already agitated Amelia, who had expected to enjoy the entirety of her mother's quarters after the wedding for at least a little while and would now be confined to a small space adjacent to the new dormitory ahead of schedule.

'What am I supposed to do?' Amelia said, waving a piece of paper in the air.

'About what?' said Hope. It was a fait accompli as far as she could see. Turning girls away for lack of accommodation was never a pleasant task; the extra beds would be welcomed.

'This!' Amelia thrust a folded piece of paper at her.

'Ah,' said Hope. It was a letter, an invitation to tea two weeks hence, in the company of Amelia's mother. Fine penmanship, good quality paper. 'It's all very proper. Do you want to go?'

Amelia's shoulders had drooped. 'I don't know. He seems all reight. I thought he liked Alice.'

'Then you evidently thought wrong. Who is he?'

'His name's Barnaby Greaves an' he's partner in a cab company wi' Alice's mother. She – Alice, I mean – invited me round the other day an' I met him then.'

'So, it was just the three of you?'

'Aye.' Amelia shrugged. 'We played Charades.' She folded her arms. 'It was my afternoon off, tha knows.'

'Alice is quite the matchmaker considering she's resisting marriage for herself,' said Hope.

Amelia went to the hall mirror and fussed with her hair as if Barnaby Greaves was about to follow his letter into the house. 'We've got nowt in common,' she said. 'What will we talk about if I do go out wi' him? He's educated. I'm not. I mean to say,' she turned towards Hope, 'apart from the learnin' I got from you. I don't know what to do!'

'Sleep on it,' said Hope, 'then decide. There's no rush, although I shouldn't wait too long.' She laughed. 'Don't allow a month to go by. And remember, it's only afternoon tea with your mother. He's not marching you down the aisle.'

'Got enough o' that sort o' shenanigans goin' on,' Amelia grumbled. 'Hetty's a tinder box lookin' for a Lucifer. Can't hardly get a word out of her these days. I swear she'll explode before she even gets to the big day.'

She held out her hand for her letter and marched off down the hallway.

Then, just after midday, Hope shared the kitchen table with four residents of the house. Two of the women had been found jobs nearby and could barely spare the time to return halfway through the day for a hot dinner. They had become friends and were searching for lodgings to share. Also present was a girl of fourteen who was in ill health, palely complexioned and as thin as a rake. An orphan, she had been moved from pillar to post and, too frail for the servant training school, was destined for the workhouse. Miss Barlow had arranged for her to be seen by the doctor but he couldn't find what ailed her. Cook had taken pity on her and brought her pastry treats that the girl left crumbed on her plate.

Seated at the end of the table was a stranger to the town, a young woman who had needed a bed for the night and was waiting for her brother-in-law to collect her from High Bradfield. He was a widower and was bringing her to his farm to cook and clean and look after his large brood of children. It had all been arranged by her parents, she told Hope, anxiety written across her face.

'I'm sure you'll settle in, and your nieces and nephews will be excited to see you,' Hope had told her. She wondered if the girl would be expected to step into her deceased sister's shoes in every respect. 'Write to me,' Hope said. 'Tell me how you're getting on.'

Angus had turned up not long after dinner, admitted by Clara who warned him he was interrupting a staff meeting even as she showed him into the front parlour where Miss Barlow, Hope and Amelia were poring over the warden's ledger and housekeeping journal. The three women contrived to meet for an hour once a week, although it wasn't always possible. The warden was due to present her monthly report to the trustees and wanted to go over the admission and discharge figures again.

'It's funny,' Amelia had remarked. 'You'll be signing a different name at the foot of the page in your next report. Mrs Bertrand Wallace.' She had laughed at the stricken look on the warden's face. 'You're not goin' to your doom, Hetty.'

'You're starting a new chapter in your life,' Hope had said, 'not closing the book.'

Miss Barlow had given her a grateful look.

Then, just when her final meeting of the day was winding down, Angus had appeared in the doorway, apologising for the interruption, Clara smirking over his shoulder. 'Look what the cat dragged in,' she said, before closing the door on his heels.

'Ladies, hullo!' he said.

'Yes, you have our attention,' said Hope.

Angus laughed. 'No, no. I'm using the telephonic vernacular. "Ahoy" was suggested for a greeting but we can't have the Queen sounding like a sailor, can we? Although I've heard she's partial to a tot of rum in her morning coffee.'

Amelia gaped. 'Is that true?'

'It's a load of rubbish,' said Miss Barlow. 'He'll say owt to bring the dimples out in Hope's cheeks.'

Hope blushed. 'We're having a meeting,' she told him.

'We can conclude it,' said Miss Barlow. She got up and gestured to Amelia to follow her out of the room.

Angus waited until their footsteps had receded down the hallway then sat beside Hope and took her hands in both of his. 'I'm sorry for the rude interruption. I would have been happy to wait out on the doorstep if need be.'

'Yet it seems waiting is the one thing you're not capable of,' said Hope.

To soften her words, she leaned towards him to kiss him chastely on the cheek, as a sister would, but Angus turned his head so it was their lips that touched. Heat flooded her body like glowing coals. Obeying her instinct, Hope leaned closer, her hands resting on his chest. The kiss lengthened and a moan escaped her throat. Angus broke contact first and when he spoke his voice was hoarse.

'Do you remember when we first met?' he asked.

Hope met his gaze. 'Of course I do. I'd been here a week and you drove me to my interview at the police station. It was snowing.'

'And you were being chaperoned by that frosty old lady.'

'Mrs Shaw.' Hope smiled. 'The secretary of the trustees keeps us on our toes.'

His grip on her hands tightened. 'I recall she helped find a home, for your son.'

Hope looked down, at their entwined fingers.

'Why would you raise that? Do you know where he is?' she said.

'No.' The surprise in his voice seemed genuine. Hope hated to think he possessed knowledge about her son that she did not. 'What I'm trying to say is that your past life is of no consequence to me, that I admire you, for all you've been through, and how you've handled your woes, and how kind you are to everybody. You're such a good soul.'

Hope bit her lip. He had wounded her, telling her that her past was of no consequence. How wonderful it must be to be able to brush it away.

'You're kind to everybody,' said Angus, driving home his point, 'except yourself. Marry me, Hope. I'll make you happy, I promise I will.'

The past was an immovable boulder that blocked her path. Would a simple *yes* help her navigate her way around it? She did not believe it could be so easy.

'I enjoy my job here,' said Hope.

'Then keep the job,' said Angus. 'I'm not averse to having a wife who has a calling. I'm not your father. Let's continue the sport of annoying Mr Robin Hyde by keeping you employed here. I'm all for it.'

The questions crowding her mind all had yes for an answer. Did she love him? Was he offering a fresh start? Would her father give his blessing? *Yes, yes* and *yes*. But what about his family? Would she ever earn their respect? If he was unbothered by her past, so should they be. There was no denying that she wanted him by her side.

Hope took a deep breath. 'Then I will marry you, Angus Deveraux,' she said. 'On one condition.'

He dropped to his knees before her, his expression serious. 'Name it.'

'We keep this between ourselves until after Miss Barlow's wedding. You've waited this long, you can wait another week.'

She wasn't aware she was crying until he gently rubbed the tears from her cheeks with the side of his thumb. Touching her face now, where he had wiped away her tears, she recalled his tenderness.

And finally, Alice. Dear, headstrong Alice, had appeared in the early evening, seeking Hope out. Every room in the house was occupied so they had gone for what Alice inaccurately promoted as a stroll to the church grounds. Hope could barely match her stride.

'You met Ginny, the other day,' said Alice, marching along, 'at my cousin's house. All I'm trying to do is help repair her relationship with Isaac, and I had the idea, well, I thought it was a good idea, of delivering the two halves of the silver dollar to him, joining them together. D'you see?'

'Silver dollar?' said Hope.

Alice explained.

'Ah, I see,' said Hope.

'He swept them onto the floorboards' – Alice demonstrated, hitting the iron railings they were passing with the edge of her hand and cursing – 'and threatened to throw me down the stairs. He said he was sick of my interfering.'

Hope was trotting to keep up. 'Are you all right?'

Alice rubbed her hand. 'Aye.'

'Did he really?'

'What?' said Alice.

'Threaten to throw you down the stairs.'

Alice laughed. 'I'm laying it on a bit thick. No, not exactly. But he did tell me to get out.' Her expression soured. 'He said it was none of my business and to leave it alone, and he was...' She gulped. 'He was sick to death of the lot of us, and he called me a scheming woman and said I should leave him be. So that's what I shall do.'

'Oh dear,' said Hope. She could see that Alice was on the verge of tears. 'Let's find somewhere to sit.'

Alice tossed her head. 'I'd rather keep walking.'

'All right, then.'

She allowed Alice to lead her on a circuitous route that ended back at the foot of Paradise Square. Alice pointed to the window above the butcher's shop. 'He'll be in there feeling sorry for himself.'

'Do you want to go to him?'

Alice shook her head. 'I think he's best left alone,' she said. Her eyes filled with tears. 'And I'm afraid he'll refuse to open the door to me.'

They walked at a more measured pace back to the House of Help. Alice paused on the doorstep. 'Thank you for listening, Hope. I'm sorry to have blethered on.'

'Not at all. Are you coming in?'

'No, I'd best get home.'

Hope smiled to cover her relief. She was glad Alice had marched her temper away, but the episode left Hope needing a moment of solitude.

Now, she rose from her chair and went to the window, looking down on the square where the lamplighter was going about his work, a shadowy figure in the evening's dusk. She had an hour before she was due to be collected and returned to Tylecote, an hour she intended to spend in Miss Barlow's company, going over the arrangements for the following week's wedding celebration. Hope left the classroom, gently closing the door behind her, and stopped to allow two of the residents of the second-floor dormitory to ascend the stairs, wishing them a good night, and pausing still, her hand on the banister.

She stood on the edge of a precipice, torn between her past and the future, knowing she would have to give up one to embrace the other.

Chapter 13

The side room above the Vestry Hall on Cemetery Road lacked a fireplace, the plaster walls giving off a chill that made Alice shudder. She had left her mother chatting to the driver and come up to practise her opening remarks, facing a room that would soon be filled with warm bodies.

She stood at the front, beside the lectern that had been provided, and looked out over a battalion of empty chairs. By the door, a trestle table held a collection bucket for the House of Help, teacups and saucers, sandwiches Alice had made that afternoon, wielding the butterknife as she practised her speech, and a large metal tea urn borrowed from Greaves's cab company. Alice focused on the gleaming instrument, her hands clutching notes that shook slightly in her grip. She gulped air and began to speak.

'Ladies and gentlemen, and distinguished guests, welcome...'

The door swung open. The frisson of excitement and apprehension that heated her cheeks faded when Alice saw who was entering: Aunt Harriet, her mother and Hope. They waved to her and looked tentatively around the room, as if all the chairs were already occupied, then found seats together in the third row. The door gaped open, showing part of the narrow dingy corridor and the bottom edge of the black rectangle of a skylight. It was already dark out; the nights were drawing in.

'You can sit closer,' said Alice.

'We're all right here,' her mother replied. 'Posh folk'll want the front, I expect.'

'Good luck,' said Hope.

'We're very proud of you,' said Aunt Harriet.

Alice beamed. 'Thank you. I was just... oh, good evening.'

She immediately recognised the clerk from the Gower Street library, the young man she had nicknamed Mr Billy Goat. He smiled and nodded shyly at her and took a seat across from the three women, who all inclined their heads and cut their eyes towards him. Alice ignored the broad smile her mother gave her. She examined her notes for something to do, but knew she was as prepared as she'd ever be. A moment passed that seemed to Alice to last a lifetime before the next arrival, a middle-aged woman, well-dressed, heavily bosomed. She took a seat in the back row, her stern gaze roving across the room before coming to rest on Alice. It occurred to Alice that she ought to have greeted people at the door, out of politeness and to learn who was attending. There was a ledger and a sharpened pencil on the table next to the tea urn. She had brought them with the intention of inviting her audience to leave their name and address, with a view to establishing a new committee devoted to female enfranchisement. She must remember to make that request. Perhaps the book could be passed around while she spoke.

Had she time to step from behind the lectern for a moment? Her cheeks burning, Alice hurried over to retrieve the book and the pencil, handing them to Hope and bending to whisper in her ear. Hope took possession of the items with an encouraging nod and smile. 'I'd be happy to help.'

147

Back at the lectern, Alice shuffled her notes, pretending to examine them. Time ticked by. Where was everyone? She tried not to acknowledge the trickle of doubt in her mind that would end in a humiliating flood of tears. The words she had so carefully crafted danced on the page, mocking her. Finally, Aunt Harriet broke the silence, remarking that the blustery weather that was stripping the trees of their leaves might deter people from venturing abroad. Alice met her eyes and tried to smile. Hurried footsteps on the floorboards of the corridor matched the pattering of her heart. A man entered, rain dripping from his Mackintosh. It was the reporter who had helped her put together an advertisement in the *Sheffield Independent*, making good on his promise to attend. He had called her plucky. The reporter winked at her as he removed his waterproof and slung it over a chair at the back, across the aisle from the stern-faced woman, who now had her lips pressed together in annoyance.

It was ten minutes past the appointed time.

Alice stood before her small assembly of three, not counting family, her face burning. Nobody was coming, not the member of parliament, not the town aldermen and their wives, nor any of the working women she had thought to enlist. How many of her posters had gone on the fire? Like the paper they had been printed on, her ambitions were going up in smoke.

The sound of rain pattering on the skylight was loud inside the room. Her voice was small, reedy in her ears.

'I haven't the audience I'd hoped for,' said Alice, 'but if you'll indulge me, I'd like to tell you what I've learned about female enfranchisement and why the movement that was started here in this town should not be allowed to fade from our memory, and why a new crusade must be launched.'

She paused, grateful her voice had strengthened as she spoke, giving her the courage to raise her eyes to the room. Her mother was studying her, an expression Alice couldn't read on her face, and there was an enquiring tilt to Mr Goat's head. Aunt Harriet and Hope sat with their hands folded in their lap, waiting for Alice to continue, looking for all the world as if the event was not a complete disaster. The reporter was writing in his notebook. 'Hear hear,' he mumbled, without looking up.

'We see women in the workplace now,' said Alice, glancing at her mother, who was nodding encouragingly, 'doing a hard day's graft alongside the men. Why should they not—'

The woman sitting at the back interrupted her. 'Excuse me, love. As there's so few turned up, shall we have a discussion instead?' She didn't wait for a response. 'What I'd like to know is how much more you want? Girls can get a proper education now. You sound like you've had one. We can own property. I do mesen. Isn't that entitlement enough? We should be running the home, not the country, and raising children, not merry hell.' She glanced across at the reporter. 'Don't write that last bit down.'

Louisa twisted to glare at the woman. Alice spoke quickly, to avoid the humiliation of having her mother come to her defence.

'There are women working *and* running the home,' she said. 'But there's a larger point. There's a fundamental question to ask. Why shouldn't women be allowed to vote when we are governed by the same laws that govern men?'

'I'm sorry,' said the woman. She sounded anything but. 'It's not as simple as that, love. What do women know of war, of diplomacy, of empire and the running of our nation's great industries? I'll tell you, nowt at all. It would be farcical to seed parliament with a female's level of ignorance of world affairs.'

Alice was rattled. 'You talk as if you are not a woman.'

'I know my place, love. Women have their sphere.' The woman scraped back her chair. 'Why mess with nature?'

One-third of Alice's audience had turned out to be anti-women's rights, a heckler come here only to mock. And now, like this woman, the reporter was getting to his feet. He offered Alice an apologetic smile, picked up his coat and slipped from the room.

'And another thing I'd like to know,' said the woman, hands on hips. 'Why do you want to set man against wife by bringing political differences into the domestic arena?'

'I don't,' said Alice. 'Men and women can...' She searched for the word. 'Can coexist while holding opposing views.' For some reason, Isaac's face swam into her mind. 'We must respect and value another's opinions and beliefs, if we cherish that person, if they – if they are the person we love...' She trailed into silence.

'And if we are lucky,' said Aunt Harriet, coming to her rescue, 'we find like-minded souls to share our lives with. I imagine, madam, that your husband has similar views to your own, about keeping women in their place. Seen but not heard, together with children.'

She had spoken mildly but the woman's cheeks flushed with rage. 'You'll find,' she said, 'that I carry the weight of public opinion, and this child' – she pointed again at Alice – 'is going against the laws of nature. In my day, she would have been put in the stocks for all to laugh at.'

The librarian raised his hand. 'There are men who support female enfranchisement,' he said.

'Then tell me, where are the men tonight? I count one.' The woman's sneer inferred that Mr Goat barely merited his sex. 'You're preaching to an empty room,' she said to Alice and, with a triumphant nod, swept out.

Alice took a few faltering steps down the aisle, her notes in her fist, with some idea in mind of continuing the argument. She was halted by her mother's hand on her arm.

'You don't allus have to have the last word, love,' said Lousia. 'An' you won't change that one's mind.' She tugged on her arm. 'Sit down by me.'

She slumped into a chair. Hope reached across to pat her knee.

'How about a cup of tea?' said Aunt Harriet. Alice watched as the others ate the sandwiches she had made.

'It's the weather,' said Aunt Harriet, 'putting paid to good intentions.'

'It's my fault,' said her mother, 'for pickin' an out o' the way venue. You'd have done better in the middle of town, above a pub or summat.'

'But here we are on Cemetery Road,' said Mr Goat, amusement in his voice. Alice had not been paying attention when introductions were made so remained ignorant of his name.

'If you dare say anything about this room being quiet as a tomb,' said Alice. 'I shall have to tip my tea over your head.'

'To the stocks with you,' Mr Goat declared. Hope laughed, and thus encouraged, he went on. 'Do you know, we have a stocks, a flimsy prop only, but it does the job, at the theatre where I am a member of the amateur dramatics group.'

'I do love the theatre,' said Harriet. 'Tell me, have I seen you perform?'

'Well, that depends on what you've seen.'

The two of them began a conversation. Hope moved her chair closer to Alice.

'Don't be disheartened,' she said.

'I'm not!' Alice set down her cup on the floor. 'In fact, I'm more determined than ever.'

'God help us,' said Louisa. 'What next?'

Alice smiled. She was bruised, but not broken. Her mother had provided the solution. The heart of town was where she needed to be. She rubbed the toe of her shoe over the notes scattered at her feet. What use were words if nobody was listening? It was deeds that mattered. An empty room, indeed. She would take her campaign out to the people if they wouldn't come to her. She would make her mark, and Mr Goat had given Alice an idea of how this might be achieved.

The following day, Alice found herself grooming the horses, sweat tacking the faded shirt she was wearing to her body. Her mother had sent her to the yard, declaring she would put her to use, partly to cheer her up and partly, Alice suspected, to keep her busy. Grudgingly, she could admit — to herself, though certainly not to her mother — that the physical labour distracted her from the previous evening's failure and her misery over Isaac's continuing absence. She had not expected to feel so bruised by it. The heat draped a suffocating blanket over her head and over the poor foam-flecked animal she was brushing down. Alice licked dry lips and was imagining how lovely a drink of bitter lemonade with a sprig of mint would taste when one of the cab drivers came along and pressed a cloudy glass into her hand.

'Here tha goes. Sup up, love,' he said.

Alice took the glass gratefully and sipped at the contents. It was beer, tart and earthy at once, but she was so thirsty she drank half the measure down in one gulp. This, she imagined, must be how Ginny's life had been in the western region of America – horses and ale and no standing on ceremony. Men and women on equal footing, and the sun always shining, no cloud or smoke stack to stain the wide-open skies.

The driver interrupted her reverie.

'Yer mother wants thee at home,' he said. 'Tha'd better trot on.'

The kitchen of the cottage smelled deliciously of stewed fruit and sugar. Louisa was putting the finishing touches to an apple and rhubarb pie, expertly cutting out and moulding a corona of pastry leaves for the middle and crimping the edges. 'I'd save a slice for Isaac,' she said when Alice entered the kitchen. 'It's his favourite, but I've not seen hide nor hair of him and nor has his mother.' She straightened up. 'What's goin' on, love? Have the pair o' you had words?'

Alice sighed. 'We argued, I told you, an' I've not seen him since. You know, we're not kids any more, in each other's pockets. P'raps we've nowt left in common.'

She swallowed the lump in her throat.

'I've asked that nice young man Edward Shelton to tea,' said her mother. She pointed at the pie. 'This is for afters, if he's a sweet tooth.'

'Who on earth is Edward Shelton?' said Alice. 'Not another one of your—'

Louisa held up a floury palm. 'Don't start! I thought you'd be pleased. He's your friend, in't he? Came all the way to Cemetery Road to see thee speak?'

She was talking about Mr Goat. Alice smiled. 'Oh aye. Sorry, the heat has addled my brain. Yes, that's a lovely idea.'

Louisa beamed. 'He'll end up runnin' that library, he's a smart lad.'

'Mother.'

'An' not bad-looking behind them spectacles. Your aunt was taken by him.'

'*Mother.*'

Louisa laughed. 'All reight. Go an' get theesen washed an' change into summat nice, like that blue stripe. Or is that too fancy for a bit o' tea, I don't know.'

Alice left her mother still chattering away to herself, allowing the smile that twitched at the corners of her mouth to widen as she bounded up the stairs. Deeds, not words. She had a deed in mind, and would enlist the help of Mr Goat to realise her plan, as well as the gentleman from the press, whose premises she intended to visit the following day. Anticipation fluttering in her chest, Alice closed her bedroom door and leaned against it, her palms flattened against the smooth pine.

Now she was decided, she saw no reason to delay.

Chapter 14

The road fit for carts, named the Wagon Way, once ran past the gates of a fortress. Waingate was now the street that steepened from Lady's Bridge over the River Don up to the bustling marketplaces of the town. The sky was blue on this Wednesday morning, striated by dark plumes of factory smoke, a nip in the air. Isaac lifted his coat collar as he emerged from the shadow cast by the Royal Hotel at the top of Waingate. He waited for a heavily laden omnibus to clop past and crossed towards the looming bell tower and clock of the town hall.

He had been assigned to a crew installing telephony wires at the hotel and, when dinnertime arrived, volunteered to fetch the sausage-meat pastries from the street vendor favoured by his gaffer, rather than sit and chew the fat. The truth was, he was still smarting from that morning's encounter with Silas. The two men had bumped into each other, Silas on his way to the Yorkshire Bank further up town, and after an awkward exchange of pleasantries, his father had laid into him. *Stop this nonsense. Tha's sulking like a little bairn. Come home, make peace with tha mother and get theesen back to work.* Isaac had stuffed his shaking hands into his pockets and told his father he had a job and was on his way to it now. Silas had stared at him for a moment, incomprehension furrowing his brow, before turning and stalking away. He didn't look back.

He'd almost reached the pastry shop when a hoot of laughter drew Isaac's attention to a crowd that was gathering outside the town hall, a few hundred yards down Waingate. There was some spectacle at the judges' entrance, hidden from view by townspeople who had formed a rough semi-circle that spilled over the pavement and onto the road. A passing wagon was reined to a halt, the driver standing on his box for a better view. Curiosity got the better of Isaac. There was no harm in wandering down to see what all the fuss was about. Perhaps a famous, or infamous, character was being brought to appear at court and forced to run the gauntlet of popular opinion, although Isaac read the papers and couldn't recall an ongoing salacious case. Alice would know. She devoured the town's news. He drew closer, lingering on the outskirts of the crowd. Over the scarved heads of the women standing in front of him, he could see a man fiddling with a camera on a tripod. The device looked like a squeezebox. Isaac shouldered his way closer, his gaze flitting to whatever was being recorded for posterity.

His eyes fell first on a banner being held in the air by a short, bespectacled man wearing a tufty goatee, who looked discomforted standing with his arms stretched about his head. A child, a barefoot boy, was hopping up and down by his side, his thin arms and fists raised in a boxer's pose, making as though to jab him in the stomach. The man studiously ignored him. Isaac smiled as he read the words on the banner. *Is it a crime to want equal rights?* Alice would agree with that sentiment. He wished she was here, by his side, to enjoy the spectacle. Every time he thought of Alice his chest ached with guilt and longing.

He'd chased her away and so it fell to him to make amends. Poor Alice, who had only been trying to help.

Isaac's gaze dropped to the pavement, to the bare-headed woman sitting legs outstretched behind a flimsy set of plank wood stocks, strands of loose blonde hair blowing across her face. Her stockinged feet – narrow, delicate feet – poked through the twin round holes. Isaac laughed along with the rest when a shout went up. 'Escaped from the madhouse, has tha?' Another joined in. 'Easier ways than this to get a foot rub, love!'

The woman in the stocks lifted her chin and swept her hair aside. Her eyes fell on Isaac and lit up in recognition. She returned the smile that had frozen on his face with her own smile of delight. 'Isaac!'

The crowd swivelled in his direction. Was there more fun to be had?

Isaac elbowed his way forward, unwilling to believe what his eyes were telling him. He needed to get a closer look, for confirmation that he was mistaken. This was a girl who resembled her, yes, but could not be his Alice, sitting in stocks, under a banner being held in the air by a man Isaac now recognised as one of the clerks from the Gower Street library.

The photographer put out his hand to stop Isaac getting in the way of the shot he was framing. 'Mind yourself,' he said, then recoiled when he saw the look on Isaac's face and held up his hands in a gesture of surrender, although his smirk remained. 'Is this your lass? She's got some gumption. Want to be in the picture?'

Isaac took hold of the squeezebox – it was surprisingly light – and flung it to the ground, ignoring the man's protests, and only distantly aware of the eager shrieks from the crowd. He lunged for the library clerk, ripping the banner from the man's hands, the child who had been pestering the man whisked out of Isaac's way by an aproned matron, and bellowed into the man's face, 'GET HER OUT!'

The clerk leapt away, losing his spectacles, fumbling for them on the ground, whining in a high-pitched voice. 'This is a peaceful protest!' This provoked more laughter from the crowd, more goading.

Isaac, his face burning, tore away the wooden slat that trapped Alice's ankles, snagging and ripping a stocking, exposing the smooth white skin of her foot and shin. He lifted her and slung her over his shoulder.

'What are you doing? Put me down!'

There were some boos from the crowd. Alice's fists pounded his back as he strode away.

Despite everything, he wanted to laugh at the absurdity of it. A memory surfaced, of picking up a furious Alice when they had been children and sitting her on a high stone wall.

A face loomed, a burly man in his path. 'This your missus?'

Isaac scowled. 'Aye.'

The man stepped out of his way.

—

In the end, they reached a compromise, Alice mutely agreeing it would be better to be carried on his back rather than over his shoulder like a sack of potatoes. To curious passers-by, he offered excuses, hoping to break her stony silence.

'She's had her shoes nicked.'

'We're practisin' for the piggy-back championships.'

'She can't afford a horse.'

'Never marry a scold. See here? I can't get her off me back.'

Alice neither tightened nor loosened her grip or made a sound. Not even a sigh to tickle his ear.

Isaac slowed his pace as they approached her cottage. 'Alice,' he said, trying for a reasonable tone. 'That were a daft stunt. Tha could've been chucked in jail for it.'

He lowered her to her feet. Alice turned away to unlock the door.

'What were you playin' at? They were all laughin' at thee,' said Isaac. She paused in the act of turning the key. Perhaps his words were bringing her to her senses. He hoped she would allow him to follow her inside. 'An' I'll tell thee summat for nowt, if I get my hands on them two fellas, they'll never come near you again, encouragin' you like they were. It's not reight. You've made a fool of yersen.'

Alice whipped around, her eyes flaming with anger, and he sagged with relief. She would castigate him and he would apologise for manhandling her, even though it had been for her own good, and he would tell her he was sorry for sending her away when she had only been trying to help. He'd taken out his anguish and confusion over his mother on Alice. That wasn't right, either. There was blame on both sides. He would make her see it and the two of them would get back on their old footing, before he declared his love. These thoughts raced through his mind as Alice raised her hand.

The slap was a shock. Isaac resisted the urge to touch his cheekbone where she had caught him. The blow hadn't hurt, not physically.

She spat the words at him. 'Neanderthal! Brute! How dare you?' She wrenched open the door. 'Don't you ever come near me again. Don't you ever put your hands on me.' Her voice broke into sobs. 'You've humiliated me, betrayed me.' Her final words were spoken in a whisper. 'I hate you.'

Alice slammed the door in his face. Isaac recoiled, then laid a palm against the varnished wood, as much to steady himself as to maintain a connection, however futile the gesture might be, with the woman who was weeping on the other side of the door, the woman he loved but did not understand. 'Alice, I'm sorry. Will you let me in? Alice?'

After a few moments, the sobbing stopped, or Alice had gone deeper into the house. Isaac knocked gently on the door, not yet ready to walk away, to admit defeat. Who was in the wrong, here? He had saved Alice from further disgrace and humiliation. Isaac rubbed his hands over his face. She had not wanted to be saved.

' 'Ey up.'

Isaac turned to see Louisa coming up the road, a cheerful smile on her face.

'Our lass not in?' she said.

Isaac grimaced. 'She's in. I've upset her.'

'Everythin' upsets Alice,' Louisa said. 'She allus comes round.' Her eyes widened. 'Unless…?'

'No,' said Isaac. 'I've not told her how I feel. It's not that.'

Louisa frowned. 'What is it then?'

He gestured at the door. 'Best find out from the horse's mouth.'

'I'm asking thee, lad.'

Isaac stepped back into the gutter so he could look up at the windows of the house. They stared back, blankly. He looked at Louisa. 'All right, but don't be too hard on her. Neither one o' us comes out of it well.'

Chapter 15

The front page of the local broadsheet was reserved for public notices and advertisements. Sitting at the scrubbed pine table in the kitchen of the House of Help, Hope noted that the School of Art in Arundel Street was hosting its annual exhibition. Angus might be interested in accompanying her. She idly turned the page. It was the day before Miss Barlow's wedding, and the house was still, as if it was holding its breath ahead of the festivities.

By this time tomorrow morning, Cook and the residents she had enlisted would be in a frenzy of preparation while Miss Barlow and Mr Wallace exchanged their vows at St Mary's church, witnessed by Hope and Amelia and a small congregation. The wedding breakfast was to take place at two o'clock at the house, a deliberately informal affair.

'We're not a blushing young couple,' Miss Barlow had emphasised. 'I'm forty and he's a widower. We both have grown children. The decision's been made.'

Hope wondered whether Mr Wallace had had a say in it. She imagined not.

Pages two and three were crammed with classified ads and a summary of the goings-on at the magistrates' court. Hope glanced over the marriage and death notices, skipped the lengthy report of the proceedings of the town council and turned the page. A boy had broken his leg playing leapfrog in Sylvester Street. Poor child. In Foreign News, the Prince of Monaco had died. Hope turned to the *What Truth Says* column. A guilty delight, it was full of catty paragraphs that began with 'I have heard…' and 'I learned lately…' and 'I must mention…' from a writer with a penchant for alliteration.

As she read, the faint smile on Hope's face faded. She put down her mug of tea and lifted the newspaper to her face and read the paragraph again.

> I learned lately that sitting down for women's rights is emphatically as ineffective as standing up for them. A young woman of this parish whose meeting on female enfranchisement I attended, considerably bulking up the audience, had herself encased in stocks outside the Town Hall to plead her case. Alas, her embittered husband effected a forceful rescue, much to his young wife's fury as she was slung over his back and carried away. I await this curious creature's next foray for the cause with ardent anticipation.

'Found this on a tip, if you can believe it,' said Clara, bustling into the room with an epergne in her arms, its delicate glass bowls streaked with dust and dirt but intact. 'Thought I'd clean it up an' we can use it tomorra, fill it wi' sweets or summat for the bride an' groom. What's tha think?' She put it down on the table. 'Hope?'

Hope shook her head. 'No, I mean, yes. That's a lovely idea.'

'You all right, love? Look like tha's seen a ghost.'

'Hmm?' Hope folded up the newspaper and rolled it into a baton. 'Clara, will you let Miss Barlow know I have an errand to run? I'll be back before twelve o'clock.'

Undoubtedly, the unnamed *curious creature* was Alice. Hope could recall the face of the reporter who had attended Alice's meeting. But who was the man who carted her away? Perhaps that alarming aspect of the story was as erroneous as describing Alice as a young wife, included solely for the purposes of titillating the reader. Tomorrow morning, the girl would walk into the house dressed for the day's festivities, an impish smile on her face. Hope couldn't bear to wait that long.

She took her cape from the row of hooks in the porch and, clutching the rolled-up newspaper, emerged onto a square thronged with shoppers for the Thursday morning market. Hope threaded her way towards the path that led to St Peter's and the centre of town, emerging from the noise and bustle of the market onto a high street busy with omnibuses, cabs and costermongers. Frustrated by the pace of her fellow pedestrians, Hope left the crowded pavement and darted through a maze of side roads to reach the long sweep of Pond Street.

Her knock on the door was answered by Louisa, an older and more careworn version of her daughter, but with the same lively blue eyes and bow-shaped mouth. Her blonde hair was loose on her shoulders, as if Hope had fetched her from her bed.

'Good morning, Mrs Leigh,' said Hope. 'I hope I'm not disturbing you. We met at—'

'The Vestry Hall, aye,' said Louisa, coming outside so that Hope had to take a step back. 'It were only the other day, weren't it? Seems ages since.' She squinted up at the steel-grey sky and back at Hope. 'Looks like rain. What can I do for thee?'

Hope took a deep breath. 'I wondered whether Alice was at home today.'

'She is.'

Louisa glanced at the baton in Hope's hand then gazed into her eyes levelly, her expression giving nothing away.

Hope gulped. 'I have heard...' She paused. She sounded like the gossip columnist. 'I wonder if I might come in?'

Her jaw set, Louisa stepped aside and waved Hope into the house. Footsteps pounded across the ceiling and Louisa rushed to the foot of the stairs. 'Don't you dare, young lady!'

Alice's face appeared over the banister.

'I told you to stay put,' said Louisa.

'Mother, at least let me speak with Hope! She wasn't involved, I promise.'

Louisa relented. 'Go up,' she said to Hope. 'Maybe you can knock some sense into her.'

Hope sat on the edge of Alice's bed and watched her pace back and forth, reading and re-reading the offending paragraph. Finally, she gave the newspaper back to Hope with a weak smile and sank into a chair.

'It's a start, I suppose.'

'A start?' said Hope. 'What does that mean? And who is this so-called husband who carried you away?'

Alice waved a hand dismissively. 'Oh, that was only Isaac, turning up to do his best to ruin my life.'

'But what were you thinking?'

'Hope, the meeting was an abject failure, we can agree on that, can't we?'

'That's harsh.' Hope picked fluff from the counterpane. 'I thought you spoke very well.'

'Aye, to an empty room.' Alice leaned forward. 'Do you remember, afterwards, Mr Goat was talking about the props his amateur dramatics group used?'

'Mr *Goat*…?'

'I call him that. His name's Edward and Mother invited him to tea, thinking I might show an interest in him. And I *was* interested, but not in the way she hoped.'

Hope pinched the bridge of her nose. 'You wanted the stocks.'

'Yes!' Alice clapped her hands. 'Mr… Edward agreed to help me.'

'But why?'

Alice threw up her hands. 'To cause a stir, to start the argument. We were all set up and I was to have my photograph taken, for the newspaper, then Isaac came barrelling in and ruined everything.' She gestured to the newspaper in Hope's hand. 'And all I get is this. But as I say, it's a start, isn't it?'

'I suppose so. What does your mother say?'

Alice pouted. 'She's left the firm in Barnaby's hands for a few days so she can keep her beady eye on me. She's threatening to go to the Gower Street library and give Edward a telling off. Ginny's been round but she took Mother's side.' Her voice trembled. 'You're with me, aren't you, Hope?'

Hope frowned. 'I can see both sides.'

'I'm not going to ask you to sit in stocks!' Alice came to sit beside her and rested her head on Hope's shoulder. Then she leapt up and went to the window. It seemed she could not be still. 'I shall miss the wedding breakfast.'

Hope went over and embraced her. 'Let me speak with your mother about that. I'll do my best to persuade her to release you for the afternoon.' She put her hands on Alice's shoulders and peered into her face. 'I have to ask, what possessed you? You might have ended up being arrested.'

'I know,' Alice whispered. 'Isaac said the same.' She shrugged Hope off. 'But my meeting was a failure. I wanted to do something dramatic, I suppose, to get myself noticed. Nobody listens to what I have to say. Nobody takes me seriously.'

Hope laughed. 'Well, you're in the papers. Unnamed, and wedded, but certainly not unnoticed.'

'A subject of gossip,' said Alice, but she didn't look displeased. 'Us agitators must start somewhere.'

That evening, on the eve of her wedding, Miss Barlow was persuaded to sit in an armchair in the front parlour while gifts wrapped in ribbon and tissue and brown paper were placed at her feet. 'There's no need,' she said, unpinning her warden's cap and setting it down on a side table. 'No need at all.'

'This is from Alice who is sorry she can't be here this evening,' said Hope, handing up a large, round hatbox. 'But she will be attending the wedding breakfast, in the company of her mother's friend Miss Ginny Hinchcliffe, if that's acceptable.'

'The more the merrier,' Miss Barlow said, lifting the lid of the box. 'Oh, how lovely.' Alice had gifted her a blue velvet hat with a wide red satin ribbon. 'I don't know when I'd ever wear something so striking as this. What beautiful colours.'

'Don't fret, I'll borrow it, save it collecting dust,' said Amelia.

'Haven't you enough hats?' said Miss Barlow.

'Here,' said Amelia. 'This one's from your artistic stepdaughter-to-be.' The flat rectangular package was wrapped in thick paper, tied with string. 'I'll hazard a guess it's an umbrella.'

'Where's the sewing tin?' said Miss Barlow.

'I came prepared,' said Amelia and handed her a pair of embroidery scissors.

Miss Barlow snipped the string and opened the paper. 'Oh my goodness.' She turned the frame for everyone to see the watercolour scene of Paradise Square at night, all the windows of the House of Help lit with a welcoming glow. 'I'll put it in the hall, alongside the other painting she gave me,' she said. 'Flora is clever, isn't she?'

Amelia pulled a face. 'People will start mistakin' us for an art gallery.'

One of the younger residents, a fourteen-year-old orphan named Mabel, was bouncing up and down on the faded chaise longue. 'Open ours next!' she said. 'That flat one there. It's not a paintin'. It's summat better.'

Miss Barlow obliged. The residents had given her marzipan fruits. The tiny and exquisitely crafted bananas, oranges, apples and pears were all made, Mabel announced, by themselves with only a little help from Cook. The box was passed around. Hope took an ersatz orange and popped it in her mouth, relishing the nutty sweetness. She wondered whether her son had ever tasted marzipan, and rubbed at the ache at the base of her throat.

Clara came into the room, tying a scarf under her chin. 'That's me done for't day. Here,' she said, shyly thrusting a tin at Miss Barlow.

'Ah,' said the warden, warmly. 'Pontefract cakes, my favourite.'

'Sorry it's nowt fancy,' said Clara.

'You shouldn't spend your money,' said Miss Barlow.

'Oh, I din't. I've a friend works at Bassett's.' Clara pulled a face. 'She din't steal 'em.'

'I'm sure not,' said Hope.

'She gave them me, but I don't like them.' Clara hurried to the door. 'Anyhow, see thee all tomorra.'

Miss Barlow opened Hope's present next, a delicate silver brooch shaped like cupped hands and a silver sixpence.

'To put in my shoe,' said Miss Barlow. 'What a lovely thought.' She explained to the younger residents that she would slip the coin into the heel of her shoe when she walked to the altar, to bring good luck and fortune. 'Not just for me,' she said. 'I'll be thinking of the house and all its residents, past and present. Good luck and fortune to all.'

When she smiled at Hope, there were tears in the warden's eyes.

'Mine next,' said Amelia, rising from her seat to deposit a froth of pink tissue paper in her mother's lap.

Miss Barlow parted the flimsy sheets and shook out white linen pillowslips. 'Why, they're lovely,' she said. 'How much have you spent on these?'

'No expense spared for the marital bed,' said Amelia, to laughter from the residents.

'Amelia, really!' said Miss Barlow.

Her daughter stuck out her tongue. 'There's summat else in there.'

Miss Barlow re-examined the tissue paper and brought out the folded square of a handkerchief. The corner of it was embroidered with roses and the words *To my precious Mother from your Amelia*. The tears she had been holding back slid down the warden's cheeks.

'An' that's what the hankie's for,' said Amelia.

Hope watched the two women embrace, all their past grievances forgotten, or, if not forgotten, laid to rest, while Hope remained dissatisfied, fearful she would be unable to commit herself to a happy life with Angus, wanting only the one thing that was set to remain forever out of her reach.

—

The wedding breakfast guests put down their sherry glasses and obediently trooped, on Amelia's command, from the front parlour into the kitchen where, they were told, they should serve themselves from the feast on the table. This was the informal celebration the new Mrs Wallace had requested and Hope was glad to see the satisfied expression on her superior's face. Cook stood by proudly, her hands clasped, as the guests exclaimed over the tongue, salmon, ham, buttered bread, fruit compotes, cheesecakes and blancmanges that left no part of the tabletop bare. The epergne Clara had retrieved and cleaned sat on the dresser, full of nuts and sweets. Beside it were half a dozen bottles from the crate of sherry Mr Wallace had had delivered. He had been thoughtful enough to provide lemonade for the younger residents of the house. The newly-weds were served first, by Cook, and carried their plates back to the parlour where two chairs had been decked out like thrones with cushions and flowers. Mrs Wallace's cheeks were flushed. Hope kissed her cheek as she left the room.

'You can enjoy the rest of the day now, Mrs Wallace.'

'I don't like bein' the centre of attention.'

Hope squeezed her arm. 'I know.'

Mrs Shaw, the secretary to the trustees of the House of Help, stood slightly apart from the people crowding around the table, clutching her plate as if she was going to her death by food poisoning.

'But where are we to eat?' she said.

Hope took the woman's elbow and guided her closer to the feast. 'In here,' she said, indicating the chairs ranged around the room. 'Or in the parlour, whichever you prefer. Use your lap for a table. The cutlery and napkins are over there.'

The older woman gave her a look. Hope knew what she was thinking, how Mrs Shaw had once chaperoned, to a police interview, a frightened girl who had turned up on the doorstep of the House of Help, how terrified this girl had been, and how she was now deputy warden of the house and reassuring her rescuer over the abandonment of wedding breakfast etiquette.

'It's all very bohemian,' said Mrs Shaw. 'I'm sure the gentlemen in Mr Wallace's company will find it...' she paused, clearly wanting to say they would find it beneath them and finally settling for 'confusing.'

Two of Mr Wallace's gentlemen friends strolled past with piled-high plates on their way to find seats in the parlour.

'They do seem to be coping quite well,' said Hope. 'Will you partake, Mrs Calver?'

Mrs Calver, a handsome, white-haired woman wearing a haughty expression and a hat dripping with feathers and gemstones, swept a haughty gaze over the table. She was one of the houses trustees, a former hospital matron with the formidability to match, and it was common knowledge she had set her cap at Mr Wallace only to discover he had eyes only for Hetty Barlow.

'An unconventional celebration to follow an unconventional ceremony,' said Mrs Calver. 'I was just informed that Amelia delivered her mother down the aisle.'

'Merciful heavens,' said Mrs Shaw.

'And where are they honeymooning?' asked Mrs Calver, rhetorically. 'In a fisherman's cottage on the Humber estuary?'

Hope smiled. 'The property belongs to Mrs Wallace. It's going to be sold and she wants to retrieve any sentimental items. Mr and Mrs Wallace will be staying in a suite in a fine hotel in Grimsby.'

Neither woman had anything to say about this and the polite smile on Hope's face was growing stiff. 'Will you excuse me, ladies?'

She had spotted Alice sitting in the corner of the room with a meagre portion of salmon mousse and salad leaves. Alice smiled wanly as Hope approached her.

'Thank you for persuading her to release me,' said Alice, 'though it's straight back to jail after this. One small mercy is that Mother has returned to work so won't be glued to my side.'

'She only wants you to be happy,' said Hope, 'and to find somebody to share your life with, as Mrs Wallace has. Doesn't it gladden your heart to see two people declaring a lifetime bond?'

Alice shook her head. 'I don't think I shall ever wed, not if I'm required to swear obedience to a man.'

'Mrs Wallace followed tradition but I can't see her husband ever demanding she obey him, not in day-to-day life,' said Hope. 'It's only part of the ritual of words spoken.'

Alice frowned. 'My uncle Silas likes to say he's the head of the family but my aunt is the neck, and the neck turns the head yay or nay. Which is all very well if men act according to the wishes of their wife, but it's a world apart from women having a vote in their own right.'

'Goodness,' said Hope. 'We've got onto this subject again.'

'I'm never off it.'

Ginny plonked herself down in the empty seat on the other side of Alice, swallowed the remains of her sherry and dropped the glass to the floor where it rolled under her chair, mercifully intact. She took her spoon to a large slice of cheesecake buried under a blanket of blancmange. 'This is delicious,' she said. 'Where's your plate? Hope, isn't it?'

'Yes,' said Hope. 'I will eat once everyone's settled.'

'The perfect hostess,' said Ginny. 'I remember you from a while ago. You came to the house, didn't you?'

Uneasiness squirmed in Hope's gut, although she couldn't say why this woman should have such an effect on her. Perhaps it had been the circumstances of their previous meeting. 'Yes,' she said. 'I was looking for Alice.'

'That's right.' Ginny smiled knowingly. 'Weren't you lookin' for someone else, though, really?'

Hope forced a smile. 'I don't take your meaning?'

'Oh, just summat Alice told me.'

Alice had been picking at her food and looked up at the mention of her name. 'What's that?' she said. 'I'm sorry, I wasn't listening.'

'Poor love,' said Ginny. 'Louisa'll come around. Won't she, Hope? I tell you what, go and fetch me another glass of that sherry an' I'll tell you all about that mother o' yours. What I know about our Louisa Leigh will put your little escapade in the shade.'

Alice perked up immediately. 'They were friends, long ago,' she explained to Hope. 'Ginny's forever promising to tell me about my mother as a young woman. Don't you dare change your mind again, all right?'

'I won't, love. I'd say this sherry's loosened my tongue enough.' Ginny moved into the seat Alice had vacated and leaned against Hope's arm. 'I know summat,' she whispered, her voice slurred. 'I know summat about you that you don't. Shall I tell you? We'll have to be quick before herself comes back.'

Hope hesitated. Could she stand to have her suspicion confirmed by this unfeeling woman? She glanced around the room. Three of the younger residents of the house were sitting cross-legged in front of the range, making a picnic of the occasion. Angus's grandfather, whose frequent donations to the coffers helped keep the wolf from the door, was deep in conversation with the vicar. The new Mrs Wallace had given up her seat in the spotlight to return to the kitchen and was chatting to Mr Wallace's daughter, Flora. Hope could hear piano music coming from the front parlour but it seemed most of the guests had chosen to remain in the kitchen.

Hope looked into Ginny's eyes, saw herself swaying on the edge of the precipice. 'All right.'

'We've all got pasts, love, things we'd like to forget,' said Ginny. 'But when it's shoved in your face, what can you do?' She shrugged. 'That little boy, Teddy. It's only right you should know the truth of it. I think you already do know, don't you?'

Hope's voice trembled. 'I should like to hear it spoken.'

'He's your son. There.' Ginny smiled. 'Don't be too hard on Alice. She let it slip.'

'Does everyone know but me?'

'I've no idea, love.'

The cold gleam in the woman's eye pushed her over the edge, sent her flailing into the void. Ginny was speaking but the sound came from far away. Somewhere, a woman was wailing. Hope was on her feet, pushing her way through the bodies in the room, trying to escape from the terrible noise, and now she was outside, in the yard amongst the laundry hung out to dry, but her legs would no longer carry her. She sank to her knees. Then hands were on her shoulders, stroking her back, and there was a murmuring like distant waves. Hope pushed her face into the crushed russet satin a tiny part of her mind recognised as Mrs Wallace's wedding gown.

Chapter 16

'That was cruel.'

Alice sat beside Ginny on a bench in the grounds of St Peter's, her clenched fists hidden inside her muff, the cold air tickling her nose. She watched Ginny pour sherry into the mug she had liberated from the kitchen of the House of Help, along with a half-empty bottle swiped when the party was broken up and the two women taken to one side by Amelia and asked to leave. The request had been gently made but Alice had reeled as if she'd been slapped in the face. She wanted to apologise to Hope, on Ginny's behalf and her own. Would she ever get the opportunity? Every action she took seemed to close her off further from the world. Polly Bramall was dead, Hope distraught, Isaac lost to her and her mother now her gaoler.

'You're just worried Hope'll be cross with you.' Ginny burped. 'I got drunk. I still am. Did I ever tell you about the time—'

Alice cut her off. 'That's no excuse.' She looked over her shoulder. The narrow path behind the church was deserted, the only movement the occasional leaf falling from a tree, and a high stone wall blocked the view from the street. 'If someone comes, you'll get us both arrested.'

Ginny laughed. 'So says the woman who openly invited the police to throw her in jail. Good job Isaac was there to cart you away, eh?'

Alice hunched her shoulders. She didn't want to think about Isaac.

'Poor Hope,' she said.

'Listen, dear,' said Ginny, 'while you were all tiptoeing around the girl, she already knew the truth of it. I confirmed her suspicions, that's all.'

'But it wasn't your place. It certainly wasn't the time.'

'The truth will always out,' said Ginny, 'one way or the other. You all should be grateful to me.' She tipped her head back and drained the contents of the mug.

Alice stared at her in wonder. The skin of Ginny's throat had been tanned by a different sun, hotter and brighter than the one Alice knew. This woman had travelled alone across half the world, or so she claimed. Had she really returned for her son or, as Uncle Silas reckoned, had she nowhere else to go and known her family would not deny her? Perhaps Isaac knew his mother better than anybody, certainly better than Alice knew hers.

'What do you have to tell me about my mother?' said Alice. 'While you're in a confessional mood.'

A slow smile spread across Ginny's face. 'I knew her before you were born,' she said. 'Not for long, but long enough. She took me under her wing, introduced me to Joseph Crookes, the one everybody calls a bad 'un, a crook by name and nature.'

The questions tumbled out.

'*Was* he a crook? Why did you leave him? How did my mother know him? Do you know who my father is?'

Ginny shook her head. 'Tell me first, did you work your charms on Isaac? Will he talk to me?'

Alice shook her head. 'I'm sorry, Ginny. I did try.'

'Then you need to try again.'

'That won't be possible.' Alice's voice thickened with emotion. 'Ginny, our friendship is ruined.'

'No need for tears.' Ginny poured more sherry into her mug. 'I'm the one should be cryin'.' She gave the mug to Alice, who hesitated before taking a sip and handing it back. 'Louisa's got me workin' this job I never asked for. Need to earn my keep, says Harriet. Always was the Goody Two-shoes, your aunt.'

'What about my mother?' Alice leaned forward, away from the damp slatted wood that had seeped cold through her thin cloak and best silk, chilling her bones. She shivered, cupping her elbows. She ought never to have gone to the wedding party. Hope should not have had the truth confirmed in such a brutal fashion. Perhaps Alice could do without Ginny's promised revelations about her mother. Perhaps Ginny knew nothing at all and was simply teasing her.

The older woman's breath was sour when she put her arm around Alice and leaned close. 'You should come away with me, love.'

Alice pulled away. 'You're leaving?'

'Aye, I've been thinkin' on it. Could use some company. Two heads are better than one an' all that.' Ginny took a swallow of her drink. 'D'you have any savings? How far would they take us, do you think? I've no money left.'

Alice tried to keep the contempt from her voice. 'I think we'd better go. I can walk myself home, all right?'

'Wait.' Ginny put her hand on Alice's arm, serious now. 'I'm ramblin' on, aren't I? It's this.' She swung the mug in the air, splashing Alice's cloak with sherry. 'Oops. Sorry, love. Tell you what, let's go for a bite to eat at The Angel while we're all tarted up. It's a bit of a walk but it'll help me sober up, an' I'll tell you all about your mother, and your father, too.'

Ginny tripped over her skirt negotiating the step into the restaurant at the end of the hotel block in Angel Street, her exclamation as she fell to her knees causing every head to turn towards them. She sniggered as Alice helped her up.

'This was not a good idea,' hissed Alice. 'We should leave.'

A woman she vaguely recognised came forward, wearing the cap and bib of a serving girl.

'It's Louisa's lass, in't it? Wantin' a table for you and your friend?'

Alice's cheeks reddened. 'I'm sorry to land on you like this.'

'Don't be daft. How's your mother? Tell her I asked after her.'

'I will.'

'It's Franny, tell her. My father works for her cab firm.'

'Yes, I'll tell her.' Alice took Ginny's arm. 'Shall we have a pot of tea?'

'I'm starvin',' said Ginny.

The serving girl smiled. 'I'll bring you a scone. No charge.'

'Thank you,' said Alice.

The din of chatter resumed as they were led to a small lace-draped table in the far corner of the room. Ginny fell into her seat and rested her chin in the palm of her hand, tapping her fingers against her cheek. She regarded Alice through half-closed eyes.

'Don't you nod off on me,' Alice hissed.

'I have a headache,' said Ginny. 'An' my ears are buzzing.'

She slowly tipped forward until her forehead rested on the table. Alice yanked her upright and smiled tightly at the server, a different woman, who was carrying over a tray with a teapot, two cups and saucers, a jug of milk and a bowl of sugar. The woman set them down with a tight smile. A second server, a man this time in a starched collar, delivered plates of scones, jam and cream.

'Are we all right, ladies?' he said.

'Yes,' said Alice. 'Thank you.'

Alice poured and encouraged Ginny to drink. After a while, she seemed able to focus her eyes on Alice's face. 'I'll tell you what,' she said. 'That place, that house for destitute girls, your mother could have done wi' having somewhere like that to go to, back in the day. But then, she wouldn't have you to dote on, would she? She'd have been saved, first. Every cloud an' all that.'

'What happened to her?' said Alice. She imagined her mother in a similar situation to Polly Bramall, or to the young girls abandoned by their families for lack of money, or simply too poor to furnish herself with the clothes that would secure her a job.

Ginny spread jam and cream on a piece of scone and nibbled at it. 'I hope Harriet's done one of her goulashes for tea,' she said.

Alice waited.

'You know your mother was a scullery maid, dreaming of marrying a gentleman one day and livin' a life of comfort an' ease.'

'Yes,' said Alice. 'She's told me that much.'

She clasped her hands in her lap, trying to still her excitement. Finally, she would learn something about her parents. She was wise to the idea that Ginny might exaggerate or feed her false information but the gist would be there. Alice was confident of that.

'So, she's caught up in the great flood, nearly drowns.'

'Yes, I know all about that. I'm named for Aunt Harriet's cousin who died.'

Ginny burped. 'Pour me more o' that tea? It's a lovely brew.' Alice did. 'I didn't know her then, I came to town later. She'd started drinkin' by then.'

'But she doesn't touch...' Alice trailed off. 'I see. Go on.'

'She's rentin' a cottage, a tiny place. I went there, in Barker Pool. She kept it tidy enough, but by this time she's in wi' a bad crowd.' Ginny pursed her lips. 'I allus wondered whether my Joe had doings wi' her. I suppose I'll never know. He said not. She's denied it, a'course, but coin is coin.'

Ginny's eyes were distant, and her voice had altered too, losing the twang she'd picked up on the other side of the world. She sounded, with every passing second, more and more like Louisa.

Alice swallowed. 'But Joe was your beau. You ran away together, didn't you?'

'Aye. We wronged her, an' I've apologised for it.' Ginny shrugged. 'Water under the bridge now, at least so far as I'm concerned. Louisa's been a bit off wi' me, for no reason I can fathom. Bygones. What was I saying? I've lost the thread.'

'She drank,' said Alice.

'She did more than that, love. A girl in her line o' work could've used somebody like you to take her to that house, that's what I was sayin', how she earned a crust before good old Jemima Greaves took her under her wing.'

'What line of work?' said Alice.

Ginny licked cream from her fingers. 'Men,' she said. 'Customers, who called on her. She had no choice. She'd 'av starved otherwise, an' in those days she were too proud to go to Silas for help. I can't tell you everythin' she did, back then.' She sighed. 'Maybe she will, one day.' She yawned. 'Do you know, I think I've sobered up but now I'm tired out.'

Alice sat back and stared at the white cloth on the table. 'You're saying that my mother…'

The words would not come. Ginny nodded and nibbled at her scone.

'Why are you telling me this?'

Ginny spluttered crumbs onto the table. 'You asked! Were you expectin' a fairy tale? D'you think your mother's secretly a princess? The truth is always more prosaic, love.'

Alice looked around the room. Nobody was paying them any attention. 'But what about my father?'

'He were no prince, I can tell thee that much, or that little.'

'You knew him?'

'Well, this is the thing, love.' Ginny sipped her tea, carefully replacing the cup in its saucer. 'An' don't shoot the messenger.' She tilted her head, her eyes roaming over Alice's face. 'He could be anybody, a gentleman gone grubbing in the gutter, or a rogue, or a regular. Could be my Joe, but I don't see a resemblance. I'm sorry, love. The bare truth is, you'll never know.'

She sat by the fire in the front room, still wearing the fine striped silk her mother had bought for her, stockinged feet kneading the fabric of an upholstered stool – the same stool she had once cut the fringes from with a pair of kitchen scissors and then been sent to bed without her supper – when the front door opened and closed, the key was turned in the lock and the bolt driven home. Alice's heart had already begun to pound before Louisa called out.

'You back, love?'

She didn't reply. She couldn't, through a throat raw and rough as sandpaper. With some effort, Alice swallowed the sob in her throat. She had not thought there were any tears left to shed but the sound of her mother's voice undid her all over again.

Frozen in place, she listened to the familiar sounds of domesticity coming from the kitchen, the rattle of the kettle on the stove, a cupboard door being opened and closed, curtains swishing together. Then, footsteps softened by the hall rug.

'Alice?'

She leaned forward in her seat, poised, her breathing quick and shallow.

'Oh, you *are* back. You should hang that dress up.' Her mother closed the front room door behind her. 'Glad you got the fire goin', at least. It's brass monkeys tonight. So how was—'

Alice didn't allow her mother to finish her question.

She leapt up from her seat and rushed at Louisa, enfolding her in a tight embrace, burying her face in her mother's neck. After a moment's pause, Louisa patted her on the back, the palm of her other hand pressed against the top of Alice's spine, an enquiring touch. Throughout

Alice's childhood, this was how her mother tested for a fever. It had been a while since she'd felt those exploratory fingers.

'Are you poorly? Don't cry, love. Tell me what's up.'

When Alice moved back, Louisa took hold of her elbows. Her eyes were wide, alarmed, and, beneath that, a look of such anxiety and fierce protectiveness that Alice's breath was taken again. 'Did summat happen, at the party?'

'I have to tell you,' Alice said, 'I have to tell you something, that I never knew 'til now.'

Louisa's forehead was creased with concern. 'You'd better say. Whatever it is, I'll allus be your mother, so spit it out.'

'I never knew,' said Alice. She gulped. 'I never understood how much you've done for me, or how much you do for me now. I've been so ungrateful. I want you to know that you're a wonderful mother. The very best. I wish I'd been a better daughter. I will be.'

'Steady on,' said Lousia. She laughed uncertainly. 'You must've done summat terrible to be sayin' all this. Best come out wi' it.'

'No.' Alice was calmer now, the storm of emotion ebbing away. She sniffed. 'No. It's only that I realised I don't appreciate you enough. I wanted to let you know, I suppose, that I understand why you want the life you want for me.'

Louisa cocked her head, her eyes narrowed. 'All right, then. I suppose we'll leave it at that, though I'm very glad to hear it.' She smoothed Alice's hair away from her sticky cheek. 'Your barnet needs a good brush. Have you had your tea or are you full of party food?'

Later, sitting across from each other by the fireplace, Alice reading, her mother gazing into the flames, Louisa leaned forward and tapped Alice's knee. There was a twinkle in her eye.

'You know you said you wanted to be a better daughter?'

Alice raised an eyebrow.

'Does this mean you're goin' to give up on this daft crusade for women's rights?'

'Oh no,' said Alice. 'No, Mother. I'd say I'm more determined than ever.'

Chapter 17

A chill November dusk was falling, along with a misty drizzle that diffused the glow of the single streetlight and softened the edges of brick and tile and chimney pot. Isaac raised by an inch or two the brim of the cap he'd been wearing low on his forehead and rapped once more on the door. Fires had been lit in every dwelling on Love Lane, columns of smoke rising like pale ghosts against the darkening sky. That was, except for the house Isaac stood outside. He might have given up by now but for the faint glow that shone through the gaps in the shuttered window.

He glanced sideways towards the sound of approaching footsteps. A bulky shape was emerging from the gloom. Returning his gaze to the rough timber door, Isaac curled his hands into fists, tensing his body. There was a rattly cough at his back, and a few mumbled words he didn't catch, then the footsteps receded down the lane. Looking left and right, he knocked gently again. Immediately, catching him off guard, the door was opened a crack and a female voice whispered through it.

'Who's there?'

The voice was young, tremulous. Isaac had been expecting the cracked tones of the brothel keeper.

He cleared his throat. 'I've come to see Dolly. She in?'

'She's not here.'

Isaac frowned. He knew that voice. 'Dolly, is that you? What're you playin' at?'

The door widened slightly. A slim hand snaked through and found his sleeve. Isaac allowed himself to be pulled inside. He took in the lack of furniture, the blankets piled in a corner, cold ashes in the hearth. 'What's going on?'

Dolly closed and bolted the door and turned to him, wrapping the thick shawl she was wearing more tightly around her shoulders. 'The police came, the other day, and took Ma an' told me an' the other lasses to clear out. Then yesterday a girl appears wi' a man an' a cart an' tells me Ma's been charged wi'' keeping a disreputable house, and the pair of them take the settee and table an' chairs. They ransacked the kitchen, an' all. Rent collector says he'll knock the door down if I don't open it to him in the mornin'.'

Her eyes were wide with fright in the flickering light from the candles tilting in pools of wax on the mantelpiece.

'Tha'll burn the place down wi' them,' said Isaac.

'It's all they left me, a few candles and a box of matches.'

'An' you've nowhere to go?'

Dolly lifted her chin. 'I'm not goin' back to the workhouse. I'd rather take my chances on the street.'

Isaac took off his cap, pushed his hand through his hair, and replaced it. There was no reason for him to feel responsible for this girl, but he did, just the same. 'Tha can't stay here tonight. Come wi' me. I know a place.'

—

He watched from a distance as Dolly was ushered inside the House of Help. When the door closed behind her,

187

Isaac strolled away across the square. It struck him as curious, how the two of them had left the house in Love Lane, and walked side by side, a shared reticence keeping him from offering his arm and her from speaking, all pretence dropped away. Isaac had been in this woman's bed but they were strangers to one another. He hoped she would be well cared for, and smiled at the notion of telling Alice he too had become a do-gooder, saving women from the streets. Then he remembered Alice had sent him away.

Isaac trotted across Division Street. Was he as pig-headed as Alice reckoned him to be? Wasn't she just the same, and full of daft notions to boot? He turned the corner into Wellington Street. Perhaps she had been right about one thing, but he knew he'd never open his heart to Ginny. The damage had been done. Taking out his key to open the front door of his parents' house, Isaac shook his head and smirked at the idea of accepting advice from a girl who had made such a spectacle of herself. How many weeks had passed since he had delivered her home on his back, her stockinged feet swinging at his sides? He had found it comical but should have taken her fury seriously. The problem was, he couldn't reconcile himself with Alice's crusade, and she knew it. All their lives, she had been his staunchest ally, and he hers. Now they were staring at each other across opposite sides of a widening chasm. Pausing on the threshold, Isaac rubbed his hand over his face and wondered how long he would carry the weight of their estrangement in his heart.

Teddy toddled out of the front parlour, dragging a blanket behind him in one fist and studiously sucking at a wheat and sugar rusk held tightly in the other. The boy shrieked with delight when Isaac lifted him into the air and sat him on his shoulders.

'Where's the baby? I can't find him anywhere,' Isaac said, ducking into the room where his mother was drinking tea with the two spinsters who lived next door and the wife of the local grocer. He'd heard the women's voices and had hoped one of them belonged to Alice. It was really for her benefit Isaac was monkeying around.

Harriet got to her feet. 'Watch his head on that doorframe!'

'Whose head?' said Isaac. 'Oh! How'd you get up there, Ted?' Deflated, he set Teddy down on the carpet and brushed at his shoulder where the boy had deposited some of the crumbly paste he was eating. 'Sorry to barge in.'

The women smiled at him.

'It's lovely to see you,' said his mother. 'What a pleasant surprise.' She stretched to kiss Isaac's cheek and bent to lift Teddy into the baby cage Silas had made from battens and canvas. Isaac knew she would have hugged him fiercely were it not for the company, and he ached with guilt. 'Will you stay until your father gets home?' asked Harriet, and in answer to his unspoken question: 'Ginny is upstairs.'

She gave Isaac a meaningful look. There was evidently more his mother wanted to say but she was, once again, constrained by the company. Teddy began to wail.

'I should get this one off to bed,' said Harriet.

Her hint worked. The other women made a show of looking at the clock and declaring on the lateness of the hour. Isaac slipped from the room during the protracted farewells and went to the kitchen to see what he could find to eat. He was lifting the lid of the biscuit tin when Ginny walked in, humming a tune. She had on the same wide-brimmed hat she was wearing when she had turned up out of the blue, the same jacket too, under a thick wool cape he recognised as belonging to Harriet. Isaac nodded a greeting and replaced the tin on the top shelf of the dresser, taking a bite from a ginger snap.

'You always had a sweet tooth,' said Ginny.

She was fond of making these claims on him, reminding him that once he had belonged to her. She'd lost the right to reminisce over his infanthood when she ran away. Determined not to show her how riled he was, Isaac confined himself to a shrug. He dropped into a chair and swallowed the biscuit, its sharp edges lodging in his throat.

'Goin' out?' he said in a hoarse voice.

'Goin' away,' said Ginny, lightly.

Isaac snorted. 'Oh aye? See thee in another twenty years, then?'

'Sooner than that, I hope.'

He looked away, not wanting to acknowledge the hurt in her eyes, and was relieved when Harriet came in, concern furrowing her brow.

'Has your mother told you?' Harriet said.

'*Ginny* reckons she's off again,' said Isaac.

'Don't talk as if I'm not here.'

Isaac shrugged. 'Well, you haven't been all these years.'

'That's enough,' said Harriet. 'I have to say, Isaac, it's been a long time since you graced us with your presence, or you'd be aware of what's been going on. Your mother is going to Bridlington, first thing tomorrow.'

'How does that concern me?'

Ignoring this, his mother explained Ginny would be staying the night at the Royal Victoria ahead of the next morning's early train. Uncle James, Harriet's brother, a London banker whom Isaac had never met, had purchased a property on the coast and wanted a live-in caretaker to keep the place aired in summer and warm through the winter. It was his intention to holiday there with his family.

'All right for some,' muttered Isaac.

'It's a job, an' Lord knows I've been nagged to death to get another one,' said Ginny.

'The cab company didn't suit you?' said Isaac.

Ginny sighed. 'I couldn't be doin' with the hours. An' have you tried talkin' on one of them telephone machines? All I could hear were other conversations and humming noises. I was forever cutting people off, an' Louisa sure wasn't happy about that.'

'I'll bet,' said Isaac.

'Well, I'm sure you all will be glad to see the back o' me.'

'Ginny, we have never begrudged you anything,' said Harriet. 'It's your actions that have given us such a—' She broke off. 'Never mind.'

Isaac's mouth twisted. 'Another flit,' he said, 'an' no thought o' the son you supposedly came back to see.' He turned to Harriet. 'Why am I allus kept in the dark?'

Harriet threw up her hands. She opened her mouth to speak then closed it again and took a breath. 'I'm going to make sure Teddy's settled,' she said. 'Ginny, let me know when your cab arrives, please. Hopefully, Silas will be home in time to bid you a safe journey.'

She stalked out.

'Takes a lot to vex my mother,' said Isaac, 'but tha's managed it.'

'I could say the same to you,' said Ginny. She sighed. 'Isaac. Can I say something, before I go? Something I should have said a while ago?'

Isaac folded his arms. 'Not payin' me off with another broken coin, are you?'

He watched her master a fleeting expression of annoyance. 'Let me speak.'

Isaac relented, nodding his head for her to go on.

'I want to say I'm sorry, for leaving you when you were a bairn. I was in difficult circumstances, well, Joe was, but I'm not making excuses for myself. I went with him.' Ginny put out her hand, as if to touch him, then withdrew it. 'Will you let me apologise now, so we can part on better terms, and hopefully meet again somewhere down the line?'

He couldn't meet her eye. It was better − easier − to be at loggerheads with her than to acknowledge the deep, unhealed wound of her abandonment. She was waiting for his answer. Isaac's voice was thick with emotion when he finally spoke.

'You abandoned a tiny little boy then came back as if it were nowt.'

He backed away when Ginny moved towards him. She stopped. 'Like I say, I've no excuse. I'm sorry, love. I really am. But you are my boy, for better or worse.'

There was a rap on the front door. Isaac cocked his head. 'Seems like your cab's here.'

Ginny had left her valise at the foot of the stairs. Isaac picked it up and carried it outside while she and Harriet said their farewells. He waited by the step of the cab as she climbed inside. Ginny paused and turned to face him, sticking out her hand. After a moment's hesitation, Isaac shook it.

'I will see you again,' said Ginny. 'And hopefully we can be kinder to one another. I'm not so far away this time.'

'Aye,' said Isaac. He stepped back onto the pavement. 'P'raps I'll come an' take a breath o' fresh sea air one day.'

Ginny's face lit up. 'I'd love that,' she said.

He watched the cab disappear into the night and followed his mother into the house to retrieve his cap and coat, telling her there was a jar of ale with his name written on it at The Crown on the corner of Wellington Street and Rockingham Street.

'I thought you might stay at home tonight,' Harriet said. 'Don't go back to that dingy room.'

'How do you know it's dingy?'

Harriet reddened. 'I think Alice might have alluded to it, a while back.'

'Wasn't up to her high standards, then? She's spoiled rotten, that one.'

'Oh, don't say that. Alice has a heart of gold. Are you two still at odds?'

Isaac kissed her on the cheek. 'I'm off.'

'But you'll miss your father.'

Isaac laughed. 'We'll see about that.'

The leaded windows of The Crown gave the merest glimpse of the crowded interior, but he immediately picked out Silas turning from the bar, a pint in his hand, and walking away towards the back of the room. Pulling open the door, Isaac plunged into a fug of beer fumes and pipe smoke. He carved a path between noisy groups of working men to reach his father, who had wedged himself onto a banquette.

' 'Ey up.'

Silas had the grace to look shamefaced. 'Has tha been round?' he said.

Isaac nodded. 'She's gone.'

'Good.' Silas took a long drink. 'I thought I'd make mesen scarce, didn't want to be wishin' her a good riddance by accident. How's your mother?'

Isaac frowned. 'Tetchy.'

'She'll have been glad to see thee. It's been a while.'

'Work's been busy.'

Silas grunted.

'Is it wrong,' said Isaac, 'that I'm glad the other one's gone? Relieved, like.'

'No, son. I'd say not. Get theesen a pint an' I'll tell thee the real reason why she's upped sticks again. Get me another, while you're at it.'

There was no seat for Isaac so the two men ended up standing at the bar. 'Can't swing a cat in 'ere,' said Isaac.

'Allus busy, this place,' his father said. 'Good ale. I'm sorry about her, your mother, Ginny.'

'She said she were sorry, an' all.'

Silas reared back. 'Did she, now? Wonders'll never cease.'

'What's been goin' on?'

'I threw her out.'

Isaac spluttered beer. 'Tha did not.'

'Aye, well, it weren't quite as quick or simple as I make it sound.' Silas put his glass on the mantelpiece and tamped tobacco into his pipe. 'There were a weddin', an' Alice were allowed to it, so long as she were in Ginny's company. Seems like she's been a bit o' an imp, our Alice.' He lit the pipe with a spill from the coal fire and drew on it until smoke curled from the bowl. 'I heard about your fallin' out, lad.'

'She were sittin' on the pavement wi' her feet poking through stocks.'

Silas rubbed a hand over his mouth, trying and failing to hide his mirth. 'So, at this weddin'', he said eventually, 'our Ginny tells this young lass all about Teddy.'

Isaac frowned at the unexpected direction the conversation had taken, and wondered how long his father had been hiding in the pub from the women. 'What's Teddy got to do wi' owt?' he said.

'This young lass, she's Teddy's mother. We had no idea but the lass had her suspicions. Alice knew and she let Ginny in on it.' Silas's expression was serious now. 'I reckon Ginny were jealous o' Harriet, bringing up two boys not her own, an' doin' a good job of it, an' all. But her sort don't need a reason to meddle.'

'Wish I'd been a fly on the wall at that weddin'.'

'Aye, she caused ructions. An' the upshot was I lost me temper a little bit. Told Ginny she weren't wanted.' He paused. 'She's a stirrer, I allus knew that, but this time she went too far. I wasn't havin' it, for Harriet's sake, but your mother wouldn't let me put her out.' Silas shook his head. 'To be fair, I wouldn't have seen her on the street.'

'So, this Bridlington thing were contrived.'

'Aye,' said Silas. 'Ginny's kept hersen quiet in the meantime. Summat else went on between her an' Alice, but nobody's sayin' owt.'

'Oh aye?'

'I know nowt. Alice'll probably tell thee herself, once the pair o' you have got over yourselves.'

Isaac decided to ignore that remark. He swilled the dregs of his beer around the glass. 'I know she's my mother, an' I might even visit her, one day, but reight now I'm glad she's gone.'

'Me an' all.' Silas's gaze roved around the room. 'She's left a mess behind her, though. This woman, Teddy's mother, she wrote to us and Harriet wrote back – tha knows what tha mother's like, too soft-hearted – and the upshot is she's now asking to see him.'

He nodded when Isaac groaned. 'I know, lad, I know. Trouble is, your mother's too soft to say no.'

Chapter 18

The early morning sky was a wintry blue, the hammer blows and chatter of construction workers beyond the square amplified in the crisp clear air. Hope stood at the window of the front parlour, her back warmed by the fire Clara had lit. The chill that penetrated the glass pane held her clasped hands in a cold embrace. She was dressed in the simple black broadcloth, lace collar and cap she wore when performing her duties as deputy warden. To an observer, she gave off every appearance of being calm and composed. The maid back at Tylecote would have a better idea of her real state of mind as soon as she entered her bedroom; as if a whirlwind had torn through, every surface was festooned with bodices and skirts that Hope had picked up and discarded in a frenzy of indecision.

She had been standing in the middle of the room, still in her woollen chemise and stockings, when she heard her transport rumble onto the gravel drive. Finally, her host knocked on the door to enquire whether Hope would be travelling to the House of Help today. Her throat aching with suppressed tears, she asked for a few more moments. But the brief exchange had helped clear her mind. She was going to her job and would dress accordingly, as if this was any other normal day.

The House of Help was, relatively, quiet. Those residents with jobs and those in training had left, some for the day, some to return at dinnertime for the day's hot meal. There were two thirteen-year-old girls in the dorm above the parlour. Hope could hear them chattering and the occasional patter of feet. A street walker who had arrived at the point of starvation was confined to one of the beds in the new dorm beside Amelia's room and the warden's office. Mrs Wallace was delivering a girl to the servant training school and had promised to return well before ten o'clock. Two residents were cleaning the dorms with duster and broom, and a third was in the scullery, helping the laundry woman. Amelia had said she would deal with any visitors to the house. Clara was preparing the tea things for when the guests arrived and Cook had baked her famous carrot cake.

Hope was grateful, but all this attentiveness, the many small kindnesses she was being shown, left her with nothing to do but fret.

She walked to the fireplace and stretched her fingers towards the flickering yellow and orange flames, guilt and fear stirring in her gut. The clock on the mantel showed there were twenty minutes until the appointed hour. Staring at the ticking hands would not make time fly faster. Remaining still was impossible.

Marching across the room, Hope wrenched open the door and hurried down the hall, pausing at the top of the steps that led to the kitchen to fix a composed smile to her face. Inside, the kettle was whistling. She took a breath and entered the room.

Amelia sat at the kitchen table, writing on a piece of paperboard, and acknowledged Hope with a smile and a nod.

Clara gestured to the tray at Amelia's elbow. 'Four o' thee, right?'

'Yes,' said Hope. 'Thank you.' She picked up a cup and put it down again on its saucer. 'That cake looks delicious. Where is Cook?'

'Shoppin' for dinner,' said Amelia. 'Took one o' the women with her. I'm holdin' the fort, like I said I would.'

'I hope I'm not inconveniencing anyone,' said Hope.

'Don't be soft,' said Amelia. 'Look.'

She folded the paperboard in half and held it up for Hope to inspect. Stencilled across it in bold letters were the words *Do Not Disturb*. An arrow pointed sideways.

'I'll hang this over the picture in the hall, once you're safely tucked inside,' said Amelia. 'It's nowt fancy, but it'll do the job. Don't want people thinkin' they can just go blunderin' in.'

'That's kind of you,' said Hope.

'Go on, now. Shoo!' said Clara. 'I'll carry this lot up in ten minutes, then the tea'll be mashed for when they arrive.'

Hope mumbled her thanks and returned to the parlour. She sat in one of the ladderback chairs that had been decorated for the bride and groom, now shorn of its flowers and ribbons, and straightened the bow of her collar and curled her hands in her lap. Unwanted memories were washing into her mind, a tide she could not stem, come to drown her. She squeezed her eyes shut. Here was the field where she lay on her back, crushed under the weight of him, and here was the threshold of the House of Help in the dead of night where she cowered, numb with fear. And here, months later, she lay curled on her side, head pillowed, listening to murmured words of consolation that failed to soothe. The bassinet was gone, leaving behind a void that had swallowed her child and her heart.

Hope's eyes flew open at the sound of a gentle rap on the door. She flexed her hands, which had been gripping the arms of the chair, and swiped at her cheeks, and tried to smile as the warden entered.

'Worried I wouldn't be back in time?' Mrs Wallace's nose was red with cold. She examined Hope's face. 'It'll be all right, love.'

'Will it?' She waited for the warden to sit. 'Mrs Wallace, I feel so much guilt. This is so unfair on the people who took him in. And everything I've tried so hard to forget is back, as fresh as yesterday. I don't deserve your regard, or Angus's. I'm still making a mess of everything.'

'No,' said the warden. 'What you're doing is being overly harsh on yourself. I'm sorry you ever overhead our conversation' – she flapped her hand when Hope tried to protest – 'or had dealings with that troublemaker, Ginny. I hear from Alice that she's gone and I say good riddance. I don't doubt Mr and Mrs Hinchcliffe will be saying the same about that woman.'

Hope shook her head. 'What will they be saying about me? They've cared for him almost from the day he was born. They must loathe me.'

'Don't be silly. They're good people.' The warden patted her hand. 'I wouldn't have let him go to them were it not so.'

A gentle knock on the door set her heart pounding. Hope sat up straight and clasped her hands in her lap, but it was only Clara coming in with the tea tray. She set it down and left, closing the door behind her.

The mantel clock chimed the hour.

–

'I fall,' said Teddy, solemnly. He rubbed at the sleeve of his green and brown checked dress – a child's Sunday best – and gazed up at the man he called his father. 'Make better?'

Silas Hinchcliffe had taken up position behind his wife's chair, his hand resting protectively on her shoulder. He duly bent and took the boy's arm in his hand and kissed it. 'There,' he said.

'He's not used to these new boots,' said Mrs Hinchcliffe. 'He's growing so fast.'

'He's certainly a good talker,' said Mrs Wallace.

Mr Hinchcliffe nodded proudly. 'He's a clever lad, no doubt about it. Turns two in the spring.'

'Yes,' said Hope. 'In May.'

Her heart shrivelled. She had wanted to join in the conversation and had not meant to sound accusatory. In the awkward silence that followed, they all watched Teddy plonk himself on the carpet and set about trying to unfasten his button-up boots.

'Just look at the state o' his hair,' said Mr Hinchcliffe. 'Did you cut that fringe, love? Steepest angle I've ever seen. Better slope than the one on Blake Street.'

His wife laughed. 'He wouldn't keep still for me!'

Hope managed a tremulous smile, grateful for this moment of levity. She was gathering the courage to make her plea. When the Hinchcliffes arrived, the warden had immediately apologised for the indiscretion that had placed them in this unfortunate position, but they would have none of it. Alice had fully explained to them the circumstances that had resulted in Hope turning up on their doorstep in the summertime. Ginny, whom Mr Hinchcliffe referred to more than once as 'that blasted woman', had been the catalyst.

Hope agreed she might never have acted on her suspicion and Mrs Hinchcliffe had smiled at her kindly. 'But always wondered, never to be content?' she asked, bringing tears to Hope's eyes.

Teddy gave up his mission to divest himself of his boots, got to his feet and side-stepped towards the tea tray, where earlier he'd given Cook's carrot cake a wide-eyed stare. He turned his dimpled smile on each of the adults in turn, speculatively, finally settling on Mrs Wallace and asking her hopefully: 'Mine?'

'Shall I pour?' said Mrs Wallace. 'Can Teddy eat a bit of cake?'

'Aye,' said Mr Hinchcliffe. 'A tiny bit.'

Hope declined the cup and saucer offered by the warden. She was afraid her hands would betray her nerves. Mrs Hinchcliffe scooped up Teddy.

'Might he sit on your lap?' she said. 'I warn you, he'll cover you in crumbs.'

Hope nodded mutely, overcome by the woman's generosity. She took Teddy from Mrs Hinchcliffe's arms, relishing the solid weight of him. He leaned against her body, his head nestled under her chin, in a display of trust that made her heart soar. Hope held the sliver of cake on the palm of her hand and watched Teddy's chubby fingers pick at it. He held up a crumb for her inspection and she laughed and nodded and he put it in his mouth.

Mr Hinchcliffe came around to sit in a chair. 'Reight then,' he said, running a finger under his stiff white shirt collar.

Holding Teddy on her lap gave Hope the courage as well as the means of expressing her wish. She bent to rest her cheek on the boy's head.

'Teddy, will you call me Aunt Hope?' she said, and looked up, heart in mouth, into the eyes of Harriet Hinchcliffe.

—

She had one more task to perform.

The following day was a Saturday, bright but cold, and Angus had arranged to collect Hope from Tylecote and take her for a late breakfast at the home of his parents in Whirlow, an affluent district where the town's wealthiest resided. The Grange was an impressive double-fronted stone building sitting in extensive and well-manicured grounds. Hope had visited once before, for a supper held to celebrate her engagement to Angus, where she sat at a dining table as large as the four-bed dorm at the House of Help, and wondered how many women in need this mansion could accommodate.

There was no opportunity to speak to Angus privately before they set off, as she had intended, and, once settled in the carriage, Hope found herself tongue-tied.

They drove along the edge of the new park at Endcliffe, created, Angus told her, to celebrate the Queen's golden jubilee two years earlier. Hope breathed in the cold, clean air, watching the tops of evergreens sway against the blue sky, and was overcome by an urge to walk amongst the trees.

'If it stays dry,' she said, 'might we take a stroll in the woods after breakfast?'

Angus looked across at her and smiled. 'She speaks, at last.'

He thought she was anxious about this meeting with his parents, where the wedding arrangements would be debated. Hope had requested a quiet ceremony, held locally, and had been – until yesterday – dreading having to explain why she no longer went by the name her parents had given her. For legal reasons, Emma Hyde would have to return from the dead for the wedding ceremony. Angus knew her history and loved her regardless. But for Hope, answering to the name of her past self was an unbearable prospect. Yet, her earlier resolve was ebbing away, the motion of the carriage lulling her down a road she had already decided she could not take.

Hope put her hand to her mouth, fighting a sudden nausea. 'Can we stop?' she said. 'Please, stop now.'

Angus reined in the horse, and the gig slowed to a halt by the side of the road. 'What's up?' he asked, concern written across his face. 'Are you ill?'

'Not ill.' Hope bit her lip. 'Can we walk now, please?'

'What about breakfast? My parents are expecting us.'

'I need a moment.' Her stomach rolled. 'I need to breathe.'

'Of course. You're pale.' He jumped onto the pavement and helped Hope down. 'Really, there's no need to be nervous. My parents have fallen in love with you. I obtained your father's blessing, and he has written to Mother and Father. They'll show you the letter. All is well. Shall we find a bench?'

Hope shook her head. 'Can we walk?'

'If you're up to it.'

'I am.' Her eyes slid away from his gaze.

They followed a trail through the woodland north of the Porter Brook that wound through the park, their breath clouding in the cold air. Finally, Hope stopped and removed one of her gloves to spread her hand against the trunk of a large oak. The rough bark was reassuringly solid. 'I wonder how old this tree is?' she said.

'Older than we are,' said Angus. 'Older than we'll ever get.' He took her naked hand and encased it in his two hands. 'You'll catch a chill.' The leather of his gloves was cold, like a dead animal. She shuddered. 'Hope, what's wrong?'

'Angus.' She laid her hand against his chest. 'I can't—'

He seemed to know what she was about to say and stopped her with a kiss, a gentle brush against her lips.

'I don't care if we're seen, or by whom,' he said. 'I love you, Hope.'

She stepped away so her back was against the tree. There was nobody on the path they had taken. 'I can't marry you,' she said. 'I'm sorry.'

She looked away from his stricken eyes, focusing on pulling her glove over her fingers and straightening the cuff. 'I'm going to be in my son's life, it's been agreed. He'll know me as his aunt but one day he might learn the truth and that won't be fair on you or your family. Things will become… complicated.'

Angus was slowly shaking his head.

'I mean it, and I am sorry, but Teddy is my world now. Teddy, and my work.' Hope laughed, a bitter sound. 'I'll be at odds with my parents again, but I've become accustomed to that.' She met his gaze and put as much conviction into her voice as she could muster. 'I won't allow you to be fodder for the town gossips, Angus. It's better if we part now, on good terms, and I hope we can remain friends.'

It was done, but there was no relief, only a hollowness that numbed her heart.

Angus took her hands in his. 'Have you finished?' he said gently.

Hope nodded miserably.

'Then perhaps you'll allow me to speak.'

He didn't relinquish his hold when she shook her head and peered over his shoulder down the winding path, which thankfully remained deserted. The sky had clouded over, a milky cast that leached the landscape of all colour. A sob rose in Hope's throat.

'Please drive me back to Tylecote.'

'No.'

Infuriated, Hope tore her hands from his grasp. 'No?'

'It's my turn to speak.' Angus reached for her. Hope crossed her hands behind her back, and, to her astonishment, he laughed. He hadn't taken her declaration seriously.

'Do you love me, Hope?'

'That's not the—'

'Do you love me, yes or no?'

He rested his hands lightly on her shoulders as if he was afraid she would bolt. Hope stared miserably at the ground until Angus gently raised her chin with one finger. She watched his lips when he spoke again in a whisper quieter than the breeze.

'Yes or no?'

She couldn't move, couldn't tear her eyes from his mouth. He dropped his head so that their lips were almost touching. 'I've loved you for so long,' he murmured. 'But I will step aside only if you will tell me you don't love me in return.'

Hope's lips parted. She would tell him she was only trying to save him pain, that he deserved better than what she had to offer, that the reason she wanted to save him from the ignominy of her situation was because she loved him. She loved him with all her heart.

Instead, her lips touched his. They kissed, Hope tasting her own salt tears.

Angus pulled away first, cupping her face between his hands. 'I shall be Uncle Angus and everything shall be all right. That's my promise to you.'

She searched his eyes. Could she dare to believe him? When Angus bent his head to kiss her again, the sound of a throat being noisily cleared came from the path above. A middle-aged man wearing a waterproof overcoat, a pair of sturdy boots and carrying a walking stick nodded an acknowledgement as he passed by.

'Good morning,' said Angus.

'Mornin'.'

Hope, who had turned her face away, released a breath when the man disappeared around the next bend. 'How can you possibly know that everything will be all right?'

'Because we'll be travelling this road together.' Angus laughed and pulled her back into his arms. 'Making it up as we go along. I want to make you happy, Hope, if you can bear that burden. Do you think you can?'

He was telling her she deserved happiness and even though she did not, in her heart, believe that, there was only one truthful answer to his question. Hope took a deep breath.

'I do.'

Chapter 19

The word was daubed across six of the twelve panes of glass in the front parlour window of the House of Help, filling the bottom half of the sash with a crimson letter per square, except for the final square where two letters had been crammed together.

HARLOTS

Alice laughed but her voice shook when she spoke. 'Ruins the aesthetic, that last pane. Could they not come up with an equally offensive six-letter word?'

The warden, jaw set, steered her away from the handful of onlookers that had gathered. 'Constable Goodlad's gone to pay a call on our friend Alfie Bramall. He's the likeliest candidate, the police reckon. The paint was reported nicked yesterday from the Albert Hall.' Mrs Wallace shook her head. 'Clara got the fright o' her life when she opened the curtains this morning. She thought it was blood.'

'That horrible man,' said Alice. 'I hope he's got paint all over his hands. I wish I could see him being put in cuffs.' Indignation burned in her chest. 'He should be locked up for life for what he did to Polly, but he's not in jail, is he? He's at large, allowed to bully women.'

'Aye, well, we should let the police deal wi' him.' The warden went back to the window to shoo people away.

'Excitement's over. This isn't the first time we've had trouble an' I'm sure it won't be the last.'

Clara, her face stony, and Amelia, whose mouth was pressed into a thin line, came out of the house, wielding between them a tin bucket filled with steaming liquid. Clara went back inside, returning with a large terrycloth that she balled up in her fist and dipped in the bucket, screwing up her nose against the pungent stench.

'We boiled up some vinegar,' said the warden in response to Alice's unspoken question. 'Should do the trick.'

Amelia came over to them. 'I never heard a thing, and I were sleeping a few feet away.' A shudder rippled across her shoulders. 'What if he'd tried to get in?'

Mrs Wallace put her hand on her daughter's arm. 'He didn't, though. It's a bit o' mischief and none o' us injured, except for our pride,' she said. 'The police say they'll increase the night patrol around here an' of course I'll move back in for a bit.'

Amelia shook her head. 'No need for that, Ma.' She frowned. 'Anyhow, aren't we full?'

'There's a bed in the attic,' said Mrs Wallace, 'and we've got a girl leavin' today, all being well.'

'No,' said Amelia. Alice recognised the firm voice the warden used when she would brook no argument. 'You go home to Mr Wallace. We carry on as normal, that's what we do. Keep the lasses indoors. Once Clara's finished there'll be nowt to gawp at.'

A woman wearing a heavy shawl and carrying a muslin-covered basket tapped Amelia on the arm. 'Excuse me, are you from this place?' she said. 'I was told this was the house.' She peered at the window, a dubious look on her face.

'I'm the warden,' said Mrs Wallace. 'And you are?'

'Mrs Frederick Taylor.'

'Ah, yes, please come inside.'

Alice followed them, leaving Amelia talking to the cleaner from the Q in the Corner, who had come out to offer her opinion on how best to erase the offending word, while Clara got on with scrubbing the first pane. A vinegary odour pervaded the interior of the house.

The woman looked about her, taking in the wallpaper that had seen better days and the worn stair carpet. 'What goes on here? I saw that word, in the window.'

'You're Jane's sister?' said Mrs Wallace.

The woman nodded, somewhat reluctantly in Alice's opinion.

Mrs Wallace took her by the elbow to steer her into the front parlour.

'Come with me, Mrs Taylor. We've had a bit of a contretemps this morning. Alice, would you ask Jane to come down?'

Alice found Jane Wilson sitting on her bed, fretting with the piece of sewing she'd been given to complete. A dress donated to the house had arrived with a tear in it and had been refigured into two girls' smocks. Jane had turned out to be useless with the needle but the task of hemming the smocks, that Alice could already see would need to be unpicked and resewn, had kept her occupied.

Convicted of prostitution, Jane been evicted from the room she rented and her five-year-old son taken away from her and put into an industrial school. She was twenty-two years old, an orphan unable to read or write, and unskilled. During her three weeks at the house, Alice had befriended her while the warden tried to come up with a solution, and, through gentle persuasion, learned, eventually, that she had a sister. The two women were estranged but Jane was able to recall the woman's address. After an exchange of letters that the warden described to Alice only as 'terse', Jane's sister agreed to visit the house. She was, she insisted, making no promises.

Alice led Jane into the parlour, which was gloomy with the curtains closed but warmer than the rest of the house, where the doors and windows had been flung open in an attempt to dispel the smell of boiled vinegar. The older women were in conversation against a back-drop of muffled thumps against the glass and voices on the pavement outside. Alice sat and indicated Jane should sit beside her. The girl began to sniff and Alice handed her a handkerchief, unsure whether she was distressed or reacting to the eye-wateringly sharp stench.

'And what does your husband do, if you don't mind me asking?' said the warden.

'He's at the Norfolk colliery,' said Mrs Taylor.

'A well-paid position?' said Mrs Wallace.

'Aye.' The woman was guarded. 'Fred does all right. But I've eight bairns and I can't be feeding another mouth. An' I've not seen hide nor hair of this one,' she gestured towards Jane, acknowledging her presence for the first time, 'for six year o' more. Never met my nephew.'

'An' won't now,' said Jane, under her breath. 'They took him.'

Her sister snorted. 'Well, what did you expect?'

'Unfortunately,' said Mrs Wallace, 'we haven't been able to place Jane at the servant training school, but our deputy warden has been encouraging her to learn to read and write. Miss Hope is an excellent teacher. Jane might even return here, to continue with her letters and numbers, if she wishes. We'll waive the charge for non-residents.'

Mrs Taylor shook her head. 'I wun't bother. She were never the sharpest tool in the box, this one.'

Alice took Jane's hand. The girl smiled at her gratefully. 'Where are your children today?' said Alice.

'Left 'em with a neighbour, so I can't be long.' She touched the basket at her feet with the side of her foot. 'Thought I might as well get the shoppin' done. The fruit's cheaper from the market, so there's that.'

The warden smiled. 'We're grateful you've spared the time, Mrs Taylor. Sounds like you've a lot on your plate.'

'Aye. Not enough hours in the day.'

'Why not employ Jane to shop and cook and clean in return for a roof over her head?' said Alice, as if the idea had only just occurred to her. 'She can help with the children, too.'

Mrs Wallace nodded. 'That sounds like a fine solution.'

'So long as she's not helpin' herself to my husband,' said Mrs Taylor. 'I know what she is.'

Jane curled her lip. Alice squeezed the girl's hand to prevent her from saying whatever it was that lay on the tip of her tongue.

'She's paid the price for her mistakes,' the warden interjected smoothly. 'Wouldn't you say?'

'Everybody deserves a second chance,' said Alice. She shifted in her seat. For some reason, Isaac invaded her thoughts. She cleared her throat and brought herself back to the present moment. 'I'm sure Jane would benefit from an older sister's guidance.'

Mrs Taylor made a disapproving noise and pursed her lips. 'Come to think o' it, I'll be able to tell the neighbours

I've a servant to boss about. I'll be the lady o' the house. She'll be the skivvy.'

'She is your sister,' said the warden, reproachfully.

'I'm only jestin'.' The woman had exchanged the scowl she'd had on her face ever since her eyes fell on Jane for a small smile. 'All right. I'll take her off your hands. I know you want rid. She'd best behave hersen.'

'I will,' said Jane in a low voice. She looked at the warden. 'Unless there's owt else for me, owt else at all.'

Her sister laughed. 'There's allus the soldiers' barracks.'

'You'll be best off with your sister and your nieces and nephews,' said Alice. 'But come back and visit us.'

Mrs Taylor got to her feet. 'I've only one son, an' seven daughters, God preserve us. Jane won't have time to come gallivanting up here.'

Outside, Clara was holding the soaked cloth against the letter O and chatting over her shoulder to a couple of women who stood on the pavement. She asked Alice to find Amelia and fetch a fresh bucket of soapy water to scrub the panes she had cleaned, which were smeared where the letters RL had been erased.

'Comin' off easier than I thought,' said Clara.

'I'll find Amelia,' said Mrs Wallace.

Alice bid the sisters farewell and remained on the door-step until the two women were out of sight. Jane, now carrying the basket, cast a glance back at the house before turning the corner. Alice had her misgivings but hoped sisterly love would prevail. She lingered for a moment longer, looking across the square at the window above the butcher's shop. Thinking of Isaac gave her a sick feeling in the pit of her stomach. She supposed she missed him. Still, she could never forgive him for what he had done. Even now, the humiliation of being flung over his shoulder like a sack of potatoes, the laughter and jeers of the crowd, and her own helplessness, stirred her to anger. He was no better than Alfie Bramall.

A small voice in Alice's head, behind the outrage, told her she was being unfair. Isaac wouldn't hurt a flea. She had always known so. Alfie Bramall had driven his wife to her death. Still, Isaac had betrayed her.

Alice shook her head briskly as if it would clear her mind and shuffle her thoughts into some sort of sense, and retreated into the house, moving aside to allow Amelia and one of the residents to pass by with a bucket full of suds. The warden was sitting at the kitchen table, checking the weekly menu card. Alice peered over Mrs Wallace's shoulder. The list began with the following day's menu: bread and lard for breakfast, a roasted joint at dinnertime – the bones would be boiled for a broth for dinner on Monday – and potatoes, with carrots and turnips that Cook mashed with salt and pepper and a pinch of nutmeg. There would be a sliver of cake after the weekly bible reading in the parlour, and bread and jam with cocoa before bed.

The warden held up the card. 'Pin that to the dresser for me?' she said.

'What did you think?' said Alice. She meant, about Mrs Taylor.

Mrs Wallace shrugged. 'It's a bed freed up.'

Amelia came in while the warden was tying her bonnet under her chin, preparing to return to her new home.

'Well,' said Amelia, 'we've got it all off. I'd like to tan the hide of the miserable beggar.' She held up hands that were red raw. 'I can't feel my fingers.'

Mrs Wallace warmed each of Amelia's hands in turn between her own. 'I'll stay if you want. You've had a nasty shock.'

'We'll be reight,' said Amelia.

The warden nodded. 'Well, we've two beds going begging if any waifs or strays turn up, one in the attic, one in the first-floor dorm. Constable Goodlad will be knocking on the door around nine o'clock tonight, to make sure all is well, an' I'll see you for the bible reading tomorrow.' She frowned. 'That's if you're sure you don't want me to stay?'

'I'm sure,' said Amelia. She kissed her mother on the cheek. 'Don't fret.'

'Are you walkin' out with me, Alice?' said Mrs Wallace.

'I'll keep Amelia company for a bit,' said Alice.

'Don't be abroad after dark, will you?'

Alice nodded. 'I won't stay long.' After the warden had left, she offered to put on the kettle. The two women took their mugs of tea and sat, wrapped in shawls, in the peace and quiet on the stairs that led to the attic, agreeing that once Clara and the resident helping her had finished cleaning the window, and Alice had left, Amelia would lock and bolt the door and, saving the arrival on the doorstep of a girl or woman in need, admit only the constable.

They gossiped good-naturedly about Hope, her son and her engagement to Angus Deveraux. 'It feels strange,' said Alice, 'talking to Teddy about his Aunt Hope, but I'm sure we'll all get used to it. I hear there might be another engagement on the cards before too long. Am I sitting with the future Mrs Greaves?'

Amelia blushed. 'Your poor mother,' she said, instead of answering. 'She'd lined Barnaby up for you.'

'I know.' Alice laughed. 'Don't worry, though. She hasn't given up. I've just learned to take all these staged meetings with suitable young men in my stride.'

'And what about your crusade?'

'Oh! Yes, I must tell you.' Alice set down her mug and clapped her hands together. 'I've been writing to the papers, although I haven't yet had any of my letters published. I'll keep trying. And there's a ladies' discussion society that I hope to speak before, although the secretary hasn't yet responded to my request.' She paused. 'I should write again.'

'Not havin' much luck, then?' said Amelia.

'Ah, but I haven't told you yet about my latest endeavour. I've got up a petition calling for equal voting rights that I'm going to ask factory workers to sign, both men and women, and it's my intention to present it to our member of parliament.'

'How will you get the signatures?' said Amelia.

'At the factory gates,' said Alice, 'if that's what it takes.'

–

Walking home, Alice allowed herself a wry smile, recalling how her leaflet had been received by the working women into whose hands she had thrust it. Discarded, unread. The lack of interest in the meeting on Cemetery Road stung, still. Alice would have to be more persuasive if she was to detain workers leaving their shift. The women would be hurrying home to continue their work cooking and cleaning, while the men would have their sights set on the nearest public house. Would there ever come a day when the scales that weighed the sexes were not so freighted in the favour of men?

Her mother had not yet returned home from work. Alice refilled the coal scuttle, built the fire in the sitting room and laid kindling and coal in the small fireplaces in both her and her mother's bedrooms. She lit the stove and set the kettle on to boil.

By the time Louisa arrived, the cottage would be warm and cosy, the bread rising and the goulash bubbling in the pan. Alice could reconcile the enjoyment she found in simple domesticity and her passion for equal rights for women. She had told Isaac this when he teased her about how good she was at making home, back when she was able to respond in good grace, before he had revealed his true colours and shown himself to be no more advanced in thought than a caveman.

Over their shared meal at the kitchen table, Louisa told her about her busy day. Two of the drivers had got into a scrap and Barnaby, of all people, had stepped in and defused the situation. 'His mother would be proud of him,' said Louisa. 'I gather your friend Amelia has set her sights on him.'

Alice laughed. 'It's the other way round.' She spread butter on a chunk of bread. 'I went to the house today.'

'Oh aye? What for?'

She decided in that moment to say nothing about the venomous word scrawled on the window. It had been scrubbed away and should be forgotten about. That wasn't the only reason to remain quiet. Her mother might forbid her returning to the house.

'A resident, one who'd been there a little while, was moving on and I wanted to wish her well.'

'Where's she going?'

'To her sister.' Alice frowned. 'I hope she's all right.'

'I'm sure she will be if she's wi' family. Listen, Alice.' She paused. 'I wanted to say summat about Isaac, an' your fallin' out, but I've not had the chance. I take it you've not made amends wi' him?'

Alice put down her spoon and stared at her mother, incredulous. 'It's not up to me to make amends!'

Louisa held up her hands. 'Don't get a monk on wi' me, love.'

'You know what he did, though.'

Her mother tipped her head to the side and gazed at her. 'Be that as it may, I'm goin' to tell thee summat. I should've said it sooner, but, well, I thought you'd make up an' he'd get to say it himself.'

Alice folded her arms. 'If he's tryin' to get you on his side, Ma...'

Louisa laughed. 'There's no sides in this, love. Or too many. I can't fathom it out, so I'm tellin' you, an' it's the truth.'

Alice lifted her hands impatiently. 'Tell me then.'

'Isaac wants to marry you.' Louisa sat back in her chair. 'There it is. He loves you.'

'As a cousin,' said Alice, but she was thinking of the kiss he had given her on her twentieth birthday. She had thought she would swoon, it had been so unexpected, and so unexpectedly lovely, but then he had laughed it off. He had been teasing her, playing a joke on her. If she recalled correctly, she'd been cross with him afterwards, and unsettled for a while, then it was all forgotten. Why had she been cross? Was something awakened in her by that kiss, only to be extinguished by Isaac's seeming dismissal of what had happened?

'No,' said her mother, 'not as a cousin. He came to me, before you had your upset, an' asked me whether I'd give my blessin'. I told him to go back to work at his father's.'

Alice frowned. 'Why?'

'Job security. I want to see thee well looked after, set for life.' Louisa shrugged. 'You know that much already.'

Alice stroked her fingertips across her lips, dropping her hand when she saw the look her mother was giving her. 'What did he say, when you told him that?'

'That if you would have him, he'd go back to Hinchcliffe's in a heartbeat.'

Chapter 20

Five thousand men, or so the Monday newspaper would report, all streaming in the same direction, Isaac and Silas among them, collars turned up and caps pulled low against air that was sharp as scissors.

'Ground'll be frozzed,' said his father. 'I'll bet thee owt.'

Isaac grunted in reply. Father and son had reached a compromise of sorts. Silas still wanted him back at the firm but was keeping his counsel. For his part, Isaac bit his lip whenever he felt the urge to blether on about John Tasker and his amazing electrical light and telephony company. An uneasy truce had been made, for Harriet's sake.

The pubs were emptying out as they approached Queens Road in the centre of town, dinnertime drinkers filling the streets, jostling, cat-calling and whistling as they were stirred into the crowd. Hinchcliffe and son were allies here, at least, united in support of the Wednesday club. The thought brought a smile to Isaac's face.

He paid them into the Olive Grove ground. The Wednesday were up against Sunderland Albion and favourite to win. Isaac and Silas found a place to stand on the wooden planking about halfway up the tiered kop, shoulder to shoulder with fellow supporters stamping their feet against the cold. A cheer went up when the players ran onto the pitch, which was a buckled, frozen sea. One of them tripped and fell, to jeers and laughter from the crowd.

'Told thee,' Silas shouted in Isaac's ear. 'Want to lay bets on broken ankles?'

'Cost us five grand, that steamin' pile o' shite,' said the man on Isaac's left. 'Never should've built o'er a stream.'

The man standing in front of Isaac turned and glared up at the speaker. 'Nowt to do wi' it, tha daft sod. Blame the weather if tha's blamin' owt.'

Isaac looked back at the pitch, where the referee was conferring with both teams. 'Should've stuck wi' Bramall Lane,' he said. 'At least it'd save the players havin' to get in an' out of their kit at the Earl of Arundel.'

Now he was on the receiving end of the man's aggressive stare.

'An' pay United for the pleasure o' playing?' the man said. 'We're a professional club now an' need to be actin' like one, wi' our own pitch.'

'A changin' room would be nice, though,' said Isaac. 'It's not askin' much.'

'Shurrup, then,' said Silas. 'I came to watch me team not listen to tha pair gabbing like old women.'

Isaac laughed. The man spat on the ground and turned away. Then the players fell back into position and a shrill whistle signalled the start of the game.

–

Silas got the round in at the Earl and the two men stood beside the fireplace, as close to the roaring blaze as they could get without catching alight. Several of the players were accepting drinks and some good-humoured ribbing. The Wednesday had won – and by a creditable four goals to Sunderland's one – but the result would be disqualified from the Football Alliance league because of the poor condition of the ground.

'It's not a patch on Bramall Lane,' said Isaac morosely.

'But it's ours,' said Silas. 'That bloke were right. We were long overdue goin' professional. I still shudder to think o' that seventeen nil game against Halliwell.'

'That were two year since!'

'At my age, lad, it were the day before yesterday.'

They supped their ale, surveying the room. Isaac's father nodded towards a forlorn-looking man sitting at a small table by the door, counting the change in the palm of his hand, an empty pitcher by his elbow. 'That daft sod bet his week's wages on a trouncin' for Wednesday,' said Silas, 'an' now he can't afford a pot to piss in an' he daren't go home. His missus'll have his guts for garters.'

Isaac laughed. 'You an' your stories.'

'What's your story then, lad? Still above the butcher's shop?'

'Aye, but not for long.' Isaac gulped his ale. 'I'm movin' tomorra, in fact. Found better lodgings off Fargate. Nearer to work, an' all.'

Silas grimaced. 'Tha knows tha can come home at any point, son.'

Isaac nodded and tried not to let the irritation he felt show on his face. He took his father's empty pint pot from his hand. 'One for the road?'

'Aye, why not?'

When Isaac returned, Silas was sitting at the table the alleged gambler had quit, tamping tobacco into his pipe. Isaac took out matches and a cigarette from his pocket. They smoked in silence, Isaac's gaze following the curl of smoke from the glowing tip of his cigarette to the mottled, yellowed ceiling.

'I were just thinkin' back to that first floodlit game we went to,' said Silas. 'Who'd have thought you'd end up workin' for Tasker?'

'Aye,' said Isaac carefully.

'He's had to reduce his rates a bit, tha knows.'

'Oh aye?'

Silas's eyes flashed with humour over the rim of his pint pot. 'Cheaper to send a boy across town wi' a message than pay twenty pound a year to use a telephone exchange, even wi' a free advert in the directory. So, I knocked his salesman down to fifteen.'

Isaac's jaw dropped open.

'An' now I've one o' your clever devices on me desk.' Silas winked. 'Got to move wi' the times, son. Are tha tryin' to catch flies?'

Isaac snapped his jaw shut.

'There are people,' said Silas, pausing for a sip of ale, 'that reckon the telegraph sped up life too quick, an' this is worse still. I can tell thee I'm not one o' them. It does mean I'll be at every bugger's beck an' call but we'll see how it goes. I can allus dip out once the contract's up.'

'True enough,' said Isaac. He couldn't keep the smile from his face. 'You got a 25 per cent discount?'

'Proud o' the old man? I thought tha'd like that,' said Silas. 'I'll have to practise me telephone etiquette, eh?'

Isaac laughed. 'So will the operators. I'm told some o' the young lads get a bit rowdy, rude to customers, cuttin' people off mid-conversation, or joinin' in wi' a few choice words, that sort o' thing. Girls do better at it, but that's day shifts only.' He shrugged. 'It's new to us all. There'll be bumps along the way.'

He left the Earl with a spring in his step. It was dark by the time they reached the street where he would part ways with his father.

'Come for Sunday dinner, tomorra,' Silas called over his shoulder as he walked away.

'I'll try,' said Isaac. 'I can't promise owt, mind.'

His father didn't turn around but raised his hand in salute.

Late that night, Isaac gathered his few possessions together. He'd left behind in Wellington Street his good suit and moleskin trousers and the blue silk-lined waistcoat his mother had given him, which he'd hardly ever had occasion to wear. They were still hanging in the wardrobe of the room he still thought of as his. He shoved his work clothes, britches and braces, spare shirt and trousers and flannels into a burlap sack. Into a box went the few kitchen items he'd purchased, along with his razor, brush and soap. There was a crack in the shaving mirror he'd hung on a painted-over nail in the wall. Seven years back luck. He hesitated, then lifted it down and stowed it in the box. It might be a couple of days before he'd find the time to buy a new one.

Isaac put the sack and box by the door. There wasn't a lot to show for the five months or so he'd lived in this mean little room above the butcher's shop.

Vowing to make his next accommodation more homely, he went to the window and hooked back the curtain. At first, all he could see was the glow from the gas lamp in the middle of the square, then details emerged from the surrounding dark: a faint wash of light in an upstairs window, a shadow flicking over gleaming cobbles, a sliver of a cloud-wreathed moon. The spire of St Peter's loomed a deeper black on the dark sky, rising behind the rooftops of the houses at the top of the square. Isaac thought fleetingly of Dolly and whether she had been saved by the House of Help. The idea of asking Alice what had happened to her brought a sardonic smile to his face.

Finally, chilled by the cold air that penetrated the glass, he turned away and went to bed.

—

Isaac jerked awake, certain his mother had been repeatedly calling his name. Breakfast would be on the table. He was late for work again, and Silas would be on the warpath. Flinging the blanket aside – it was scratchy, where was the sheet, the counterpane? – he put his feet onto bare boards where a rug usually lay. Rubbing his hand over his face, Isaac sighed as realisation sank in. A pale light infiltrated the room – he'd left the curtain hooked up – along with the peal of church bells calling parishioners to the Sunday services at St Peter's and St Paul's, St George's and St Mary's, a competing clamour for the attention of their individual flocks.

Shivering in his nightshirt, Isaac went to the window to look down on the people traversing the square. At the top, a woman emerged from the House of Help and his heart quickened, but it wasn't Alice. The woman hurried out of the square, no doubt off to church. Above the rooftops and chimney stacks, the sky was a cold, washed-out blue. Unable to bear the chill any longer, Isaac pulled on a pair of trousers and a shirt and found his cigarettes. He was content to remain for a few moments at the window watching the comings and goings, reflecting on his conversation with Silas. He was undecided over whether to go home for his dinner or eat at the Q in the Corner. A meal at the Q would be less complicated. None of the patrons cared a fig about where Isaac worked or who he was pining for, and the landlord wanted only his coin. Home was a different kettle of fish entirely.

His father probably knew about the rumour that was circulating regarding Tasker's business. A takeover of the telephony side by the National Telephone Company, that was mopping up services throughout the provinces, was on the cards. Already, several firms had been brought under this company's umbrella. Isaac could go there, provided he could secure a job, or stay with Tasker in the electrical works division. He wanted to discuss it with somebody. Not his father, though. Silas would use it as an excuse to nag him to return to Hinchcliffe & Son. No, the person he wanted to talk to was Alice, and that was impossible.

He made up his mind. He'd eat at the Q and then walk to his new lodgings.

Isaac drew on his cigarette and exhaled slowly. The air was still, coalsmoke from every chimney in the square rising implacably towards the sky. A single coil of smoke rose lazily from behind the roof of the House of Help, darker than coalsmoke, darker by several degrees. His eyes followed it into the blue, then he returned his gaze to the roof to see a second languid coil mingle with the first. Now it was a black serpent, thickening and growing.

'Somebody's burnin' summat rotten,' Isaac muttered to himself.

But where had the fire been set? There was no land behind the square with space to burn rubbish. It could only be a house fire. Isaac gasped, the cigarette falling from his fingers. He hastily stamped it out, cursing. No one in the square seemed aware, yet, of the danger. Nobody was looking up. Isaac began to push up the sash so that he could shout a warning into the square, then changed his mind, grabbed his greatcoat, and ran.

Chapter 21

Alice strode purposefully towards Paradise Square, hugging to her chest a folder containing the petition she intended to ask Hope to examine before it was committed to the printing press. A spelling mistake or grammatical error would destroy any credibility that she had. It was difficult enough that she was labouring under the condition of being a mere woman. Although Alice had checked and double-checked the text, it would do no harm to have it scrutinised by a fresh pair of eyes, and Hope was the most well-educated person she knew. She had considered showing the petition to Barnaby who, now he no longer had her mother's beady eye on him, had become a good friend, but was worried he might scoff, as Isaac had scoffed, and tell her to train her focus on womanly things, like baking or sewing or practising her piano, or securing a husband.

As Alice reached the foot of the square she slowed her pace, wrinkling her nose. A pungency hung in the air, sharper than coalsmoke. A woman dressed in her Sunday best was hurrying three children along, all bundled up in coats and scarves, late for the morning service, and seemed oblivious to the stench. An elderly man hunched over a walking stick passed by at a snail's pace, a little dog at his heel, and smiled at her. A dewdrop hung precariously from the end of his nose. 'Jack Frost's got us in his grip, Miss.'

'Can you smell that?' said Alice, but the man shuffled on serenely without responding.

It wasn't her imagination. The air was acrid, as if she was standing in the deep bowl of the town where the steel factories belched out the residue of their industry. Alice looked around the square. She could detect nothing peculiar. Her gaze roved to the top of the square.

Alice inhaled sharply. She could barely comprehend what she saw. Isaac Hinchcliffe was running breakneck down the pavement, directly at her, his head bare despite the chill, his dark hair flopping. She laughed uncertainly. What on earth was he up to? Then he stumbled, and almost fell, his arms pinwheeling. It was then she truly saw, and her blood ran cold.

The man she had mistaken for Isaac was Polly Bramall's husband. Alfie Bramall was running towards her with a wildness on his face that froze Alice to the spot.

She was helpless, unable even to draw a breath. An older couple who had been strolling ahead of her – Alice had almost caught them up as she reached the square – flattened themselves against the barred door of the chinaware shop to avoid a collision, the man gesticulating but only half-heartedly as Alfie Bramall was already past him. He was almost upon Alice.

A shout went up, one unmistakable word bellowed in a man's deep voice from across the square.

'*FIRE!*'

At the same time, Alice realised that Alfie Bramall was not running at *her*. There was no recognition in his eyes, which were fixed on the middle distance. He was hell bent on escaping, but from what? Now, shouts of alarm rang across the square, figures moving hastily in her peripheral vision. But Alice kept her eyes locked on the running man. Any moment now, she would be knocked flying. It was the idea that he must not escape that finally galvanised her to action.

Alice cried out, dropping her folder, and flung herself at Alfie Bramall, all the pent-up rage in her body giving her a strength she hadn't known she possessed. Caught off guard, he fell backwards and they crashed down together onto the pavement, his body under hers, cushioning her fall, his face a mask of shock and confusion.

He recovered quickly, digging his fingers into her upper arms and flinging her away from him as if she weighed nothing. She landed on her back, sprawled across the edge of a stone doorstep, the shock taking her breath away. Adrenaline gave her the strength to scramble onto her hands and knees before the pain of impact lanced through her body. An iron boot scraper was inches from her face. Alice stared, sickened, at the dried dirt on the blade of it. Her skull might have been smashed open like a grapefruit. Whipping her head around, she saw he was rising to his feet, blocking out the sky.

His feet slipped on the pages from the folder she had dropped and she thought he would go down again. While Alice was still forming the thought that she should attempt to crawl out of the way or be squashed like a bug, he steadied himself against the wall, leaned down and closed his fist on her woollen bonnet. The lace fastening jerked and tightened against her throat, choking her, before, mercifully, coming apart.

Alfie Bramall dropped the bonnet to the ground and pulled Alice to her feet by her hair. His eyes widened with the shock of recognition, then his lips spread in a wide grin and he barked out a harsh laugh. Alice moaned in pain and revulsion as he brought his face close to hers, twisting her neck. She flattened her hands against his chest and pushed. He was immovable, a wall. Struggling against him only emphasised the horror of her helplessness.

He panted in her ear, his breath damp and rank, his grip on her scalp agonising.

'That place full o' women? I've burned it up, love.'

When he moved back and his hold loosened, she closed her eyes, anticipating the strike of his fist, the bones of his knuckles connecting with the bones of her face. He might kill her and there was nothing she could do.

The strike never came.

Alice opened her eyes. He was gone.

Only a few moments had passed since she had first seen him running from the top of the square and mistaken him for Isaac. A tiny part of her triumphed. Alfie Bramall had set a fire and admitted to it. This would be his downfall. Then her knees weakened and she sank to the ground, falling forward, her hands hitting the pavement, instinct saving her from headbutting the ground. The pain in her back and scalp and neck threatened to spin her out of consciousness. *The house. He'd set fire to the house.*

She had to get up. Alice focused her eyes on a crack in the pavement, which was then obscured by the polished black toe of a man's boot; a fragment of a children's nursery rhyme came into her mind: 'step on a line, marry a swine'. She breathed in shakily and accepted the hand offered to her and was pulled to her feet. Alice assured her rescuer, a gentleman who was looking over her head towards the top of the square, that she was all right and he patted her shoulder and trotted away.

Retrieving her bonnet, Alice saw that a crowd now filled the square. Black smoke was erasing the blue sky behind the House of Help and the discordant clang of a fire cart's bell filled her ears.

–

Isaac ran to the top of the square, the acrid stench of an open-hearth furnace filling his nostrils. Before he reached the door of the House of Help it was flung open and women poured out. People were also emerging from the adjacent houses and gathering on the cobbles, joining a growing crowd of onlookers. He approached a young woman who appeared to be trying to shepherd the residents of the house into one place so that she could carry out a head count.

Isaac took her arm. 'Where's the fire?'

'Kitchen!' She turned away, casting about her. 'I can't see Annie... there you are! Has anybody seen Maggie Price? Maggie?'

'She went out, Miss Barlow,' someone called. 'A bit since, to church.'

'That leaves us with eleven, then.' She went around, counting. 'Will you all stand still or do I have to fetch a sheepdog?' She waved to a woman wearing a maid's uniform. 'Clara! Had we any visitors?'

'Miss Hope an' Alice Leigh were supposed to come round this mornin',' said the maid. 'But I don't think they'd got 'ere before we all came out.'

'What?' said Isaac. 'Do you know if they were in that bleedin' house or don't you?'

The woman named Clara put her hands on her hips and opened her mouth to retort, then gasped and stumbled backwards, away from him. 'It were thee!'

She shook the sleeve of the woman still attempting a headcount and pointed at Isaac. 'He were hangin' about when I pegged out the washin' earlier, pushin' a barrow full o' pitch. I saw him peerin' in the yard after I'd gone back in.'

'What's tha on about?' Isaac spread his hands as if to demonstrate the absence of a wheelbarrow. 'Is Alice in there or not?'

'Amelia, I'm tellin' thee it's him. That Bramall fella.'

Both women were now staring at him.

Isaac turned and ran towards the house.

He'd reached the threshold when he glimpsed her standing on the edge of the square, scanning the crowd, her hat dangling at her side, her hair dishevelled, the most beautiful sight he had ever seen. Their eyes met and she ran towards him. He crushed her into a tight embrace, then held her away from him and laughed to see the expression of astonishment on her face.

'I thought tha were in there,' Isaac said, touching her face with his fingertips.

Alice clutched his arms. 'We have to tell the police.' She looked past him, wildly, around the square. 'Alfie Bramall set the fire.'

'Who?'

From the depths of the house, a child wailed. Isaac's blood ran cold.

'Go an' get someone,' he said.

He waited for Alice, whose eyes had widened in shock, to nod, then turned and ran into the house, following the sound of a child's cries down a hallway filling with acrid black smoke.

The crowd was being herded towards the foot of the square. Alice spotted Constable Goodlad in animated conversation with Clara and Amelia.

'I'm tellin' thee, he just ran in the house,' said Clara. 'He's set fire to the back an' now he's settin' fire to the front!'

'I've two girls missin',' said Amelia. 'Eliza an' Mary. What if they're still in there? Alice!' She gulped. 'Alice, I can't find the little girls.'

'There is somebody in there. We heard them. Isaac went in,' said Alice. 'We have to help him.'

Constable Goodlad gestured to another officer. 'The fire crews are round the back. Go and tell them we need a couple of men.'

'Hurry!' cried Alice.

'It were that fella,' shouted Clara. 'I hope he burns up.'

Alice rounded on her. 'It was *Isaac* ran in.' She turned to the constable. 'But Alfie Bramall did start the fire. He's the one you should be chasing after.'

'I'm tellin' thee,' said Clara, but now she looked uncertain.

'They resemble each other,' said Alice. 'Even I... never mind. But for goodness' sake, Alfie Bramall ran straight into me. Constable, that man told me he'd set light to the house. He *told* me. What more evidence do you need?' Tears began to fall and she swiped at her cheeks, cross with herself for appearing weak when the only emotion she felt was anger. 'Find *him* and arrest him! Isaac's just trying to help.'

She whirled around and ran back to the house, ignoring the constable's calls for her to stop. Tendrils of smoke curled around the doorframe. Alice stepped over the threshold into the haze of smoke that pervaded the ground floor of the house. She reached the foot of the staircase and stopped, gripping the banister. Might the children be hiding upstairs, too terrified to come down? Had Isaac gone up? She shouted his name.

There was no reply. Alice glanced towards the back of the house, where the hallway ended in a wall of dense smoke. Beyond it, the clatter of metal and men's voices filtered through as well as a sound that could be rain, or flames.

The stench was a suffocating blanket. Alice shouted Isaac's name again and again and backed away, towards the door, burying her mouth and nose in the sleeve of her dress, her eyes stinging. She cried out when Isaac emerged through the smoke at the back of the house, staggering under the weight of the unconscious girl in his arms. He lay the child at her feet, a girl of ten or eleven wearing a pinafore and wrinkled stockings, and remained bent over, his hands on his knees, his breath coming in ragged gasps. 'She were on the floor in the water closet,' he finally managed. 'We need to get out o' here.'

Alice risked a breath of the smoke-saturated air. 'Was there another one?' she said, clutching his arm. 'Another girl?'

Isaac shook off her hand. She wanted to tell him to wait, that help was coming, but she couldn't stop coughing. She could only watch in horror as he disappeared back into the shrouding smoke.

Alice dropped to her knees and put her face close to the girl's. She couldn't tell whether she was breathing but the air, mercifully, seemed clearer close to the ground. Alice risked a deeper breath but began to cough again, gulping on the foul air. The choking fit passed and, dizzied by it, she decided she would rest her head on the girl's chest, for just a moment, before she attempted to pull her outside. How wonderful it would be to stand in Paradise Square and fill her lungs with fresh air. First, she would rest. Her eyelids were unaccountably heavy. Would it hurt to close them?

She felt the slap sting her cheek. Alfie Bramall was back, come to finish her off. Let him. Alice had no fight left in her. But it was the rugged face of an older man, sporting the bushiest moustache and beard she had ever seen, that swam before her blurry eyes. Then she was being lifted.

'Let's get thee out, then. Tommy, you've got the little lass?'

Somehow, she found the strength to put her arms around the man's neck and press her face against his woollen tunic. She opened her mouth but there was no air to breathe.

'Isaac,' she croaked.

—

Arms outstretched, he felt blindly around the room he'd found the first girl in, a deafening pounding sound – his own heart? – filling his ears and pulsing behind his streaming eyes. Where was she? His head was buzzing with the effort of taking only the shallowest of breaths, his ears whining a monotone that threatened to drown out his reason. Isaac knew he was moments from collapse.

He stumbled back into the hall and had taken a handful of steps – laboriously slow, heavy steps that sapped him of his remaining strength – before, terrifyingly, the ground disappeared from beneath his feet. Isaac pitched forward into a torrent of water and utter darkness. Or were his eyes closed? He couldn't tell the difference. Struggling to his hands and knees, he realised he was, impossibly, in a pool of water, the knees of his trousers and cuffs of his coat sodden. Spray was hitting his face.

It must be a waterfall. He was in a pool behind the curtain of a waterfall. How could that be? Somebody was shouting, more than one person. People were searching for him, roaming the craggy hills. They would never find him because he was hidden in the rocky chamber behind the waterfall and hadn't the energy to burst through it. Isaac's shoulders buckled, and a hard surface came up to meet his head. Now he was submerged, water in his nose, in his mouth, and no strength left.

His final thought, a dazzling moment of clarity before the darkness took him, was that he had never told Alice he loved her.

Chapter 22

The child, Eliza, sat cross-legged on the cobbles, playing with the ringed chin strap of the fireman's helmet she held in her lap. Alice was on a bench nearby, beside Hope, huddled in a shawl some unknown person had placed around her shoulders.

Eliza seemed none the worse for wear. She had awoken a few moments after being carried from the house, clutching at her throat as she huddled against Alice and finally fetching up a sticky, black mucus onto the pavement. The other girl, Mary, never had been in the water closet. During the evacuation of the house, she had run out of the square, terrified, and been found in the next street and returned to Amelia, who had hugged her tightly, too relieved to be angry. Mary now crouched on her haunches beside Eliza, inching ever closer, trying to persuade her to let her try on the brass helmet.

'He gave it me,' said Eliza, tangling her fingers more tightly in the strap.

The man who had carried Alice out of the house, who had seemed to her to be a giant at the time, taking seven-league strides in his leather boots, laughed. 'I'll be needin' it back,' he said. He offered Alice a cigarette. 'I allus think this helps, after, Miss, even if tha wouldn't normally partake.'

Alice shook her head. Her limbs were gradually turning to stone in the cold air. The numbness was welcome. If her mind would grey over, become fossilised, she might forget the sight of Isaac being brought out of the house, his limp form suspended between two firemen who had him by the ankles and shoulders. They had dropped him onto a stretcher laid on the pavement, none too gently, picked it up and carried him away.

He had saved a little girl's life. Was he still under suspicion?

'Where's Alfie Bramall?' Alice had whispered when Isaac was brought out, dredging the name from her raw throat. Nobody was listening.

The burly fireman who had given his helmet to Eliza to play with had started a conversation with Hope, a lit cigarette cupped in his hand.

'He come out an' must've gone the wrong way,' the man said. 'Fell down the steps into the kitchen, an' one o' the men who were dousing the room saw him, lying there, but nobody could get in the back, not safe enough.' He took a deep drag of his cigarette and blew a plume of smoke into the air. 'They just had to keep waterin' him 'til a couple o' men could run round the front o' the house an' fetch him out.'

'Goodness me,' said Hope, faintly. 'How did it start?'

'I shouldn't really tell thee wi'out the chief's say-so, but looks to me like some daft bugger dumped a wheelbarrow load o' pitch on the back door step an' set it alight. It's arson, no doubt about it.'

Alice coughed. 'Alfie Bramall,' she repeated. 'And not daft. Evil.'

The man gave her a look. 'Well, that's for the bobbies to sort out.'

'Amelia has gone to fetch the warden and then we must find accommodations for the residents,' said Hope. 'What do you think, Alice? Amelia can stay with the Wallaces. They might have space for a couple of the women, too. I'm taking Eliza and Mary back to Tylecote for now.' She sighed. 'What a terrible thing, to have to say our door is closed. I wonder if this is the end for the house.'

When Alice didn't respond, Hope turned back to the fireman.

'What's the extent of the damage?' she said. 'Are you able to say?'

'We kept it to the kitchen, else the whole place would've gone up. But there's smoke damage, a lot o' that right up to the rafters.'

'When might we be up and running again?' said Hope.

'Weeks, or months. Can't say, love.'

Alice stared wearily at the house, which looked, from the outside at least, untouched, as if the events of that morning had never happened. Had she really tussled with Alfie Bramall? It seemed an age ago. Had that really been Isaac slung between two firemen like a sack of flour? She could not believe it was so.

Hope leaned forward to look at her, gently pulling Alice's hair away from her face. 'Shall we go inside the Q and I'll braid your hair?' she said. 'He's opened up his premises for a shelter. Look, there's hot tea and whisky doing the rounds. Shall I get you some and we'll go inside?'

Alice shook her head.

The fireman rubbed his hands together. 'They're goin' to start doling out the puddin's and potatoes meant for today's payin' customers.'

'That's kind,' said Hope. 'What the landlord loses in revenue he'll make up in goodwill.'

Alice looked away. None of that mattered if Isaac was dead.

Hope put her arm around Alice's shoulders. Her voice was artificially bright. 'You must be chilled to the bone. Please come inside and let me fix your hair. I'm sure we can borrow a brush from the landlady.'

The black smoke was dispersing now, trailing off into the washed-out blue of the sky. She wondered would she ever get the terrible stink out of her nostrils. 'Isaac,' she whispered.

Hope bit her lip. 'He's been taken to the infirmary. All we can do is wait for news.'

'I know,' said Alice. She tried to take a deep breath and coughed and coughed but could not clear her chest. 'I know what you're thinking.' She gulped cold air past the knives in her throat. 'By the time I get there he'll be in the morgue.'

Hope didn't reply, which was answer enough.

In front of the house, Mrs Wallace and her husband were deep in conversation with several uniformed men. A child, a young boy, was playing in the water that gushed down the pavement from the gennel, hopping backwards and forwards over the stream, thoroughly absorbed in his game. The square had begun to empty of people. Alice supposed this was because it was too cold to stand about. After a time, a gig rattled onto the cobbles and Hope got to her feet. 'That's my driver,' she said, and raised her voice to call to the two young girls. 'Eliza. Mary. Come with me.'

She reached down to take Alice's hand. 'Will you come, too? I can draw you a bath. You can borrow fresh clothes.' Her grip was tight. 'Please, Alice. Please come with me.'

She might as well. Alice got to her feet and swayed and would have fallen if Hope hadn't snaked an arm around her waist. Perhaps she was not made of stone, after all.

—

Alice sank lower in the warm water until it reached her chin and trailed her fingers over the curved porcelain rim of the bathtub. She lifted back into place the lace strap of the thin white chemise Hope had given her, inhaling the scent of rose oil. The maid who had carried up pans of hot water to fill the bath returned to lay a fresh set of clothes on a chair. Hope had told her the bath would be a tonic and Alice had agreed, for politeness' sake, that the water would soothe her back and neck that were already stiffening where Alfie Bramall had thrown her onto the steps. During the scuffle, and unnoticed until now, two of her fingernails had been ripped and were throbbing painfully. The pain was welcome. She would rip out all ten nails, if Isaac lived.

'How is that?' said Hope. She was sitting in a chair behind the bath, washing the stench of smoke out of Alice's hair.

'Much better,' said Alice. 'Thank you.'

She twisted her neck to one side, then the other, and stared at the porcelain until it swam out of focus. Where was Alfie Bramall? He must know the authorities would be looking for him. Alice closed her eyes so that Hope wouldn't see the tears in them. She would have him escape justice, run away and never come back, never be answerable for any of his crimes, if Isaac lived.

She pushed herself up, unable to pretend any longer. 'I'm better now, thank you. I should go home.'

There, she would escape to her room and sob silently into her pillow. Then she would forsake her campaigning and be the daughter her mother wanted her to be, if Isaac lived.

—

Alfie Bramall was apprehended after two days on the run. Acting on information received, the police had broken down the door of an upstairs room in the Orange Branch and dragged him out of his hidey-hole. He had freely admitted the crime. Mrs Wallace didn't tell Alice that he bragged about what he'd done as the cuffs were fastened on his wrists.

'He'll live out the rest o' his days staring at the four walls of a prison cell,' Mrs Wallace said. 'We shan't see him again.'

Three days after that, and accompanied by her mother, Alice knocked on the door of the Hinchcliffe residence. Sarah Hodgetts, their cook, answered, her face drawn. 'Come in, love,' she said. 'How do, Miss Leigh?'

Louisa smiled and rubbed Sarah's arm. 'Fair to middlin'. How's thee?'

'Mustn't grumble.'

They followed her into the kitchen. 'I'll put the kettle on,' Sarah said.

Alice sat and took off her gloves and hat, placing them carefully on the table where she had eaten count-less Sunday dinners. Today, she felt like a stranger in this house, an interloper in someone else's pain. 'It's lovely and warm in here,' she said, with barely a hint of a quaver in her voice, 'and what's that delicious smell?'

'I'm baking cheese scones,' said Sarah. 'Lord knows Mrs Hinchcliffe needs summat inside her. She'll waste away.'

'Where are they?' said Louisa.

Sarah pointed at the ceiling.

Alice made a conscious effort to calm her breathing. 'And Teddy?' she said. 'Where's Teddy?'

'He's all reight,' said Sarah. 'Knows summat's up, so we've had a few tears an' tantrums. He's wi' his Aunt Hope. She took him for the night.' She paused. 'To be honest wi' thee, I prefer havin' him about, for a bit o' noise, a bit o' normality. Quiet as the— I mean, too quiet here, wi'out him.'

She turned her back on the women to reach for the teapot. 'It feels like two minutes since Isaac were runnin' about in this kitchen, gettin' under me feet. No sooner had he had his tea, than he were beggin' for summat else to eat. Had me wrapped round his little finger, I don't mind admittin'.'

Alice's hands squirmed in her lap.

'Can she go up?' said her mother.

Sarah put the teapot on the trivet and folded her lips together. 'Let me go an' check.'

Alice stood up as soon as Sarah left the room. Her mother put out a warning hand. 'She'll be back in two shakes, love,' said Louisa. 'Let's see what Harriet says, all reight?'

'Yes, but I have to move. I can't bear it.'

She went into the front room and paced about, stopping to peer at the framed family portrait on Aunt Harriet's piano. Ginny had admired this photograph, taken to celebrate Isaac's tenth birthday, although her twisted mouth told a different story. Aunt Harriet sat on a chair, Uncle Silas standing beside her, his body tilted towards her. It was as if he had been attempting to stand up straight but was drawn like a magnet to his wife. Isaac was posed stiffly in front of his father, the top of his head level with his father's pocket watch. They all wore serious expressions and looked unlike themselves, the faintly blurry black and grey tones failing to capture the vibrant red of Harriet's hair, or Silas's keen green eyes or the warm olive tones of Isaac's skin. The more Alice stared, the more they resembled colourless mannequins, got up to look like real people, or, worse, like the pictures of the dead commissioned by grieving relatives.

'Alice.'

It was Isaac's voice. She whipped around, her hand at her throat.

Silas leaned on the doorframe, the expression of utter weariness on his face bringing tears to her eyes. He held out his hands and Alice rushed over and took them.

'You can see him now, love. Come wi' me.'

The curtains in Isaac's bedroom were drawn, the air warm and stuffy. His mother got up from the armchair by the crackling fire in the little hearth and embraced Alice, murmuring a greeting, then returned to her chair and sat with her hand over her mouth. Alice perched gingerly on the edge of the bed that as a child she had bounced up and down on to aggravate Isaac, always with the aim of landing on his stomach or head. Now, she dared not reach out to touch any part of him. He lay under a blanket, his head exposed in profile. Alice was glad for the dimness of the room, which was filled with the sound of his harsh, ragged breathing.

'He asked for thee,' Silas whispered, 'more than once, but he's gettin' his rest now.'

Alice reached with trembling fingers to caress Isaac's face. His skin was warm under the rough stubble on his jaw. Leaning closer, she lay her hand lightly on his chest.

'Can I stay?' she asked, searching for Harriet's eyes in the gloom. 'I mean, will you allow me to stay here with him until he wakes?'

'Aye,' said Silas. He turned to Harriet. 'Come on, love. You could use the rest. Alice is here now. Let her look after him.'

Chapter 23

Hope returned early the next morning, knowing Teddy was needed however reluctant she might be to give him up. The little girls had, the night before, been enchanted by the infant, insisting on helping get him ready for bed and almost drowning him with his cup of milk. As dawn broke, Hope had taken him in to see them in their shared bed, her heart brimming to see their innocent joy. She helped Mary dress in a plain woollen smock and clogs that were too big for her narrow feet. Later that day, the girl was due to be collected by a nurse from the orphanage. A pinafore and stockings had been conjured from somewhere for Eliza, who was a little older than Mary and would remain at Tylecote, an apprenticed servant. Eliza was already at work when Hope left the house, tasked with cleaning the chamber pots the maid had emptied and shoving them back under the beds, so only Mary waved Hope off.

'Be a good girl,' she said, choking on the words.

On the doorstep of the Hinchcliffe residence, Harriet wordlessly took Teddy from her arms and buried her face in his neck. When she looked up at Hope her eyes were raw from lack of sleep. 'Will you come in?'

Hope didn't know this woman well enough to be able to tell whether she was wanted or not. 'Only if I'm not disturbing you,' she said.

In reply, Harriet turned and walked away and, after a second's hesitation, Hope followed her down the hall, Teddy gazing at her sleepily over Harriet's shoulder.

'I'm sorry about the house,' said Harriet in a toneless voice.

Hope shook her head. 'It's only bricks and mortar. We'll get back on our feet soon enough.'

In the kitchen, Sarah Hodgetts was toasting and buttering pikelets for breakfast. Silas Hinchcliffe stood at the range, stirring broth in a pot. Sarah gave Hope a wan smile.

' 'Ey up,' Silas said. It seemed to Hope he had aged ten years overnight. 'Take a pew, love.'

She sat down at the kitchen table.

'I was just sayin' that today is Saint Lucy's Day,' said Sarah. 'A day of light.'

Silas grunted. 'It's also Friday the thirteenth.'

'I prefer Sarah's interpretation of the day,' Harriet said, settling into the armchair by the range, Teddy content to remain on her lap. Hope realised with a pang that he must have missed her terribly. Harriet patted his back. 'Tell us about Saint Lucy.'

Sarah gave Hope a buttered pikelet. 'We're waitin' on the doctor,' she said quietly. 'I took a cup o' tea to Alice. She's been sittin' up wi' him all night.'

Hope nodded. 'You know your saints days?'

'I'm Catholic.' Sarah laughed and pointed the butter knife at Silas. 'Mr Hinchcliffe, if the wind changes, your face will stay like that. Saint Lucy is the patron saint of the blind.'

'Blind leadin' the blind, eh?' said Silas.

He looked to Harriet, clearly expecting to receive a telling off, but she was feeding porridge to Teddy, and seemed completely absorbed in the task. Silas sighed and continued stirring the broth.

'Go on, then,' he said. 'Let's have it.'

'Saint Lucy was killed by the Romans for her Christian beliefs,' said Sarah. 'She'd deliver bread to the poor hiding in the catacombs at nighttime, and would wear a crown o' candles to light her way.'

'What's wrong wi' an ordinary torch?' said Silas.

'She could carry more food if she had both hands free.'

Silas snorted. 'It's a wonder she didn't catch hersen on—'

He stopped himself and grimaced at Hope, who gave him a sympathetic smile.

'Well,' said Sarah, 'all's I say is she brings the light. Hope and light durin' the darkest time of the year. It's traditional to put up the Christmas decorations on Saint Lucy's day.'

'Then that's what we'll do today,' said Harriet. 'Bring a little cheer into the house.'

The doorbell's jangle was a jarring sound in the silence that followed. Silas dropped the wooden spoon he was using to stir the broth into the pan and cursed.

'That'll be the doctor,' said Sarah, wiping her hands on a cloth. 'I'll go.'

'Nowt much he can do,' said Silas. 'He can take the broth up, if he likes.'

'How is Isaac?' Hope finally dared to ask.

Silas ladled soup into a bowl. 'He got over the knock to the head quick-sharp but they can't say how much damage has been done to his lungs, and there's nowt they can do about that, so he were discharged swift an' all.'

'His own bed is the best place for him,' said Harriet.

Silas clamped his lips together. The tacit implication was that Isaac had been brought home to die.

Isaac tapped his football into the front room and upset the tin soldiers Alice was patiently lining up on the rug in preparation for a bloody battle. Glancing at the grown-ups sitting around the card table, she threw one of the figures at his head. Isaac caught it deftly and pocketed it.

'Can I go down Port Mahon?' he said, retrieving the ball.

Alice scrambled to her feet, her heart knocking in anticipation. She knew what the answer would be. The same as always.

'If you take your cousin, then yes,' said Aunt Harriet.

Isaac scowled. Luckily for Alice, his mother's word was final. It all depended on how desperate he was to go to the common. Alice had tagged along before on similarly warm Sunday afternoons when the walls of the house couldn't contain Isaac. He was popular with the other boys – he owned a leather football – so they tolerated Alice's presence and sometimes even let her stand in goal, although the ball was hardly ever allowed to come near her. Instructed to watch her by his parents and her mother, Isaac never actually paid her any attention, unless it was to tease her. But Alice watched him. She watched him carefully place balled up shirts for goalposts, and kick the ball around in a game she couldn't follow, although when Isaac celebrated so did she, and she chased after him in tag even when she wasn't it. She wanted to be like him, strong and unafraid, and allowed to get mucky. The last time they'd come down, he'd refused to give her a drag on a filched cigarette when it was passed around. 'Eight is too young. Also, you're a girl,' Isaac explained. Alice had begged and begged and promised not to tell, and finally accused him of being afraid of getting a battering from his father. Isaac had made her sit on a rock until it was time to go home.

She wouldn't make that mistake again.

There was a dog running loose on the flat part of the common. The boys chased it off and set about picking sides for their game *of football. Alice sat on the grass a short distance away, making daisy chains with a couple of older girls she knew from Sunday School. Now the same dog that had pestered the boys stood at the base of one of the perimeter trees, barking at the canopy above. Alice got up to investigate. She knew this tree. She'd watched Isaac climb it, hand over hand, when the ball got stuck in its boughs. It was an easy climber. Even Alice could probably swing herself onto the lowest branch. She tried it out, and succeeded. Near the top of the tree, the object of the dog's excitement hissed at her.*

'Here, pussy,' Alice sang. She was already imagining Isaac telling her mother how brave she had been in rescuing the cat.

She climbed higher. It was easy to find handholds and footholds in the crevices between the thick branches and sturdy trunk. Just above was a messy ball of twigs and fluff – a bird's nest! Imagine if she fetched eggs to Isaac, or a tiny chick? She had only ever seen them dead on the pavement. But the nest was empty. Alice climbed on. She was at eye level with the cat now, but the animal was still out of her reach. A prickle of fear tickled the back of her neck. She wasn't sure she wanted to rescue it after all. It was a witch's cat with an arched back and sharp claws. The dog continued to bark incessantly. A squirrel ran along the bough beneath her feet, making Alice gasp in delight. Then she saw how far away the ground was and froze. The branches she had used for ladder rungs now seemed out of reach. She became aware a few kids had come to watch, their faces turned moonlike towards her. She would just have to brazen it out.

'What're you doin'?' This was from one of the girls she had been playing with.

Alice forced a laugh. 'Just havin' a rest in this tree. I'll get down in a bit.'

Far below, Isaac had the ball at his feet, running towards the goal, a small figure from Alice's vantage point. He scored and ran up and down, pumping his fists in the air. The shouts of the players scattered in the wind that rustled the treetop. This was all his fault, for not watching her.

She still had an audience.

'Tha'd best come down!'

'Are tha stuck?'

Close to tears, Alice shook her head. She pretended to examine the bark on the trunk.

'Come down then!'

'She can't! She's too scared!'

'I can see up yer skirt!'

'She'll fall an' kill hersen. Then she'll be in trouble!'

The dog barked and barked and barked.

Awakening with the sickening sensation of falling, Alice propelled herself out of the armchair and looked around, her heart thudding. Where was she? In Isaac's bedroom, where he lay supine, facing the ceiling, the faint light behind the curtains defining the shadowed angles of his face. A small groan escaped her. Massaging the small of her back, Alice went over to the bed, hardly daring to breathe. Isaac was snoring, his eyelids fluttering. Was he dreaming, too, of those carefree summer days? Sinking to her knees, Alice found a position in which she could sit relatively comfortably. She rested her head near the slight rise in the blanket that was Isaac's concealed hand.

He had saved her from the tree that day, climbing up easily and carrying her down on his back. She hadn't realised it then, of course, but this was to be one of their last adventures together. Soon after, Isaac turned fourteen and was kept busy with schoolwork and learning the ropes at his father's factory. Alice began to take piano lessons and attend a girls' school, paid for by her mother. Her tree-climbing days were over.

She recalled the relief that had swept through her when she relinquished her hold on the rough bark of the trunk and locked her arms around his neck, and how furious she had been the last time Isaac picked her up from the pavement outside the town hall and carried her away.

The bedroom door was ajar by a few inches. Someone had entered while she slept. She could hear voices from the kitchen and the clatter of cups and plates. Closing her eyes again, she let her mind wander. It had been wrong to try to force Isaac to accept Ginny. But then, he ought never to have decided he knew what was best for Alice. It had taken an act of arson to bring them back together. But they might never be reconciled.

Sometime later, a tinkling sound, like breaking glass, roused her from sleep. Alice lifted her head from the blanket and licked dry lips. Embers glowed feebly in the fireplace, no match for the bright shard of light that speared the gap in the curtains. The sound had been the doorbell. Alice pushed herself to her feet and walked unsteadily across the room. She picked up the mirror from beside the wash basin. Her image was distorted by the crack across the glass, the side of her face creased where her cheek had been pressed against the covers, her eyes bloodshot and tendrils of hair falling messily about her face. She looked like a madwoman.

Replacing the mirror on its stand, she went to the curtains and pulled them apart. Light flooded the room. Outside, perplexingly, the world went about its business.

Alice rolled her shoulders and flexed her neck tentatively. She hurt all over, particularly on her scalp where Alfie Bramall had pulled out a handful of hair. He had been apprehended. There was comfort to be had in that. She turned towards the bed. Her breath caught in her throat. Isaac was propped on his elbows, his eyes on her, the corners of his mouth turned up in a gentle smile. She rushed to him, bending to hold his face in her hands, her mouth working. There was so much to say that words deserted her. This must be another dream. She stroked the stubble on his cheeks with her fingertips. Isaac's smile widened. It was he who spoke first, haltingly, his voice croaky as a frog's.

'Alice, love, tha should see the look on tha face.'

Chapter 24

Spring, 1890

Preceding her down the aisle, the bridesmaids wore cream collars over Empire line dresses in a rich burgundy that matched the bouquet of peonies she was carrying. Through the tulle of a long silk-hemmed veil, fastened to her elaborate chignon with silver pins, her eyes darted to the altar. The glimpse was enough to show her the groom in his morning suit and topper, the cravat at his throat the same colour as her grey silk dress, and enough for her to catch the broad grin he gave her.

Before she dropped her gaze, he waggled the fingers of a hand encased in an ivory kid glove. Her lips twitched. There could be no doubt this was the tasteful wedding that both sets of parents had demanded but if anybody could put a pin in their pretension and pop it, he could.

Walking beside her, the man who would give her away nodded imperiously to the guests standing in the pews. He was making the best of it. Most of the congregation was unknown to him and that had been her doing. It was she who had insisted on being wed in the town where she had been reborn. Her mother had agreed readily enough to her request that only her parents travel north for the ceremony, no doubt relieved that extended family members and friends would not witness any barbarism.

Her father patted her hand where it rested in the crook of his elbow. Reaching the top of the aisle, he nodded solemnly to the groom and stepped back to take a seat beside his wife, who was perched in the front pew like a crow in her black dress and bonnet. Hope supposed she ought to count herself lucky her mother wasn't wearing crepe.

A small, warm hand stole into hers as she turned to face Angus. She looked down at her velvet-clad page boy and smiled. Teddy's touch gave her courage. She wanted to kiss the dimples in his cheeks but her father cleared his throat. It was time for the ceremony to begin.

The vicar opened his bible and beamed at her. 'Are you ready?' he said, kindly.

She nodded and took a ragged breath.

This was to be, she prayed, her final act as Emma Hyde.

—

The newlyweds and their guests milled around outside the church, some shading their eyes against the dazzling light reflecting from the stained glass, others turning their faces towards the warmth of the sun. Glasses of champagne were handed out, another expense her father had insisted on meeting. Robin Hyde had paid for everything and would brook no argument, the implication being he could at least salvage this tradition from the wreckage of his daughter's wilful unconventionality. Birdsong filled the air as the church bells finished pealing out the happy news. An air of satisfaction radiated from her mother. Respectability had been finally achieved and the whole thing gone off in a civilised way.

Hope was glad to have the warm breeze on her face, the mask of the veil lifted and her happiness obvious to all. One of Angus's groomsmen was galloping about, Teddy on his shoulders, the two-year-old screaming with laughter. On the road beyond the low stone wall, a handful of passers-by had stopped to have a gander at the wedding party. Carriages were beginning to line up to transport some of the guests – her parents, Angus's parents and his grandfather, the Master Cutler and town mayor and their wives, and of course the bride and groom – to the wedding breakfast. The rest would walk back to the House of Help, where Hope had insisted on holding the celebration.

She envied those travelling on foot. It was a beautiful day, perfect weather for a stroll, and to savour her new role as wife, before she returned to her duties as deputy warden, a further bone of contention with her parents but not, happily, with her husband. And that was all that counted now.

Amelia detached herself from the arm of Barnaby Greaves and came over. 'Are you back to bein' our Hope again?'

She laughed. 'Why, I'm Mrs Angus Deveraux!'

Amelia pouted. 'You know what I'm sayin'.'

'I do,' said Hope. She fiddled nervously with the antique emerald necklace Angus had gifted her. 'I'll be glad when my parents return home. Is that terrible of me?'

'I won't tell if you don't.'

Alice joined them, slipping her arm around Hope's waist and lifting her champagne glass in a toast. 'Congratulations, Mrs Deveraux! May the two of you enjoy happy and prosperous and above all healthy lives!'

'We'll have enough o' that back at the house,' said Amelia. 'Speeches an' whatnot.'

'I think Alice is enjoying the champagne,' said Hope. 'Please, while we have a moment, I must thank you for being my bridesmaids, and for everything that you have done. Now, which of you do I hand my bouquet over to, for luck?'

Both women coloured. They looked at each other and laughed. 'Oh!' said Hope. 'Seems like I'll have to divide it in half.' She looked over her shoulder. Angus was calling her name. 'My husband needs me.'

'Best obey him, eh?' said Amelia, nudging Alice with her elbow.

'You shan't get a rise out of me today,' said Alice. 'I'm in far too good a mood.'

Hope wound her way through the well-wishers, stopping to embrace Mrs Wallace and compliment her on her handsome blue velvet hat. She finally reached the lychgate where Angus stood waiting, his hands outstretched. She took them and went on her tiptoes to kiss him on the cheek. Silas and Harriet Hinchcliffe stood nearby, chatting with her parents. Teddy ran to Hope, clutching fists full of the pink blossom that had drifted into piles along the edge of the path.

'Look, Tope!' he shouted, flinging the petals into the air.

Her father raised an eyebrow. 'Tope? Yet another name for you, my dear?'

The smile on Hope's face faltered. She was perpetrating another deception against her parents, the truth about Teddy's identity. But hadn't they rejected their grandchild when he was first born? To them, he did not exist. Her mother, without a trace of guilt or shame, had already declared she was looking forward to becoming a grandmother. As ever, doubt whispered in Hope's ear. Was she doing the right thing? Could she ever allow herself to be truly content?

Angus squeezed her hand.

'Aunt Hope is, as yet, beyond the lad,' he said to her father. 'So, for now, Tope it is!'

Her father looked confused. 'How are you the boy's aunt?'

Angus squeezed again. 'It seems everyone is setting off for the house. Shall we go?'

Hope returned the pressure gratefully. There were no secrets between the two of them. Their marriage would be written on a clean slate.

The couple shared their carriage with Angus's grandfather, a benefactor of the House of Help who engaged Hope in conversation about its recent reopening. The house had immediately become full to capacity, she explained, with a truckle bed installed in Hope's classroom and two women sleeping head to toe in the same bed. The trustees were eyeing up a larger property in the square. Unfortunately, it was beyond their means. Mr Deveraux nodded. 'We'll have to see what we can do,' he said.

A few moments before they reached Paradise Square, the old man tapped on the roof with his cane and asked the driver to stop.

'I'll walk from here,' he said. 'Keep these old bones moving.' He waved away their protests. 'You two should have a few moments alone. You will be in demand at the wedding breakfast.'

He told the driver to remain in place until Angus gave the word, and walked away.

'He's a lovely old gentleman,' said Hope.

'He loves you,' said Angus. 'We all do.'

Through the slit that had been cut in her glove, Hope twisted the plain gold band Angus had placed on her finger and examined the tips of her white satin shoes. There would undoubtedly be challenges ahead but for now she was content to enjoy this day. She leaned into him and brushed blossom leaves from his lapel and kissed his cheek.

'Let's not keep our guests waiting, Mr Deveraux.'

'Mrs Deveraux, your wish is my command.'

Chapter 25

Isaac poked his head inside the front parlour of the House of Help, inhaling the room's citrusy scent. His sense of smell was almost fully restored. If only his lungs would repair so well.

Bowls of white primroses adorned every surface. A fiddler sat in the corner, his back to the room, tuning his instrument, while all around him wedding guests chattered and groomsmen went about dispensing wine. Cool fingers touched the back of Isaac's hand.

It was Alice, lit from behind where the sun streamed in through the open front door, her hair a blonde halo, her eyes sparkling. Would she ever stop taking his breath away?

'I'm going to help prepare the wedding breakfast,' she said. 'Do you want something to drink?'

'Aye.'

But he paused as Alice went ahead, cupping his hand on the rounded newel of the banister at the foot of the stairs, breathing in the heady scent of newly laid carpet and freshly varnished wood. It had been only a short walk from the church, but his weakened lungs were clamouring and Isaac was too proud to drop into one of the chairs ranged along the wall. An elderly gentleman sat in one of them, carefully eating what looked like rice pudding with a spoon. God forbid Isaac should join his ranks so soon.

One day soon, he would lift Alice in his arms and carry his bride over the threshold. Isaac smiled. She had only this morning scolded him for being impatient with his recovery.

He breathed in and out, in and out, his head gradually clearing, the detail on the walls of the house swimming back into focus. The hallway had been newly papered with a bright design of white daisies stencilled on a beige and pinprick background. After the fire, an appeal had gone out to the town's wealthier residents to donate a specific item, from the wallpaper and carpet to a new kitchen table and back door, and the townspeople had duly stumped up. Of course, he had never seen the original décor. The last time Isaac had been in the house its furnishings were obscured by roiling black smoke. If he closed his eyes, he could taste it still, a toxicity on the tip of his tongue.

He'd admitted to Alice, when he was in the doldrums, that he couldn't get the taste of ashes out of his mouth. She hadn't forgotten and, when he was able to take short strolls, had led him to the spice shop on Bowden Street for liquorice comfits. His heart had stopped when he saw who stood behind the counter.

He recalled that Alice had been delighted. 'Oh!' she had said. 'It's so lovely to see you.' She'd gabbled an explanation to Isaac while he stared at Dolly and Dolly, her dark hair tied in a neat chignon, the picture of respectability, stared back. 'Dolly came to the house. It was just before the fire. Dolly, this is my fiancé, Isaac.'

Dolly had nodded graciously, at each of them in turn. 'Congratulations. I hope you'll be very happy.'

'Are you happy?' Isaac had said, impulsively.

Alice had laughed uncertainly. 'What a strange question.' She put it down to Isaac's invalid state, explaining to Dolly his recent heroics. 'Isaac went in with no thought for his own safety and saved a young girl's life.'

Isaac had coughed uncomfortably. 'Alice, give over.'

Then Dolly had asked what she could do for them and Isaac retreated to the door while Alice bought the sweets. Perhaps it was inevitable that one day he'd see a face from his past. He was a different person now. So, too, it seemed, was Dolly. As Isaac followed Alice out of the shop he couldn't resist a glance back. Dolly lifted her hand in farewell. Isaac returned her smile and gently closed the door behind him.

The elderly gentleman had finished his pudding and sat with the bowl in his hand, a bemused look on his face as a clutch of young women hurried towards the front of the house. They were chattering excitedly, evidently awaiting the arrival of the bride and groom. Alice had told him that it was for their sake the wedding breakfast was being held in the middle of a Saturday afternoon, so those in employment could attend. Isaac understood why the house was central to the celebrations. The bride and groom had asked for cash donations for its upkeep rather than traditional wedding presents. It was, he supposed, a fresh beginning in more ways than one.

He watched a woman with a pinched face pull off her gloves as if they had committed some crime against her and drop them on the table by the door. 'Marry in May and rue the day,' she said. A man Isaac had been introduced to as a trustee of the house, but whose name he had forgotten, sighed. 'Mrs Shaw, I'm sure you could find a reason to reject every month of the year. Are there any pleasant times to wed?'

'Marry in June, enjoy a long honeymoon?' suggested Isaac.

The woman named Mrs Shaw looked affronted but the man was nodding. 'Perhaps they ought to have delayed the festivities. But here we are on this beautiful day! Come, Mrs Shaw, let's find you some refreshment.'

Alice's fellow bridesmaid hurried into the house, smoothing down her collar, telling the women the bride and groom were on their way, and only then did Isaac recognise her as the head counter from the day of the fire, the woman who had been trying to herd her charges into one place on the cobbles. She was ushering ahead of her a girl dressed in a clean white pinafore and straw hat and, Isaac realised with a jolt, making a beeline for him.

'Mr Hinchcliffe, in't it?' she said. 'I'm Amelia Barlow, the housekeeper. And this is Eliza who you saved from the fire.'

She spoke so briskly it took him a moment to absorb her words. He sat down on the stair carpet, overcome by the memory of blindly feeling about on the tile, his fingers finally closing on a small calf muscle, a warm torso, and lifting her into the air, his lungs bursting. He drew a careful breath, determined not to start coughing in front of the girl.

'What do you say?' said Amelia to the girl.

'I don't remember owt, or you, Mr Hinchcliffe, not a bit, but thank you,' the girl said. 'D'you know, I've a job now? In a fancy 'ouse.'

Isaac spoke past the thickness in his throat. 'That's grand.'

'Miss Hope lives there. I mean, Mrs Deveraux, now, in't she? An' she's movin' out, so...' Eliza looked down the hallway, and back at Isaac. 'I'm starvin',' she said.

'Well,' said Isaac, getting to his feet. 'There's a feast to be had. Why don't you lead the way.'

He followed the girl, stepping down into a kitchen he was seeing for the first time, a room he'd last plunged into in complete darkness. He was glad to have her small hand in his, pulling him along, or he might have baulked at entering. Blinking away the sensation of falling, fighting the conviction his body would splash onto a hard surface covered with freezing water, Isaac looked around the room. The air buzzed with conversation and a light breeze fluttered the net in the window. He breathed out shakily. Amelia left the girl with him and went to help Alice who was standing behind the kitchen table, serving tea and coffee and tiny wedges of cake to the guests that crowded the room.

Alice waved to him. 'There's wine and brandy in the front parlour, love.'

Eliza was staring at the food on the table, her eyes as round as saucers.

'Come on,' said Isaac. 'Why don't we ask that lovely lass o'er there to cut us a big slice o' cake?'

Chapter 26

The party was in full swing.

Alice raised her glass to Isaac who stood across the room. He was the most handsome man in it, and he belonged to her. She wondered if she was getting tipsy. Her view of Isaac was suddenly obscured by Flora Wallace, who had come to stand before her. Alice shifted over on the old chaise longue so that Flora could sit down beside Teddy. He'd made finger marks on Alice's bridesmaid's dress that she feared were permanent.

'Be careful of your dress,' she said. 'His hands are loppy.'

'And how old are you?' said Flora.

'I two!'

'Goodness!' Flora said. She produced a handkerchief to brush cake crumbs from Teddy's chin and wipe his fingers. 'You are practically all grown up.'

The boy swung his legs happily.

'I adore your art. You have such a talent,' said Alice.

Earlier, the bride and groom had been called upon to unveil two new paintings in the hallway of the house, that Hope declared were symbolic of the successful restoration of the refuge and all it stood for. They were impressionist watercolours of Paradise Square by day and by night, created by Flora to replace her earlier works that had been smoke-damaged beyond repair. Alice had learned that at the tender age of seventeen Flora had already been invited to exhibit at local galleries.

Flora frowned.

'Oh,' said Alice. 'I'm sorry, I don't mean to embarrass you.'

'Not at all,' said Flora. 'In fact, I'm nervous about approaching you. I wanted to discuss an idea that was broached to me, but I'm anxious not to offend.'

Alice was intrigued. 'Go on,' she said. Teddy pounded at her legs with his little fists. 'Ouch.'

'I hungry again.'

Alice took him by the shoulders and turned him around to face the room. 'Look, there's Amelia. She'll get you something to eat. Run to her.'

He stamped away.

Flora cleared her throat. 'It was Amelia who told me what happened when you tried to... to promote your cause.' She put a hand to her heart. 'I promise we weren't gossiping. Amelia thought I could help, perhaps. And I would love to become involved. I'm a sympathiser.'

Alice's eyes widened. Here was someone coming to *her*, asking to help, to *become involved*. She had not realised until this moment how lonely had been her crusade.

'That's marvellous,' she said. 'Truly.'

Flora laughed 'You haven't heard my proposition yet.'

'Then tell me.'

'How would it be if I provided artwork to accompany your words? You don't need to – excuse my bluntness – but you don't need to put yourself in stocks. Let me do it, with my pencil.'

'Yes!' Alice's exclamation was so loud that several of the guests turned their heads towards the two women. 'Yes,' she said again, quietly. 'Posters and placards. My own

267

efforts have been amateurish, to say the least. I write the words, you paint the picture.'

Flora stuck out her hand. 'Shall we shake on it?'

Afterwards, Isaac wandered over and sat beside her. 'You pair 'ad your heads together. What was that all about?'

'We're plotting an uprising,' said Alice.

'Oh aye?' He put his hand on her waist, sending a delicious shiver down her spine. 'Can I kiss thee in front of all this lot or shall we find a quiet corner where I can ravish thee?'

'Neanderthal man.'

'Wretched shrew.'

They smiled happily at each other.

–

Her mother never had gone to the Gower Street library to give Mr Goat a piece of her mind, as she had threatened. Once Alice had been allowed to return there, she and Edward Shelton fell over each other to be first to apologise. He had stood before her, furiously polishing his spectacles, and asked her if she might accompany him to a theatrical production. Alice told her gently that she was engaged to be married. Later, she speculated to her mother that life might be easier if she married a man who shared her ideals. 'But where would be the challenge in that?' Louisa had replied.

Now, sitting with her mother and watching Flora mingle with the wedding guests, Alice wondered whether she ought to contrive a meeting between her new ally and Mr Goat.

'Mother, wouldn't Flora Wallace and Edward Shelton make a handsome couple?'

Louisa shook her head. 'For a girl always spouting about independence, tha does seem to enjoy makin' wives and husbands.'

Alice's mouth dropped open. She closed it.

Louisa patted her daughter's knee. 'Conceding that one, then, are we?'

The celebrations went on into the evening, spilling into the square. There was uproar after the announcement was made that the newlyweds were leaving and they were ambushed with showers of rice. 'We were supposed to use it all up in the rice pudding,' Mrs Wallace wailed. 'It's everywhere. Clara will wring my neck!'

'It were the groomsmen brought their own,' said Amelia.

Hope and Angus stood on the doorstep, picking rice out of each other's hair, laughing helplessly.

'So, where's the honeymoon?' said Isaac.

Alice snaked her arm around his waist. 'You can't ask that question.'

'She's right,' said Hope, a blush rising in her cheeks. 'It's not the done thing.'

'I'm whisking her away,' said Angus, putting his arms around her waist and twirling her off her feet, depositing her on the pavement. 'She's mine now.'

Someone threw a shoe after the departing carriage, for luck. It bounced off the back wheel and landed on the cobbles and before the wearer could hop over to retrieve it a game of catch was underway. The shoe ended up hanging by its laces on the lamppost in the middle of the square and the unfortunate owner – another of Angus's groomsmen – was dragged into the Q to be consoled with ale. Several of the male guests had already sloped off to the public house, following the fiddlers, whose cheerful tunes now floated on the air.

Alice stood on tiptoe to kiss Isaac. 'We should run off to Gretna Green,' she said, 'when we marry.'

He dipped his chin so he could examine her face. 'Who's against us?'

'Why, nobody!' said Alice. 'It might be fun, that's all.'

Isaac laughed. 'Allus the rebel.'

Alice pouted. 'Well, it's something to think about.'

'What I'm thinkin' about is a jar of ale,' said Isaac. 'It'll only be a quick one an' then I'll see you and your mother home.'

'Are you sure?'

She was thinking about how pale he'd looked after the walk from the church. He would only get cross if she advised against it, so she held her tongue.

'Aye,' said Isaac. 'I need to build up me strength an' I won't do that by sittin' wi' the ladies. Tasker needs able workers, not invalids.'

She watched him walk away then went back to the house, where she found her mother and the warden sitting companionably in the front parlour over a pot of tea and the remnants of the wedding cake. Every guest had been given a boxed slice of the rich fruit cake to take away. Mrs Shaw, it was noted, had taken two.

'That's all right, though,' said the warden. 'She needs sweetening up.'

Alice popped a glacé cherry into her mouth.

'Did you ever get to talk to Mr Mundella?' said Louisa. 'I think he's sloped off to the Q with the rest o' them.'

Alice sighed. 'I tried to, earlier. Our esteemed member of parliament wanted only to talk about the good work being done here at the house. Apparently, he hasn't even had sight of my petition.'

'Maybe the time isn't yet right,' said Mrs Wallace. 'Change will come, one day.'

'Or maybe us women are too busy keepin' the world turnin' to try and change it,' said Louisa.

Alice shook her head. 'Then why have we none of the power?'

Mrs Wallace laughed. 'The men must have summat, I suppose.'

Alice folded her lips. She would keep to herself for now the conversation she'd had with Flora Wallace and the brief chat she had had with the Master Cutler's wife, who had said that through her contacts she might be able to get Alice in front of the factory girls' club. One day, she would be able to report a success. For now, all Alice knew for certain was that she would never give up the cause.

'I'll keep trying,' she said, 'even if I'm frustrated at every turn, because I couldn't bear the alternative.'

'What's the alternative?' said Mrs Wallace.

'Giving up. Admitting defeat.'

Louisa sipped her tea. 'You know,' she said, 'I am curious about summat. Why did that snooty pair, the ones that left early...'

'Hope's parents,' said Alice. 'Mr and Mrs Hyde.'

'Aye, them. I thought I were mishearin' at first, but why did they keep callin' her Emma?'

'Ah,' said the warden. 'Now that's a long story.'

Louisa settled back in her chair. 'I'm always ready to listen to a good tale.'

Author's Note

Alice Leigh's story precedes the famous suffragette campaign of the early twentieth century but I like to think she would live to see women given the vote, and that, like the Pankhursts, she and her daughters would be warriors for equal rights. The first women's suffrage organisation in the UK was reportedly established in Sheffield in 1851, with campaigning focused around pamphlets and petitions. But it was the militant campaign after the turn of the century that rattled the establishment and led to change. Alice would have been in her fifties when women were finally enfranchised – a long wait for justice through the telescope of her twenty-something self.

Acknowledgments

It takes a village, so heartfelt thanks to everybody who has helped put *The Rebel Daughter* on bookshelves. Special mention to my agent Kate Nash and editor Emily Bedford and their super teams; to my writer soulmates Asha Hick, Carly Reagon, Emma Clark Lam and Sarah Daniels for keeping me sane; my husband Al for his unwavering support and patience and my daughter Jess Cooke, my invaluable sounding board. And grateful thanks, as ever, to you, the reader.